ANARCHO GROW

ANARCHO GROW

Pura Vida in Costa Rica

by T.A.Sedlak

Illustrations by Leslie LePere

Anarcho Grow

A This Press Kills Fascists Publishing Book

This Press Kills Fascists Publishing
Madison, WI

Design by Erik and Robert Jacobson
www.longfeatherbookdesign.com

ISBN: 978-0-615-30923-1
Library of Congress Control Number: 2009938131

Printed in the United States of America

ANARCHO
GROW

This is the grass that grows wherever the land is, and the water is;
This is the common air that bathes the globe.

–Walt Whitman

2006

It was a bright June day as Ben Starosta strolled toward the exit doors of the Juan Santamaría International Airport. The smell of fried food wafted in. He was hungry but not hungry enough to settle for fried chicken and pizza. Ben fingered visa papers in his pocket giving him permission to teach English in Costa Rica for the next four months. As far as he knew, the U.S. government believed he was an honest teacher who enjoyed traveling in Latin America.

His leisurely stroll seemed to fit him, but there was a slight hitch in his gait. His shoes squeezed his feet with every step. He had just picked them up in Lima. Every other thought was about taking them off. He wore a beige suit with a burgundy shirt. His brown leather belt matched his shoes, and the hat band on his beige Stetson matched the color of his shirt. He was a bit over dressed for a simple English teacher, yet his garb was too sharp for a businessman. He felt like a fop.

Once outside, Ben was bombarded. "You need taxi?" "Hotel?" One man got so close that Ben could smell the cilantro on his breath. Ben walked over to an orange airport taxi. He was dressed well and felt he should travel professionally.

"*Where are you going?*" asked the driver. He was clean cut. Gray pants and blue button down dress shirt.

"*Heredia,*" said Ben. "*Close to the Café Britt plantation.*"

"Let's go."

The driver held open the rear door. Ben slid into the seat and began loosening his shoes.

In a taxi of another color, Ben would be riding in the front, and he would already have negotiated the price. In this car, the windows were rolled up, and the air conditioning flowed. Ben missed the aromas, but he couldn't deal with the heat in his suit.

"You here on business or vacation?" The driver looked at Ben in the rear view mirror.

"Just visiting," said Ben.

"That's nice."

Ben gazed out the window, happy that the driver wasn't trying to sell him on a hotel.

"What do you do for a living?" The driver flew through a red light.

"I teach English. Just finished in Caracas. I'm visiting friends here before heading back to the U.S."

"Oh, so you spend a lot of time in Latin America. Your Spanish is very good. Most North Americans speak none."

"I committed to learning it."

"It shows."

The driver went quiet, and Ben was happy. A different driver would be asking if he were going to meet up with any ticas. In fact, the driver may have insisted on it, even as a statuette of the Virgin Mary blessed his dashboard. There was no Virgin Mary on this car's dashboard. It was polished. If Ben were closer, his reflection would have shone back.

"Any big plans while you're here?" the driver asked.

"What?"

"Plans? Do you have any plans while you're here?"

'Oh great,' thought Ben. 'This guy's going to try to hook me up.' *"No, not really. Just hanging with friends."*

"That's cool."

The driver again went quiet. Ben stared off the highway at the tiny homes covering the valleys below. They were cheap houses, more tin than concrete. 'My people,' he thought. Eventually, they came to the intersection crowded with American restaurants. He was only a few miles from his destination. Hits from the eighties played on the radio, a pop love song. 'At least he hasn't brought that up,' thought Ben. He couldn't count the number of cab drivers who had wanted to discuss their musical tastes. He remembered one telling him how in high school he and his friends had gotten their hair cut like the members of New Kids on the Block. Not one of them had heard of Bob Dylan. Bob Marley, but not Dylan.

Soon they arrived at a modest house on the outskirts of Heredia. Like most homes in Costa Rica, a thin layer of concrete had been applied over cinder blocks, giving the walls a smooth finish. It was painted a pastel color, reminding Ben of Easter. The roof was tin. Even the roofs of the old cathedrals in San Jose are tin. The windows were screenless, and there was a black steel fence surrounding the lot.

Ben paid the driver and left him with *"¡Pura Vida!"* Though Ben could speak Spanish well, he had problems with this phrase. He couldn't flick the *"r"* well. Though he constantly used the phrase, he was aware he couldn't say it as well as the ticos. This frustrated him. Ben knew the phrase is more than a salutation. He understood *Pura Vida* is a way of life—a way that is more relaxed, honest, and pure.

"Mierda." Ben stepped into a puddle upon exiting. 'These fucking shoes,' he thought. Ben opened the gate and yelled into the doorway, *"¡Hola, Estéban! ¿Donde estás?"*

A portly tico in his forties approached the doorway. He was shirtless and wore faded blue shorts. He'd been watching soccer on television. The man grabbed an old white t-shirt off a chair inside the door. He raised his arms over his head to slide on the shirt. His body looked like a map with pale patches of skin, vitiligo induced, scattered through the sea of his bronze flesh. *"Hey, gringo,"* he yelled. *"You must be lost! The coffee plantation tour is two miles south of here."*

Ben opened the gate. *"Aren't you supposed to be picking beans?"*

"I'm not a Nicaraguan," Estéban scoffed.

"Could have fooled me."

"Hijo de puta."

"It's good to see you, too," said Ben.

They shook hands. Estéban's were small but thick. He could have crushed Ben's narrower hand. A black digital watch covered his wrist. His vitiligo was hidden behind his shirt except for a small patch on his right hand and a few scattered below the legs of his shorts.

Estéban offered Ben a seat on the porch. *"It's good to see you here safe again,"* he said.

"It's good to be here again," replied Ben. He took off his hat and hung it on a nail jutting out from a porch beam before easing into the chair.

"You're going to Quebrada Grande tomorrow?" Estéban leaned back in his chair and placed his hands behind his head.

"Of course." Ben pulled off his shoes and groaned.

"You're always on the move."

"Just got in from Caracas." Ben pulled off his dry sock, then peeled off the wet one.

"I thought you were going to Bolivia?"

"I did."

"So, you went on a mini-motorcycle diaries trip, eh?"

"Nah, my motorcycle diary trip occurred a long time ago. Finishing gathering material for my warfare book." He wrung his sock out over the concrete porch.

"What the hell did you do?" Estéban squinted at the sock.

"Stepped in one of your puddles."

"It is the rainy season."

"Yes, I can feel it." The bottom two inches of his pant leg stuck to him.

"And how is everyone in South America?"

"Could be doing better in Peru. I was there during the election when Humala was edged by a couple points." Ben stretched out his bare feet.

"Do you think it was rigged?"

"It's possible." Ben's eyes widened. *"I don't assume, though, like with the U.S."*

A group of small children ran by. Their little voices grew as they drew closer and faded as they passed.

"It does seem there are more people watching the elections down here," said Estéban.

"No doubt. But it's what the Democrats get for choosing a mark as their head corporate sponsor." Ben drew in a long breath of humid air and let it out slowly, staring at the small houses lining the street.

"So, where is Benjamin Starosta teaching now?" asked Estéban.

"Peru."

"You still have him in a country with a conservative government, eh?"

A man began to mow his lawn with a weed wacker two houses down.

"Unfortunately, I do." Ben pressed his toes against the concrete. *"Speaking of teaching, you still have close to ten library books from Quebrada Grande."* He was forced to raise his voice over the buzz of the weed wacker.

"I'll get them back. Almost finished with 'em."

"I know you'll get them back because I'll be taking some of them tomorrow. You think your library would have enough books."

"The library of Heredia doesn't have shit. Don't get me wrong, it's got some classics, but the rain puddles out here go deeper than their reading collection."

A fine mist started to fall. The man shut off his weed wacker and went inside.

"I really wish Humala could have won that election," said Estéban. *"It was like the Ticos had just lost a cup. Humala next to Morales, Ortega, Correas, and Chavez. Could have been five countries with good-hearted leaders."*

Ben laughed. *"Good people can't rule, Estéban."*

"Hogwash." He folded his arms.

"Look around," said Ben. *"Hard to find one who's not a monster."*

"Most. Hugo and his comrades are different."

"Eh, Shakespeare and Twain made me skeptical of them all."

"Ha, Shakespeare and Twain. Fuentes says we live in the place of natural man."

Ben squinted, focusing on the words.

"You remember those lines? From a book you chose for the library of Quebrada Grande."

Ben paused. *"Because the memory of the good society lies in our origins... It also lies at the end of the road."*

"That's right," said Estéban.

"I just find it hard to believe that it can happen through elected leaders, but I'll wait and see."

"I'm sure you will. Anyway, what was the main reason for your trip to that part of South America… I mean, Ryan Westby's reason? That is the name you use, no?"

"Ryan ran out of tea."

"Ahh, tea of coca leaf." Estéban licked his lips. *"You're not suffering from high blood pressure are you?"*

"No, just like good tea."

"What type of person travels to another country just to buy tea?"

Ron Numbers sat in a slick vinyl booth at a dingy cafe in Washington D.C. A thin man of average height, he was bent over reading files. His jaw sat slightly askew as he studied them, occasionally bringing a mug of coffee or piece of toast to his mouth. Crumbs fell down his newly shaved face and rested on his shirt and tie. He pretended not to notice when his assigned partner, Bill Larimore, trudged in.

Bill was dressed like Ron, a dark suit with shiny, black shoes. The aroma of smoke followed him in. He hadn't fully exhaled his last puff. His meaty, line-man-esque frame had begun to hurt over the years, and it showed in his jerky steps. The bulk that had grown around his abdomen didn't help. He blamed the intense army training for the pain he now felt.

"So, what's new in current events?" Bill grumbled through stained teeth, sliding his hefty body into the open side of the booth. His voice was as gruff as a Harley chopper.

Ron looked up from his files. "Did you read the news?" There was a hint of irritation in his nasally voice. 'He smells even worse than he looks,' he thought.

"I glanced at it."

Ron raised his eyebrows.

"I got the gist of it," said Bill. "We're going to Wisconsin."

"I'm surprised how well you were able to construct our assignment from not actually reading the report."

"I'm a magician," said Bill.

A waitress of fifty made her way to the table. She swayed her wide hips as she walked. Her green eye shadow matched her apron, and a trail of cheap perfume followed. "What can I get ya, sugar?" she said. Her hair was twirled into a beehive.

"Three eggs, bacon, and hash browns. With a coffee. Black." Bill casually leaned back.

"And how would you like your eggs?"

"Fried with the yolks as hard as you can get 'em."

'Just like his prostate,' thought Ron.

"Any toast?" She twitched her hip.

"Sure, white," he said.

"That'll be right up." She gave him a smile.

"Thanks, doll." His eyes went back to Ron. "What about Peru?"

"He's not there." Ron stared into Bill's worn face. The cracks reminded him of the sidewalks in ghettos. "I phoned Jorge in Peru. He was supposed to be teaching English there."

"Most of 'em know enough English to beg for *soles*, isn't that enough?"

"Soles?" said Ron.

"The currency of Peru."

"Peru," he scoffed. "Them and their phony pyramids."

"They're the same as Egypt," said Bill. "The Great Wall, Stonehenge… Just a bunch of rocks."

Ron crumpled up a straw wrapper and threw it across the table. He picked up his files and glanced at them. "Anyway, the person working in Lima wasn't Benjamin Starosta, but some guy… Jeffrey Roesing."

Bill's eyes narrowed. His chin dropped. "Who the fuck?" he whispered.

The waitress returned with his coffee. "There you go, sweetie."

"Thank ya." Bill gave her a grin, and their eyes connected. She gave him a wink before turning.

Ron waved at the air with his papers. "Jesus, perfume. Burns my nostrils."

Bill chuckled.

Ron slapped his files against the table. "Roesing's in custody. We'll know more soon."

"So, where's this Ben?" Bill took a swig of coffee.

Ron squinted. "Doesn't it burn to gulp your coffee like that?"

"Conditioned," said Bill.

Ron shook his head. "Well, as you should know, Ben lived in Madison. He has a friend there, Ryan something."

"Westby," said Bill.

"Yeah, Westby." Ron picked up his papers and shuffled them. "Well, judging by his passport, Ryan enjoys traveling as much as Ben. A few days ago Ryan shows up in Costa Rica. Passport says he's been in Peru, and God knows where else. However, reports come back that Westby's siding houses in Madison. Never left the country."

Bill's eyes had lit up. "Costa Rica."

Ron cracked his knuckles. "Yeah, could be the next stop. We'll see after Madison."

Bill took another swig of coffee. "Madison's a college town, right?"

"Hippies," said Ron.

Bill set down his mug. "I wouldn't mind doing some hippies." He grinned.

Ron released a deep breath and looked to the ceiling. "We fly out at 9:30 tomorrow. A driver's been arranged in Madison."

"So, what? Two days there?"

"Yeah, then Costa Rica."

"Sounds good."

"So, I'll see you tomorrow." Ron slipped his papers in his briefcase. "If you don't get a fax by tonight, give Robert a call. In the meantime, read up on Starosta." He got up and mechanically pulled out his wallet. He counted out $8.70 and slapped it on the table—his bill with exactly fifteen percent.

"Tomorrow," said Bill, mouthing the words, "captain jack off."

The waitress brought out Bill's food, and he choked it down like a snake. He added two more cups of coffee to his bloated stomach, then looked over the paper until he abruptly closed it and tossed back the rest of his coffee. 'I need a smoke,' he thought. He covered his mouth as he burped and pushed himself up. His body cracked. He reached in his pocket, pulled out crumpled bills, and threw them to the table.

"Bye, hon." The waitress waved as he left.

"¡Gringo! You better get up if you want breakfast!"

Ben rolled over and blinked until he could make out the numbers on the clock. Six thirty, it read. He could hear dishes banging in the kitchen. *"I'm coming!"* he yelled. He groaned and stretched his body. Then he opened and closed his mouth, thinking how dry it was. Eventually, he staggered out of bed and got dressed. Gone were the flashy garments of yesterday. He slipped a pair of baggy tan shorts over his boxers, grabbed a t-shirt, and headed for the kitchen.

Estéban was working at the counter with his back to him. The air was humid from cooking. Ben plopped down at the table and filled a glass of refresco. He tipped it back and downed the whole thing. He then moved his tongue around the inside of his mouth.

"Well, well, someone looks a bit tired this morning. Ten hours wasn't enough?" Estéban was already showered and dressed. He looked chipper as he set two heaping plates on the table. Each was covered with a big pile of gallo pinto, an arepa, and a thick piece of farmers' cheese.

Ben rubbed his eyes. *"I should be caught up. It's just all the traveling."*

Estéban took a seat across from him. *"Yeah, must be a bitch, seeing all the world like you do."*

"It sure can be." A couple pieces of rice shot from his mouth as he spoke.

"How's the food?" said Estéban.

"Great. Same thing I'd be served in Quebrada Grande."

"There's a farmer I met not too far out where I can get fresh milk. I make the cheese right here."

"That's cool."

Ben and Estéban ate their meal together, chatting amiably. Afterward, Ben called a cab and washed up while Estéban cleaned the kitchen. The rain had started to come down hard. A loud continuous clanging echoed from under the tin roof. They waited under the porch until a battered red taxi came into view.

"Well, it was nice to see you," said Estéban. *"I'll see you next time."* He spoke loudly to be heard over the din of the rain.

Ben looked at the corrugated roof. *"Could be a month,"* he said.

"Give everyone my regards." Estéban slapped Ben on the back.

"I will." The two shook hands, and Ben turned to leave.

"Except for that drunk, Fulgencio," said Estéban.

Ben laughed. *"It was good to see you."*

"You, too, gringo. ¡Pura Vida!"

"¡Pura Vida!" Ben darted into the rain, avoiding puddles on his tip toes. Wet pieces of dirt squeezed into his sandals. He opened the front door, hopped in, and waved goodbye to Estéban and his cozy home. The door clanked shut.

Estéban chuckled. *"He'll never get it."*

The cab ride was everything the ride hadn't been the day before. The windshield wipers waved frantically as Latin music played. The driver's mouth hardly took a rest as an image of the Madonna looked over them. He was a plump man in his mid thirties with light, shiny skin. Ben stared at his puffy cheeks as he spoke.

"Your español is very good," he said.

"I studied for many years," said Ben. *"Mostly in Costa Rica, but I've been to most Spanish speaking countries."*

"Ay, chingada. What do you think about the Spanish of Mexico."

"I thudied in Thpain for thikth weekth," said Ben. *"I like their accent*

more."

The driver laughed, and his puffy cheeks bunched up.

"Gays talk the same way in English," said Ben.

The driver's cheeks turned red as he laughed. *"Fags,"* he said. He beeped the horn and yelled out the window, *"Hola, beautiful!"*

A young woman hiding under the cover of a restaurant awning didn't look. Her belly was exposed over her skintight pants.

"So what country do you like best?"

"Costa Rica, of course," said Ben. *"¡Pura Vida!"*

"¡Pura Vida!" The driver laughed. *"And, we have the best ladies, no?"*

"Can't argue with that." Ben watched the umbrellas bobbing up and down over people.

"You've been with a tica?" he asked.

"Of course."

"How do they compare with women of other countries?" The driver made eye contact.

"Well, my girlfriend's a tica." Ben smiled.

The driver laughed. *"Ticas are good women, but I always wanted to be with a North American. Just once. A blonde, blue-eyed girl like the movies."* Ben looked at the driver's face. His puffy cheeks had dropped, and there was a distant look in his eyes.

Ben looked away, and a white Madonna stared back. Juanes's *La camisa negra* came from the radio. *"They don't have the soul of ticas,"* he said.

The car splashed through a giant puddle as they turned into the station. It was little more than a worn parking lot with a small roofed area. The driver dropped Ben under the roof by a ticket window and handed him a card. *"If you ever need anything in the city,"* he said.

"Gracias." Ben stuck the card in his pocket and hopped out. *"¡Pura Vida!"* he said.

The ticket window was closed, so Ben waited under the roof with the rest. There were about forty people, half on benches, half standing. The sound of rain hitting tin droned from above. A woman in her early thirties approached carrying a woven blanket. *"You need a blanket?"* she asked.

Ben shook his head. *"No, gracias."* He avoided her eyes and looked around. One man had cell phone cases and cords. Another, clothes. The rain had taken away their selling spirit. All except the woman's.

Ben eyed the grimy restaurant across the lot. He was thirsty but unwilling to make the walk through the rain. He turned to the other people. Few were prepared for the drop in temperature the rain had brought. They held their arms against their chests. A teenage boy in shorts and a t-shirt shivered on the bench at his right. Ben looked at the woman with the blanket and thought about buying it for him. The young children didn't seem to mind the weather. They played in front of benches where their mothers and grandmothers sat wrapped in jackets or shawls. Besides a fat man, the kids and Ben seemed the only ones unaffected. A couple of cute girls caught Ben's eye. There were two in the back corner and one on a bench nearby. 'Love that tica dress,' he thought. Two of the three wore skintight pants, the other a miniskirt. For tops they wore bantam t-shirts with sleeves barely covering their shoulders. Ben could see one of the girls' bra through her shirt. Bright plastic earrings dangled from their earlobes. He stared again at the girls' pants. 'Don't know how they get them on,' he thought, 'but I wouldn't mind taking them off.'

Ben couldn't decide the girls' ages. He figured there was a chance none were eighteen. Approaching twenty eight, he wondered if he should be looking at teens. To his left he saw a man of at least fifty eying one of the girls. He smiled. 'Can't stop animal instinct,' he thought. 'Maybe it's just my puritan roots.'

He turned to his right and noticed another tico checking out the girls. The man was tall and thin, like himself, dressed in tight blue jeans, a snug black t-shirt, and a pair of old Adidases. He seemed to be burning holes into the girls with his eyes. Ben stared past him into the rain, then squinted and rubbed his hand through his hair. 'Does he think women want to be stared down?' he thought. Ben shook his head. *'Machismo.'*

A vehicle's exhaust wailed, and a small, blue van parked in front of the shelter. Its side door slid open with a scrape, and four young tourists poured out, white college girls from the U.S. They stood in the deluge looking confused as the people under the roof stared. The driver, wearing a poncho, jumped out and ran to the back of the van. He flexed his upper body and quickly pulled out the bags. Each girls' posture collapsed as they took them. After handing off the last bag, he yelled, *"¡Pura Vida!"* and ran back to the van. The girls, hunched over under the weight of their bags, walked to the ticket booth.

"I think this is where we get our tickets," said one. She stuck her head close to the window and looked in. The rain caused her blonde curly hair to stick together.

Ben glanced at the man in the black t-shirt. He'd found a new target. Water dripped from the girls' shorts, and their shirts clung.

"No one's in there," said the blonde.

"Great. What do we do now?"

Ben walked over. "You girls tryin' to get to Arenal?"

"Yeah, we were told we could catch a bus here," said the blond.

"You were told right." He pointed at a sign. "Next one leaves in fifty minutes."

"Fifty minutes." One of the girls bit her pouty lip.

"Window's not open today," said Ben. "You'll pay the driver directly. He'll pull up ten minutes early and sit. It'll be the only bus here."

"Are you going to Arenal, too?" said the blonde. Her eyes sparkled.

"Not today," said Ben.

"Aw, we could have rode together." Her smile was electric.

Ben felt there was something linking their eyes. "Sorry," he said.

"You've been to Arenal?" said one of the girls. She was short but cute, amply bosomed.

"Yeah, of course."

"What's it like? As beautiful as everyone says?"

Americans always asked him about tourist destinations.

"Yeah, it's great. Best hot springs I've been to. You might even get to see lava flow down the volcano or maybe a toucan."

"Wow." Their eyes glowed.

'Here I am, a fucking tour guide,' he thought. The four girls stood in a semicircle around him. "The lava at night's one of the most beautiful sights. Instantly dilates your pupils." He looked at the blonde. "I hope you see it. Clouds cover it most the time."

A bus roared around the corner and pulled into the lot. It looked like a tour bus from the U.S., only a little worn. Diesel exhaust fumes wafted, and the brakes hissed as the driver released the air and slid open the door. Passengers hurried to the red taxis on the street, the dirty restaurant, or the roofed area.

"That's my bus," said Ben.

The blonde frowned, and people edged by them to get to the bus. The girls in tight pants moved as quickly as their jeans allowed. Youngsters ran, but not all of them toward the bus.

"¡Leandro! ¡No! ¡Entra al autobús!" A mother scolded her child who jumped in puddles.

"How long will you be in Costa Rica?" the blonde asked.

"At least six months," said Ben.

"We'll be here another week and a half. We should try to meet up."

Ben looked at the ground. "I'm sorry. I'm gonna be pretty busy. But you can give me your email, and maybe I can get ahold of you."

The girl dug through her backpack, searching frantically for a pen. She scribbled the address and handed it to him. "My name's Nicole. Nhemrick@u.washington.edu."

"I'm Ben. It was a pleasure to meet you."

"You, too." She blushed.

He turned and stuffed the card in his pocket. *"¡Pura Vida!"* he yelled, running to the bus.

"¡Pura Vida!" she said.

Ben gave her a smile as he stepped on the bus. He could hear her friends picking on her.

The bus driver, wearing a crisp uniform, acted like his seat was a throne. Ben handed him a couple thousand colones and felt the eyes on him as he walked down the aisle. He moved his tongue around his mouth and wished he'd gotten a bottle of water. One of the cute girls from before sat alone in the middle of the bus. Ben slid into the polyester seats across from her. Her v-necked t-shirt was a mustard yellow that Ben thought he could stare at all day. He looked at the two inches that separated the carpeted seat back from his knees and thought, 'Glad I got the direct bus.'

The bus huffed out of the lot and wound through the narrow streets. The rain faded, and Ben watched people return. He looked at the approaching mountains with enthusiasm.

Just outside of San Jose, the bus pulled over, and two men boarded. One carried a giant plastic bag filled with small bags of chips, the other a large cooler. They yelled like peanut vendors at a baseball game, and passengers reached in their pockets for money. Ben held a finger up to the man with the cooler. *"You have pineapple juice?"*

"Sí, two hundred fifty."

Ben handed the man the change, and the guy gave him a small bag filled with liquid. Beads of condensation dripped off. He bit the corner and slurped, watching the girl across the aisle eat long, salty plantain chips. The men exited, and the bus chugged up the mountain road.

Within an hour, the bus had passed from San Jose's thirty eight hundred-foot elevation to forty eight hundred. The temperature had dropped more than ten degrees, and fog hung over the lush trees. Ben lay back and sighed as the cool air swept across his body. The ticos reached up and shut the windows. A few put on extra layers. Ben glanced at the tica beside him. Goose bumps dotted her arms, and she curled her body up. 'Too cute,' he thought.

The cool mountain weather was short lived. Within a couple of hours the bus made its descent, and the temperature rose dramatically.

The windows were forced back open, ticos shed their extra layers, and everyone moved their limbs away from their bodies. Ben felt like a vegetable pulled from the refrigerator and being brought to a boil on the stove.

As the bus came to its stop in Pital, Ben rose stiffly and followed the crowd. He politely motioned to the tica across from him to go first. She blushed. Tired and disheveled, he stepped off behind her. She walked in one direction, he in the other. He leaned against a payphone and dug through his pockets. A dirt bike whizzed by. He stared at a calling card and dialed. A long beep came through the phone, a pause, then another beep. *"¿Alo?"* The voice was enveloped in static.

"Chi Cho, what's up?"

"Nothing. Where are you?" Ben could barely make out the words.

"Pital."

"I'll leave in one minute."

"What?"

"I'll leave in a minute."

"Okay. I'll be at The Internet Cafe or Jeffrey's Pollo."

"Okay. See you soon."

"Until then." Ben hung up the phone and looked at the central plaza he'd have to cross. A soccer field covered one whole block. Trees hung over the sidewalk on the main street side. Benches were scattered below, red cabs were parked in a line, and a large church sat across the street. Ben hoped to avoid acquaintances. He wasn't in the mood for making up stories. But there was one person he especially wished to avoid. Victor.

Victor took the *"pura"* out of *"¡Pura Vida!"* Ben had met him seven years ago on his first trip to Pital. Victor was a taxi driver—one a bit too friendly—shuttling Ben's volunteer group to Quebrada Grande. He told Ben, *"Anytime you need a ride, call me. No charge."* Victor invited him to meet his family. He talked with Ben, learning that he desired to teach English. Back before Ben had found his true calling. Victor told him, *"You will come here and live in my house."* He introduced Ben to a tica studying English. A chubby girl a few his years his senior. *"You can help her with English, and she can help you with Spanish,"* he said. Ben quickly realized this wasn't the case.

Ben knew Latin Americans thought he was wealthy because of his race. However, he hadn't known there were people who saw him as wealth, like Victor. A commodity.

Ben didn't blame Victor. He couldn't control the society he was raised in. It wasn't his fault that race and nationality were commodified the same way as produce, minerals, or art. Ben sure as hell didn't want to deal with him, though.

As Ben walked along the cracked sidewalk leading through the plaza, he kept his eyes peeled for Victor. The soccer field was empty at this hour, as was the church. Teenagers in school uniforms, navy pants and button down shirts, sat on the benches beneath the trees. They talked loudly and threw playful punches. A few retired folks nearby stared. Ben held his head low as he passed in front of the church, avoiding the line of red taxis across the street. A booming vehicle approached, and Ben felt like a spotlight had been shone on him. It was a truck with enormous speakers mounted to its roof. A voice called out over beats, beckoning people to a fiesta outside of town, then a sale at a shoe store one town over. Ben nodded to two piratas, illegal taxis, parked around the corner. The sun shone intensely. He guessed it wouldn't rain for at least a half hour.

Ben breathed a sigh of relief and let the aroma of fried chicken pull him into Jeffrey's. An old tico with a slick mustache came from behind the counter and shook his hand. *"Pleasure to see you. It's been a long time,"* he said.

"Yes, I was traveling." Ben didn't like concealing his life. Everyone viewed him as a playboy.

"The grand traveler has returned." Jeffrey stepped behind the counter and filled a plate. A couple pieces of fried chicken, a heap of black beans, some salad, and fried plantains.

The plate felt heavy as Ben took it. *"Gracias."* He walked toward a seat facing away from the television.

"To drink?" said Jeffrey.

"You have chan?"

"Of course."

The grease coated Ben's hands as he bit into the chicken. He shoveled in a fork load of beans, and Jeffrey set down a glass of clear, semi-gelatinous liquid filled with little seeds. *"Anything else?"*

"I'm good." Ben wiped his mouth.

Jeffrey wore a wide smile as he walked away. Ben picked up the chan and took a swig. He sloshed it around, and the seeds tickled his mouth. 'Delicious,' he thought before devouring more of the greasy food. Ben didn't take a moment to put his fork down until he stopped to ask for another glass of chan, and he didn't realize how full he was until he rose to leave. He rubbed his bloated stomach and held out a five thousand note.

"Thanks for coming," said Jeffrey.

"Thanks for stuffing me." Ben tried to keep his eyes from drooping.

"I love seeing people full."

Ben took his change and headed out. *"Hasta luego."*

"¡Pura Vida!" said Jeffrey.

A couple of dusty cars rolled past, and Ben turned left into a strip mall bordering two sides of a parking lot. Music blared from speakers outside an electronics store while a husband and wife sold produce under a tent in the lot. Ben walked into the Internet Cafe. A couple oscillating fans drowned out the music from outside. A tica at a desk looked up from her book. Despite the nearly ninety-degree temperature, she wore jeans. Ben glanced at the eight computers in cubicles to his left. *"Number six is open?"* he said.

"Sí." The woman gave him a smile.

Ben sat down and loosened his belt. The woman's eyes returned to her novel. He opened his email. 'Just the message I needed,' he thought. "Going fishing this weekend," it read. He closed it and read the headlines at democracynow.org. His mouth dropped as he read, "Burger King hired investigative firm to infiltrate tomato pickers' union. They had asked for an extra penny per pound." After ten minutes of reading gloomy headlines, Ben went to ESPN's site to feed his sports addiction. He was engrossed with a story predicting success for the Milwaukee Bucks when a hand came down on his shoulder. He twisted around like startled prey. A skinny tico of five foot nine grinned. He wore work clothes, dirty jeans, an old t-shirt, and worn out sneakers. His smile was wide enough for a quetzal to fly in, tail and all.

"Chi Cho. Hola. I didn't hear you pull up."

"You were too interested in your Bucks. We're in the middle of the biggest sports event in the world, and you're reading about basketball. Silly gringo."

Ben logged off and pushed in his chair. The woman at the desk set down her novel. *"What do I owe you?"* said Ben.

"Two hundred fifty."

"Two hundred fifty?" said Chi Cho. *"But he's white."*

The woman giggled.

"You know he has more," said Chi Cho. *"If a white person ever asks, 'What do I owe you?' you tell him, 'The gold and silver you robbed from my ancestors. The hours my grandparents spent picking fruit for you.'"*

The woman and Ben blushed, and he dropped the change into her hand. *"Gracias,"* he said.

"I'm just kidding," said Chi Cho. *"I love this gringo."* He put his hand on Ben's head and shook it.

"Gracias," she said. *"Hasta luego."* She stood and watched them through the large plate glass window.

They walked to Chi Cho's battered Toyota. The truck had once been sharp black. The sun had faded it to a light charcoal color, and reddish orange clay caked its lower parts. Its doors creaked, the two hopped in, and they jangled out of the lot. They turned onto the main street and headed north out of town, passing two piratas. A strong wind blew in until Chi Cho slowed for a rough patch in the road, a fifty foot stretch littered with potholes. He swerved to miss them, and the vehicle rattled.

'If it's ever to be fixed, we'll have to do it,' thought Ben. 'Good way to gain support.'

Mountainous hills stood in the distance, the rainforest. They were filled with monkeys, sloths, colorful frogs, poisonous snakes, inch long ants, and resplendent butterflies. Birds that caused smugglers to salivate flew through the canopy. Staring at the hills reminded Ben of the time he was lost there.

It was before he had come to know the rainforest. He'd planned to go on a hike in the hills behind Quebrada Grande, but got caught up in a soccer game. He didn't make it to the woods until a little after three o'clock and hadn't brought any water. His throat was already a bit dry. Ben stopped at the lookout tower atop the first hill and smoked a small joint. He'd decided he was only going to take new trails. Ben moved along briskly, taking one trail here and another there. He watched a cormorant fly from the weeds ahead and then realized he'd come to a dead end. He looked around and inspected the trail. 'Fuck,' he thought. 'This was rain. Not men.' He followed the trail back to where it forked but couldn't tell which was right. He chose one and followed it. Then came upon another fork and did the same. 'Fuck. This isn't it,' he thought. He went back to the fork and tried another trail. Nothing looked familiar. He went back and tried a different one, noticing the dimming light and thinking how darkness would soon come. His throat ached for water as he descended a hill. Seething with frustration, he told himself to remain calm. It was difficult as the failures mounted, and he again came to the same dead end.

Ben walked down another trail, and an eerie feeling went through him, like he was being watched. He scanned the area to each side of him when a branch snapped above. He looked up to see an animal staring. He couldn't see it clearly through the leaves. 'Is that a monkey?'

he thought. They stared into each others' eyes. Then the creature let out a roar. It was a howler monkey, capable of being heard clearly at a distance of three miles. The roar then came from all the tree tops. It was a terrible, guttural sound, far more than a howl. Ben got the hell out of there and eventually made his way back, stepping out of the forest just before dusk.

Ben looked from the truck to the terrain below. Trees once grew through the whole valley. It had been cleared long ago for agriculture. Pineapple. All the land was covered with it. Rows of dull, green plants separated by walking paths in the red clay. There was a patch with a mature pineapple atop each plant, and people worked there in jeans, t-shirts, and ball caps. They hiked down the rows with a machete in one hand and a bag over their shoulder, slicing off the fruit and placing it in the bag. One man was dumping a bag full into the back of a pickup truck.

"Why isn't your truck out there, Cheech?"

Chi Cho looked out the window. *"Slavery,"* he said. *"The owner of the field makes enough to feed his family, put some away for the future, and maybe buy another plot of land. Workers making five thousand colones a day. Kids that should be in school. All the profit goes to some guy in Europe or the U.S. The owner of the factory."*

"We'll own them all someday," said Ben.

The two passed by a field of yuca. Slender trees, six foot tall, with leafy green tops cultivated for their starchy tuberous roots. Their appearance was similar to marijuana plants in vegetative state.

"Yuca here looks better than the stuff I saw in South America."

"Why's that?" said Chi Cho. *"Bad weather?"*

Ben looked at the field. *"You should have seen it. Entire fields without leaves. A wasteland."*

"Mealy bugs?"

"That's what I thought. I asked them. 'No,' they said. 'The United States. Plan Colombia.'"

"Plan Colombia?"

"Money the U.S. gives them to fight coca growers. A billion dollars a year."

"A billion!" said Chi Cho. *"Why don't they just give it to the coca growers to stop?"*

"It might be all that's keeping their government in power."

"So the yuca was sprayed by planes?" said Chi Cho.

"Sí, U.S. planes, or those bought by them."

Chi Cho shook his head. *"Why yuca?"*

"Bombs and sprays don't always hit their mark."

"Unless that was their mark."

Ben looked to the hills. *"The yuca wasn't the only thing they got. I talked with a woman who lost a child. She said it was a hot summer day, beautiful clouds shimmering. She was hanging laundry when she heard the planes.*

"Her son had been with a friend that day. She left the basket of wet clothes and walked quickly to check on him. In the road she met the other child's mother who was looking for her own son. They asked around and learned the kids had last been seen playing by the yuca field. They ran for them, but men held them back, and eventually the other woman's son returned.

"The people waited for the dust to settle before searching the fields. When they found him, his mother said he didn't look human."

Chi Cho stared straight ahead. Ben sunk into his seat and focused on the breeze from the windows. *"You got everything ready?"*

"Sí, a hundred twenty pounds."

"Top grade?"

"So beautiful I almost don't want it leaving the country."

"I'll be the judge of that."

"You don't have to check, malperido," Chi Cho cussed him.

"You're an hijo de puta. But anyway, Daniela and I will leave tomorrow for Tamarindo, eight o'clock."

"When you coming back?"

"One week. You can't go to the coast without spending a few days."

"I'm going to have to make it out to the Pacific sometime," said Chi Cho.

"I'm sick of hearing you say that," said Ben. *"I'm going to set you and Isabel up with a place. Daniela and I can watch your children."*

"You'll quit working me like a slave for a whole week?"

"You're doing well for a slave." Ben looked out the window at people planting pineapple. *"Must beat bustin' your ass in someone's field. Ten hours a day for five thousand colones."*

"Don't remind me."

They entered the small town of Veracruz, and Chi Cho slowed for speed bumps. A couple of old men sat in front of a pulpería watching the dirty Toyota. One of them leaned forward, resting his weight on a cane. They passed an empty soccer field and numerous small cement homes, then wrapped around a corner and left town.

Chi Cho sped up but didn't get further than a couple miles. A large building owned by a pineapple company sat to the right with two big trucks out front. Chi Cho slowed to a crawl and turned onto a road behind it. It was wide enough for two cars to pass but had no real lanes. A mess of mud and large rocks. Chi Cho, at less than ten miles per hour, swerved from one side to the other. The truck shook, and to talk they had to holler. It was Ben's favorite road.

He looked out the window and inspected the pineapple fields. *"This is the next to harvest?"*

"Sí, two weeks yet."

"I should probably help."

"We got enough people. A couple more families moved in."

"Good people?"

"Never worked for the state."

"Probably not even legal," said Ben.

A truck came at them, and Chi Cho pulled to the right. There were three people in front, and two people standing in the box. Chi Cho hit the horn, and he and Ben waved. Unintelligible yells came with honks and waves from the other truck. The pair passed houses where children played outside. Most waved while some stared dumbly. After fifteen minutes they hooked a right just outside of Quebrada Grande. They bounced another two miles and pulled into the driveway of a tico home. A couple farm buildings stood behind it with a hill swelling beyond. A four-year-old boy plodded out the door and ran to Ben and Chi Cho.

"¡Daviiiid!" Ben drawled his name out like a ringside announcer. He scooped him up and carried him to the house, tickling him as they went.

A one-year-old boy on the floor stared up with interest. A girl of dark complexion in the kitchen threw down a towel and hurried over. *"¡Ben!"* she said. She looked like a college girl carrying her freshman fifteen. Ben hunched down, and they exchanged a kiss on the cheek. *"You look exactly the same,"* she said.

"Not you." He reached for her hair. *"You've lost another couple inches. Seems it's been a couple each year. Five to ten more, and you'll be bald."*

"Stop." She smacked him in the arm.

"Ay, mis tortas." Isabel ran back to the kitchen and flipped the Costa Rican pancakes. Ben picked up Miguel, took a seat at the bar, and placed him on his lap while David climbed onto a stool. Isabel reached into a cupboard and brought out four mugs for coffee. She poured David's two-thirds full and put in a couple spoonfuls of sugar, then topped off everyone else's.

"Yummy tortas." Ben clapped Miguel's hands as Isabel set a plate full in the middle of the bar.

"I suppose you're hungry, too." Isabel took Miguel and lifted him to her breast.

"I'm hungry, too," said David.

"No boob for you," said Chi Cho. *"Big boys have coffee."*

"You never stop wanting boob," said Ben

The adults laughed, and David stared blankly. He looked at his mother's breast.

"How are the local businesses doing?" Ben asked Isabel.

"Great."

"Piña paying well?"

"Sí, the company's good."

"You grow good piña." He took a big sip of coffee.

"¡Piña! ¡Piña! Papa grows piña!" said David.

"He sure does," said Ben. *"The best."*

Isabel laughed, and Chi Cho winked at David. David picked up his big mug with two hands. It covered half his face.

"Everybody's doing well with Hugo Chavez here." Isabel patted Ben's shoulder.

Ben squinted at her and grinned.

"That's what we call you now, Hugo."

"No it's not," said Chi Cho. *"It's Gringo, Gringo Chavez."* He and Isabel laughed.

David joined in, pointing at Ben. *"¡Gringo! ¡Gringo!"*

The adults' laughter doubled.

"I don't really think that's an apt nickname," said Ben.

"You set up social programs," said Isabel *"Cooperative businesses."*

"You did that. Everyone here." He nodded toward Quebrada Grande.

"You stressed participatory democracy."

'Maybe I am like Hugo,' he thought. 'A businessman with half a conscience.' *"It was already here,"* said Ben. *"Especially with the women's organization."*

"Modest gringo," said Chi Cho.

"Well, I am loved by my people. That's something."

"You just better hope the U.S. doesn't want to get rid of you." said Chi Cho.

"If I'm Gringo Chavez, the difference is that I don't have to worry about the imperialists coming after me."

Isabel slipped her breast back in and kissed Miguel on his forehead. *"Let's hear about your travels."*

"Well, I had to go to the States to take care of some things," said Ben. *"I visited my family for a week."*

"How long was it since last time?" Isabel patted Miguel's back.

Ben looked into the coffee in the bottom of his mug. *"A little over a year,"* he said.

"What did you do the rest of the time?"

"I traveled. Peru, Ecuador, Colombia..."

"Gringo Chavez must have gone to visit Evo and Rafeal." Isabel giggled.

"No, I was just out of tea."

"Tea?" said Isabel. *"Who journeys to another country just for tea?"*

As the plane's wheels touched down, Bill groggily tried to wake up. He yawned and wiped drool from his mouth. He rubbed at his eyes and stretched his body. Ron looked him over. 'I don't know which is more disgusting, watching him sleep or watching him wake.' While Bill had dozed through the flight, Ron had spent his time reviewing the case or glancing at his new book, *Between Pacifism and Jihad.* He'd occasionally stare at Bill's sleeping body, wondering how he'd gotten in the C.I.A, and why they'd kept him around. The C.I.A. was an organization that should keep only the best.

"Goodbye. Thanks for flying with us." The flight attendants nodded with plastic smiles.

"Bye," said Ron.

Bill grunted.

They stepped off the plane and walked down the long corridor. Ron walked stiffly. Bill stumbled behind, trying to shake his body from petrification. Ron waited at the gate for him.

"My hip's actin' up," said Bill.

'Great, thought Ron. 'Another thing to deal with.' He slowed his pace.

A skinny kid with long, flowing hair and a bushy beard walked toward them. He wore loose faded jeans and a Yonder Mountain

String Band t-shirt. A hiking bag slung over his back. His big toe showed through his shoes.

Bill grinned. "Want to have a little fun?"

"We don't have time," said Ron. "Someone's waiting for us."

"It'd be fun." Bill turned and watched the young man pass. Something caught his nose. He raised it and sniffed. His eyes followed the smell to a heated rack on a bar. "Oooo, brats. I need one of those."

"We don't have time," said Ron.

Bill was already moving toward them. "There's no line. I'll get it to go."

Ron groaned.

An old man in a plastic apron stood behind the counter. Gray hair protruded from his nose and ears.

"One brat, please," said Bill.

The man took one off the rack with a pair of tongs. He stuck it in a bun on a red and white checkered cardboard tray.

"Are these the famous beer brats that I hear so much about?" said Bill.

"Nope. Regular old Johnsonvilles." The company's logo popped out on his apron.

"Looks delicious all the same." Bill handed him a five, and the man gave him a dollar change. He moved to the condiments and hid the brat beneath a pile of relish and onions. Ron tapped his foot as he waited. Bill stared at the brat, like a teenager eying his prom date. He paused and took a bite. As the juice hit his tongue, his brain felt numb. Relish dripped onto his hands. He licked them and wiped them with a napkin while trying to keep up with Ron. 'You'll have to wait until baggage,' he told the brat telepathically.

They stepped on the escalator to the ground floor. An old propeller plane hung from the ceiling. Small designs were carved into the stone walls. "Is that Frank Lloyd Wright?" Ron pointed at a wall.

"Could be," said Bill.

"Place has changed," said Ron. "Last time I was here it looked like an airplane hangar."

"It's nice." Bill looked at the brat.

Within a minute they stood by the luggage carousels. Ron hung between the first two. Bill took a seat. He bent forward, legs spread to avoid making a mess of his clothes, and tore into the brat. The snap of the hog casing was to him what the spinning of the spheres was to Aristotle. He took large bites, chewing with his mouth open. 'The only way this could be better is if I had a beer,' he thought. 'Or a baseball game.' He licked his fingers clean and went over them with a napkin. A machine buzzed, and the carousel began to turn. Bill pushed himself up and threw the napkins in the trash. Ron stood against the carousel, staring. A man grabbed a small black suitcase in front of him. "That's mine," said Ron.

"Sorry."

Bill walked over just in time to grab his old brown suitcase. "Let's roll," he said. He reached in his pocket and pulled out a pack of Camel Lights, then slid one in his mouth as they walked out the sliding doors. They shielded their eyes and blinked. It was hot, sticky. Bill dropped his bag and lit the cig. Ron squinted at the cars, a few waiting and others dropping people off.

A bespectacled man got out of a blue Crown Victoria and walked toward them. He wore jeans and a polo shirt. Shiny, black shoes. His hair was silver, and his mustache matched. "You two my guys?" he said. His face was almost as rough as Bill's.

"Yes, sir," said Ron.

"Welcome to Madison. U.S. Marshal, Gerald Walls." He shook Ron's hand enthusiastically.

"Nice to meet you. I'm Ron, and this is my partner, Bill."

"It's a pleasure," said Gerald.

Bill nodded and shook his hand, blowing smoke out the side of his mouth.

"So… As I understand it, we're to go visit a Ryan Westby at his place of business." The marshal spoke slowly with short pauses after each phrase.

"Yes, sir," said Ron

"All aboard then," Gerald turned and walked to the car. Ron took the front.

They pulled out and followed a small white Toyota. It had a bumper sticker split into four squares like the spinning pay lines on a slot machine. There was an *I* in the first square, an *R* in the second, an *A* in the third, and a *Q* rolling to an *N* in the last.

"So," said Gerald. "Your boy's siding houses on the west side of town. They got a good week left on the project… So… He'll be there."

"I haven't had a lot of time to research Westby," said Ron.

"Yeah... I looked over his file." The marshal played with his mustache as he spoke. "He had some problems with alcohol. Three underages… One in a bar… One while driving without a license. Don't recall the other. No trouble for the last four years, though. He's got a wife and kid now."

'Guy speaks slower than a farmer,' thought Ron. "So he's never been in real trouble?"

"Well… Not yet."

Ron watched him finger his mustache. "It's about his friend," he said.

"I got ya."

In the back Bill listened halfheartedly. He recalled hearing that, when in office, Bill Clinton did a crossword puzzle each morning during his briefings. Bill thought he was like Clinton, bright enough to hear half a story and finish it on his own.

Bill dreamed of a world where he'd made different choices. He had married his college girlfriend, Linda. Led a quiet life, took on the occasional project, like residing his suburban home. Instead of a C.I.A. agent, he was a cop parked in a lot somewhere, playing poker on his laptop. 'Maybe I'd even be seeing kids off to college now,' he thought.

"You're pretty quiet back there. What's on your mind?" said Gerald.

Bill snapped back to reality. "Nothing, I'm just taking in the information."

Gerald took a right onto the Beltline. They cruised over a marshy area linking the lakes, and Bill stared at a shiny fishing boat on the water. The sun gleamed off its red and silver metal flake paint. A man on a high seat cast a lure into the water. "So is there much good fishin'?"

Ron rolled his eyes and looked out the window. A gray Volkswagen passed with *Buy Local* and *Who Would Jesus Bomb?* stickers on its bumper. He was happy to see a *Support Our Troops* sticker next to them.

"Oh, yeah," said Gerald. "I take the boat out there fairly often."

Bill looked at another fisherman and imagined it was he who was on the boat, reeling in slowly. "What do you catch?"

"Mostly just Bluegills... But you can catch anything, Muskie... Northern... Bass... Crappie... Sturgeon."

"Must be plenty of fishermen," said Bill. "I saw a lot of water from the plane."

"You slept the whole flight," said Ron.

Gerald chuckled.

"I see all," said Bill.

"You didn't see your fly was down when you came out of the bathroom on the plane."

Gerald's chuckle escalated into what Ron would describe as a heehaw.

"I said, 'I see all.' I never said how long it takes me to see it."

Ron shook his head and turned to Gerald. "I understand you have an interrogation office set up for us."

Gerald nodded. "Yeah, we got one."

"Very far?"

"No, we're close now. Won't be more than twenty minutes from where we pick him up."

"Splendid."

Soon they passed billboards, office buildings, car dealerships, and chain stores. One business appeared to compete with another over who could display the highest American flag. It reminded Bill of the competition between North and South Korea, which led to the highest flag in the world. Like North Korea, the Cadillac and Hummer dealership won out.

A sign showed that the three were no longer in Madison, but Fitchburg, and Gerald turned off the Beltline. He steered them into a suburban housing development, navigating through a labyrinth of streets. Each street was wide with big houses and yards lining it. The only thing separating the houses was the color of their vinyl siding. Matching mailboxes stood at the street, and miniature signs documented when the lawns had last been sprayed. Gerald parked in front of a house being resided.

The construction crew was banging away. There were two workers on the roof laying shingles, another climbing a ladder with a couple packs on his shoulder, and two others hanging light blue siding on the front of the house. The siding contrasted with the pink foam insulation underneath.

Gerald put the car in park. "Your boy's up there somewhere. I only see five. I imagine he's one of the white ones."

"Let's get him." Bill opened the car door and stepped out. He let out a huff as he stood. Ron hurried to get ahead of him.

The smell of roofing tar stretched to the street. Ron marched up the walkway in front of Bill. His posture was straight enough that the crew could have used him to level siding. He stopped behind the two workers on ground level. "Is one of you a Mr. Ryan Westby?"

A stocky bearded man turned and showed a face coated with sweat. He wore loose jeans, a t-shirt, and leather steel-toed boots. A felt tip pen rested on his ear, and he held a hammer in his right hand. "I'm him." His voice was deep.

His coworker, Ramiro, held a length of siding and looked on

uneasily.

"Could we have a moment of your time?" asked Ron.

"Yeah, what can I help you with?" He slid the hammer in his tool belt.

"Could we speak to you in private for a moment?"

Ryan scrunched his face. "Yeah... Just a minute." He finished laying the piece of siding and told Ramiro to help out on the roof. Then he followed the agents to the car. "What's this all about?"

"C.I.A." Ron flashed his badge. "We need you to come downtown. Got some questions for you."

Confusion went over Ryan's face like a winter storm over a Midwest weather map. "C.I.A.," he said slowly. "I think there's some kind of mistake."

"No mistake. We need you downtown."

"But, I'm working." He waved his hands toward the house.

"We can see that," said Ron. "But, it's imperative you come with us at this instant. It's not a request."

"I got a crew here. I can't just leave."

Bill stepped forward. "We're not asking you."

Ryan sighed. "How long will it take?"

"We have no idea," said Ron. "Deal with your crew. Send them home if you have to. You have five minutes." He got in the car. Bill remained. He looked like a thug collecting cash for the mob. Ryan stared at Bill and then turned back to the house. Bewilderment hit him hard for the second time in as many minutes. Only one employee was there working. "What the fuck?" Ryan stomped up the walkway to the blue and pink house. "Where the hell are they?" he yelled.

His employee looked down. "Took off."

"Goddammit. Why?" Ryan grabbed the ladder rungs and climbed.

"They thought those guys were here for them."

Ryan cursed under his breath.

"So, they aren't here for them?"

He stepped on the roof. "No."

"Then why are they here?"
"'Cause some dumb friend of mine thinks he's Tom Joad."
"Who's Tom Joad?"

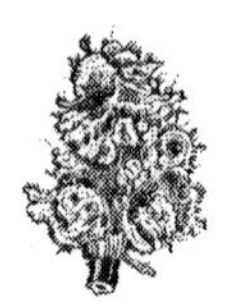

2001

Daniela dabbed sweat from her hairline and knocked at her friend's door. The air was steamy as the sun dried the puddles from the night before. The rain had been intense, but today, not a cloud. The sun caused her skin to glow, and her pants clung. Music thumped inside, reggaetón.

"¡Venga!" A woman's voice could faintly be heard yelling over the music.

Daniela pulled open the wooden door, and the music bombarded her. The bass thundered. *Como le encanta la gasolina. ¡Da me mas gasolina!* it yelled. She saw the shadow of a woman dancing in the light of the open bathroom. She made her way to the stereo to turn it down. Then she moved toward the bathroom. Her friend, a busty girl, only a hair over five feet, danced in front of the mirror while styling her hair. Daniela giggled. *"Same routine as high school,"* she said.

Her friend stopped to put mascara on her lashes. Her eyebrows had been trimmed to slivers. *"Almost ready,"* she said. Her pants, like Daniela's, were tight. A thick belt covered the top. Her midsection showed, but less than Daniela's. She was self-conscious of her belly.

"All this makeup," said Daniela. *"Are you watching the parade or are you in it?"*

The girl didn't take her eyes off the mirror. *"You have to look good. People from everywhere will be there."* She grabbed a tube of lipstick and pursed her lips, covering them with a dark red carmine.

Daniela glanced in the mirror. 'Do I not look good?' she thought. She watched her friend smack her lips. *"Luz, you look good enough. I don't want to miss the parade."*

"One second." She set down her lipstick and sprayed a cloud of perfume. Then she sanctimoniously stepped through it. Daniela coughed and migrated to the living room. Luz snapped the light off and then danced. She cranked the knob on the stereo and edged her body toward Daniela, moving her hips to the rhythm. Daniela joined in, stepping to the beat, and rolling her hips. The girls sang face to face, *"Whoa... Wha Oh... Wha Oh... Wha Oh. Boriqua, Morena, Dominicano, Colombiano. Boriqua, Morena, Cubano, Mexicano."*

Luz spun around and swayed her butt in front of Daniela. She gave it a slap. The couple laughed, and Luz shut the music off. She then picked up her purse, and they headed for the door, giggling.

Ben squinted into the wind as he stood in the back of Chi Cho's truck. He and three other boys hung onto the roll bar. Two more sat on the wheel wells, clutching the box. Isabel rode behind the stick shift in the cab, and her sister sat next to her. Only Ben and one other in the group wore shorts. The rest toughed out the ninety-degree weather in jeans. While Ben liked the fact that wearing jeans was considered dressing up, he wasn't about to do it during daylight hours.

"No piña today!" shouted one of the boys. He lifted a middle finger to the fields.

Ben smiled wide, and the wind dried his mouth.

"A day without work, I'll know what it's like to be a gringo." The kid's gelled hair stood firm in the wind, while everyone else's blew around.

Ben laughed.

One of the boys on the wheel wells spoke up. *"What do you do at Chi Cho's all day when he's working, Ben? Pork his wife?"* He was the youngest of the bunch, Fons. Just turned sixteen. He wore a baseball cap pulled low, hiding his face.

"I wish," said Ben. *"Chi Cho wears her out too much."*

They all laughed.

"We going to find some chicas today?" said Fons.

"We will, but not you," said Rico, the oldest tico in the back. *"Ya gotta have pubes to fuck."*

The group whooped.

"Hasn't stopped me yet," said Fons.

Again, they laughed.

"¡Hijo de puta!" hollered a kid by Ben. *"I'm going to get laid tonight. If I don't find anyone, Isabel's sister's lookin' good."* He thrust his pelvis at the cab while holding the roll bar tight and waved an arm in the air. *"¡Ay! ¡Ay!"* he yelled in mock female tone.

One of the boy's banged on the cab to get Chi Cho and the girls' attention. Ben turned to Rico. He was dressed in black jeans, a white t-shirt, and cowboy boots. *"So, what happens at the Saint's festival?"*

Rico turned and spit a loogie off the truck. *"Not much. They're just excited for a day in town. There's a dance up in the sports building, a big soccer game, and rodeo. The parade's just bulls and horses. Fons hopes to get lucky with one of the bulls."* He smiled Fons's way.

"Eat shit," said Fons.

"Milk that bull!" shouted the boy who had humped the cab.

Chi Cho slowed the vehicle as they entered town and turned left before the main street. He pulled up behind an old Ford Escort Wagon. The rowdy boys hopped over the side of the box, and Chi Cho and the girls slid out of the cab. One of the boys let out a woo.

"That excited over the horses?" said Chi Cho.

"Fons wants to fuck one," said Rico.

The girls snickered.

"Don't laugh," said Fons. *"You're the horses."*

They gave him an evil glare, and the group walked toward the main street. Chi Cho stepped behind Fons and gave his heel a kick. The group laughed as Fons nearly tumbled. *"Eat shit,"* he told Chi Cho.

The plaza opened up before the group as they stepped onto the main street. A few thousand people were already there.

"Let's stand in front of the church," said Chi Cho. *"It's the best spot."*

The congregation was enormous, spilling out onto the sidewalk. The group walked around them and found a place on the curb to the side of the ten-foot high doors. The words of Padre Domingo echoed out, and the smell of incense hung in the air. They looked across the street where children played on the soccer field.

The organs played, and people cleared the doorway. The group looked in to see Padre Domingo walking down the aisle. He carried a leafy branch. Four stocky men carried a bronze tub behind him. They walked through the gigantic doorway, and a man came out with a microphone in one hand and a speaker in the other. He set the speaker on the edge of the street and stared at the Padre. People filed out of the church and searched for spots on the street, many having to walk a few blocks.

"That's what they get for going to church," said one of the boys.

Commotion came from the East side of town. Padre Domingo slowly bowed his head to the man with the speaker, and the guy turned it on. *"The parade has begun!"* the man said.

Ben heard the sound of thick hooves and wooden wheels on the pavement. He leaned into the street to see a bull coming toward him. Dark objects protruded from its neck. As it grew closer, he noticed they were roses braided into its hair. It was freshly bathed and groomed. The man with the microphone raved over the beast as it passed in front of the church. His voice sounded tinny through the cheap speaker, and he walked close and waved his hand over the animal like a car model. *"Ooos"* and *"ahhs"* came from the crowd. The bulls were awarded aspersion as Padre Domingo dipped his leafy branch in holy water and shook it over their backs. The spectacle dazzled the audience, Ben included.

Three bulls had passed when Daniela and Luz edged their way into the crowd. They were in front of the soccer field, facing the church, at a slight angle to Ben and his group. *"We only missed a couple,"* said Luz.

The pair gaped at the carts. Symbols of Costa Rica, they were painted in the brightest colors, elaborate patterns covering the wheels. The designs were intricate, like la Alhambra and the sacred ruins of the new world. Once used to haul coffee and tobacco to markets, they were now ornaments. Daniela and Luz stared into the turning wheels, transfixed like tourists at Chinese New Year.

As the final bull passed, Ben and Daniela made eye contact. The priest shook the branch, and the water hung in the air between them. The sun shone through the drops, creating a rainbow.

Suddenly, a crashing sound approached.

"Yea! The dancing horses." Luz glanced at her friend, but Daniela was somewhere else. She followed her eyes to a white man across the street. Luz grinned and turned back to the parade.

Men on dancing horses trotted down the road, cutting between the pair. The crowd stared at the horses' legs as they pumped up and down. Their hooves moved quickly but took such short steps that a human could out walk them. One of Ben's friends slapped his shoulder. *"Ever seen horses like this in the States?"*

Ben and Daniela's hearts seemed to mimic the rhythm of the horses' hooves. A rider stopped directly between them. The horse stayed in place, but its legs remained in constant motion. Ben and Daniela arched their necks to find each other.

"¡Atrás!" the rider yelled. The horse slowly moved backward, its legs keeping up the hectic pace.

"¡Izquierda!" he yelled. The horse moved sideways, toward Daniela.

"¡Derecha!" The horse moved the other way, toward the church.

"They'd sooner die than disobey their masters," said one of Ben's friends. He stared into the horse's hysterical eyes, watching the drool pour from its mouth.

The rider yelled, and the horse moved forward. Ben and Daniela felt relief that the other was still there. All the horses passed, but the sound of their feet crashing against the pavement didn't. The "clack, clack, clack" echoed in their heads.

Isabel looked at Ben and followed his eyes to the girl they were fixed on. She noticed that the girl's eyes were just as steady. She tapped on her sister's shoulder and pointed to the two. She then turned to Chi Cho and showed him. He smiled and turned back to the street.

Ben and Daniela gazed at each other until a rumble tore through the crowd. The parade was ending. Once the street was cleared, the largest trucks of the area came rolling through, honking their horns. Ben later joked that it played a role in the migration of birds.

When the trucks had finally passed, Ben stepped into the street. Daniela waited, and their eyes remained fixed.

"Gringo, where you going?" Fons hollered. Ben's group of friends all looked at him.

"You didn't notice," said Isabel. *"I think he missed the whole parade staring at her."*

A crowd of people gathered in the street. Padre Domingo was showering the last of the holy water over anyone who wanted it. It soaked Ben.

"He's cute," whispered Luz.

Ben, hair wet, water trickling down his face and neck, stood in front of Daniela, who beamed. *"Hola, me llamo Ben."*

"Hi, I'm Daniela." She had an accent, but her pronunciation was clear.

Ben's eyes opened wider. "You speak English."

"Of course."

"I've never met anyone in this area that speaks English, at least good English." Ben moved his hand through his hair, flinging water.

"You hadn't met me."

Her smile overwhelmed him.

"Did you feel the need to get blessed before coming?" she said. "Needed to wash away your sins?"

"You can never be too careful. I should wash away yours, too." He moved his head in close and rubbed his hand against his scalp, spraying her as his short hair danced.

Daniela hid her face, giggling. "You look like a porcupine," she said.

"I don't know if that's good or bad."

A small stone hit the ground by their feet. *"Careful with that gringo,"* yelled Fons. *"He's a fag."*

Ben stared awkwardly, jaw moving slightly as he fumbled for words.

"That isn't your boyfriend is it?" Daniela smiled.

"I'm sorry," he said. "He's just a kid."

"It's okay. I don't want to make anyone jealous."

Ben's cheeks turned red, and the Padre walked back to the church with a few people following behind. The street cleared as people headed up the hill to the fairgrounds.

"This is my friend, Luz."

"Charmed," said Ben.

"Me, too," said Luz.

"Would you like to walk with us to the fairgrounds?" said Daniela.

"Of course."

"You two can walk by yourselves if you're going to keep speaking English," said Luz. *"I don't want to walk with two people I can't understand."*

"Spanish is fine with me," said Ben.

"We don't speak Spanish," said Luz. *"We speak Castilian."*

"Castilian's good, too."

The three started to walk to the fairgrounds. *"So, you're tall, white, and have beautiful eyes. What else is there to know about you?"* said Luz.

Ben blushed. *"That about covers it."*

"Where are you living? What do you do? Are you rich?"

"Luz." Daniela glared at her.

Luz laughed.

"I'm living in Quebrada Grande. I'm helping the people there find new markets for their crops, so they can earn a respectable wage. And, no, I'm not rich."

Daniela's eyes twinkled. *"That's so sweet."*

"Ay, he's poor." Luz looked his face over. *"Handsome, but poor."*

"Did you study international relations?" Daniela asked.

"No, English."

Daniela looked at the clouds. *"How did an American with an English degree end up working with farmers in San Carlos? And then bump into me?"*

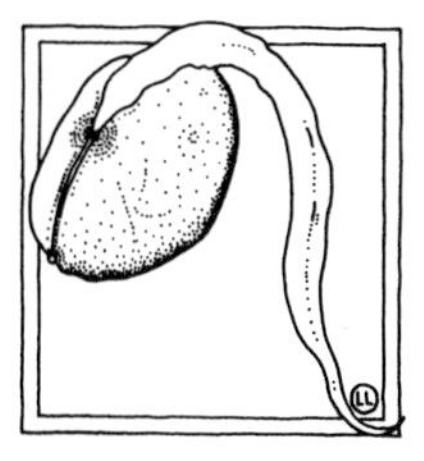

Ben cut his fried plantain and egg and mixed it with the gallo pinto. He ate a couple of bites and took a drink of agua dulce. Chi Cho and David were at the table with him, David eating his gallo pinto from a bowl. Isabel was in the kitchen while Miguel played on the living room floor. The sound of gravel snapping under tires came from outside, and the three at the table looked out the open door. A small, dark green Toyota turned in the driveway.

"*¡Daniela!*" yelled David. He dropped a spoonful of rice and beans and ran out the door.

Isabel put down her work and stared outside with the boys. A girl, slim and curvy, stepped out of the car. Her clothes were tight, showing all, as was the style. She was a comely girl of twenty six, standing five eight. The waxing crescent of her bellybutton peeked out from under her shirt. David squealed at her feet. From inside they heard the car door click and watched her hug the young boy. She grabbed his hand and skipped to the house.

Ben rose from the table as the two neared the door. He met Daniela just inside, and they threw their arms around each other, squeezing tightly. His hands slid to her hips, and her's to his thick neck. They brought their lips together for the first time in two months. Miguel let out a shrill yell, and they released. Daniela clutched Ben as she looked over his shoulder at Miguel. "*What?*" she said in a voice reserved for pets, babies, and lovers. *"You want attention, too?"* She stooped down and scooped up the young child. *"Hi, Miguel."* She kissed him on the head several times.

Isabel and Chi Cho exchanged a peck on the cheek with her. Chi Cho made a lewd gesture to Ben as he did so. Isabel then took her by the hand and led her to the table. *"You sit there. I'm going to get you a coffee, and you can tell me everything you've been up to."* She poured two mugs full and carried them over. *"It's been so long. How is everything?"*

Ben rubbed Daniela's shoulders.

"It's been good, just a little lonely."

"You can come over here anytime you want," said Isabel.

"I've been so busy teaching," she said. *"But I just gave all my students a project to occupy them for the next week and a half. I'm ready for a break."* She rubbed Ben's hand.

"Come on, Ben. Let's go check the car's fluids. Let these hens roost." Chi Cho tugged on the back of his shirt.

Isabel glared at him, and Ben laughed. He leaned forward, put his hands on Daniela's thighs, and gave a squeeze, then tenderly kissed her neck. She quivered. He ran his fingers down her arm as he departed.

"So, will you be at the coast all that time?"

Daniela sat smiling, eyes closed, for a moment before rejoining Isabel. *"Huh?"*

Isabel laughed. *"The coast, you'll be there the whole time?"*

"Sí, Tamarindo," she said.

"Ahhh, Tamarindo. I keep telling Chi Cho that the kids have to see Guanacaste."

"Have you been?" asked Daniela.

Isabel frowned. *"No. Never farther than Puntarenas."*

"Puntarenas is good." Daniela picked up her coffee for the first time. *"But we prefer Tamarindo. Ben likes the waves for surfing."*

Isabel shook her head. *"I don't think I want to try that."*

"I do it with Ben sometimes, but it's so much work. I can't do it for more than an hour."

"Then I couldn't do it for a minute."

"You'll have to go sometime. We can surf together."

"We'd love to, but I'll have to think about surfing."

Ben drove Daniela's Toyota along the dirt path that led behind Chi Cho's house. There were two buildings there of unpainted, corrugated tin. Chi Cho stood outside one while Ben made a y turn and backed in. He shut off the car, hopped out, and slammed the door.

"Ay, you gringos always bang the doors." Chi Cho pulled the building's door closed, and it grew dim. Three incandescent bulbs burned dully.

"You ticos shut the door so softly," said Ben. *"You think the car's going to fall apart. My first year here I thought a taxi driver was going to fight me for slamming his door too hard."*

Chi Cho laughed. *"Maybe we're just not used to having nice things."* He reached under a work bench and pulled out a key, then moved to a rusty steel cabinet. Ben opened the trunk, and Chi Cho carried over two enormous black duffel bags with CCM logos on the ends.

Ben walked to the cabinet. *"Where's the other one?"* he said.

"Only two are ready."

"You said a hundred twenty."

"Sí, but only eighty are bagged." Chi Cho grabbed a large digital scale, a roll of plastic, and a vacuum sealer, then laid them on the work bench. *"This way you can see it up close, make sure it's top grade."*

"I know it's top grade. I came out and smoked some last night. Didn't notice there weren't three bags, though."

"I thought I heard you out here." Chi Cho pulled a plastic mixing

bowl and a plump black garbage bag from the bottom of the cabinet.

"Thought I heard you snoring," said Ben.

"Must have been Isabel." He set the bowl on the scale.

"Yeah, right." Ben laughed as he picked up the roll of plastic and started cutting it into two foot lengths. He stuck one end in the vacuum sealer and melted it shut. Chi Cho reached in the garbage bag and lifted out the neatly trimmed marijuana buds in handfuls, tossing them in the bowl. Small buds fell on the table and the dirty floor. When the scale hit four hundred forty eight grams Chi Cho dumped the bowl into a bag and set it on the bench. Ben then stuck the unsealed end of the bag in the vacuum sealer and closed it off.

Chi Cho's hands became sticky from handling the weed, and he left THC finger prints on each bag. Ben picked up a full one, put it to his nose, and took several large whiffs. He lifted out a large green crystal laden bud. Orange hairs dotted it. He tossed it back in and put the bag to his nose.

"Beautiful, isn't it?" said Chi Cho.

"Sí, probably the closest thing you'll ever see to frost covered plants."

"I'll see snow someday."

"I hope you do," said Ben. His eyes were narrow as he brought the bag from his nose and exhaled. *"I hope you do."*

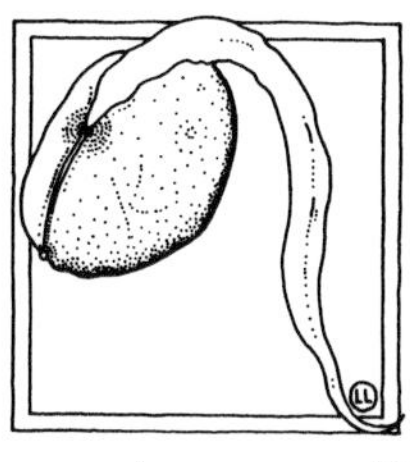

Ron Numbers and Bill Larimore sat apart during their flight between Atlanta and San Jose. They didn't acknowledge each other when passing. Ron carried a briefcase as he hit customs. Bill, wearing dress slacks and a polo shirt, waited in line. The sun hadn't yet hit its zenith, and they weren't to meet till six.

Outside of baggage, a man waved to Ron. He wore a smile above his shiny shoes and tie. He'd left the agency four years ago to work for a private firm.

"Nice to see you," said Ron.

The two shook hands.

"Likewise. Been a long time, eh?"

"Sure has." Ron looked him over. He'd expected some sort of change. Deeper voice, a scar, wrinkled face, something.

"Unfortunately, it just started to rain." The man pointed outside. "But you'll have to get used to that. I'll get the car. Come out when you see a blue Toyota."

"Thanks, Jack."

The man holding a newspaper over his head darted into the rain. His tie swung, and water flew from his heels. Ron spotted Bill approaching from the corner of his eye. He wheeled a suitcase behind and winked as he passed.

"Taxi?" said a man by the door.

"Sí," said Bill. *"Hotel Del Rey."* He handed the man his bag, and Ron watched the driver put it in the trunk of a worn out red taxi. The yellow signs on its doors were cracked and peeling.

'He could at least take one of the orange ones,' he thought.

Bill noticed a Church's Chicken and Papa John's Pizza window attached to the airport. He pointed to it, and the driver nodded. Then Bill hurried to the restaurant window.

Ron gasped at the sight and then eyed the car. '395019.' He ran the blue numbers of its license plate through his head. 'Driver: five foot five. Late thirties. Short hair, none on face. Dark blue jeans. Green button down, short sleeve shirt.'

Ron stuck a foot out the doorway as he saw the driver jump in the car. He stood listening for the engine to start.

Bill stood before the stand, eyes fixed on the fried chicken. A young man in a red and yellow uniform was behind the counter. A couple of others worked in the kitchen. *"Two pieces of chicken,"* said Bill. *"One leg and one big tit."*

The boy smirked. He grabbed a couple of pieces from the glass display and dropped them back in the fryer. He stood by with his palm on the basket handle for a minute and then brought them back up. Oil seeped from the chicken as he laid the pieces in a box.

"A Pepsi, too," said Bill.

The boy nodded and filled a paper cup, then placed the box of chicken in a bag with napkins. *"Three thousand colones,"* he said.

Bill handed him a crisp blue ten thousand note.

"Gracias."

Bill took his change and jogged to the cab. Water dampened his pant legs. He hopped in front and slammed the door.

The driver glared at the door, then pulled out. *"El Hotel Del Rey is bad,"* he said. *"I can take you to a better place."*

"I'm going to Del Rey," said Bill.

"Okay. Okay. I understand." The driver smiled.

Bill opened the box of chicken, grabbed the breast, and brought it to his lips. He bit into it, and flakes of battered skin fell on his lap. His head swam as the grease saturated his mouth. Beads of sweat grew on his brow. It made him oblivious to the driver's glare.

They cruised down the highway toward San Jose, passing the expensive airport hotels. Bill looked at a sign advertising tiny trucks for under five hundred thousand colones and cleaned the last bit of meat from the breast bone. He tossed it back in the box and reached for his soda, grabbing it with his fingers extended to avoid getting grease on the cup. He took a long sip and went for the drumstick. 'Nothing like that first bite of skin,' he thought.

"So, you've been to Costa Rica before?" asked the driver.

"Sí." Bill paused to swallow. *"Many times."*

"You a businessman?"

"Correcto."

"And you like the ticas?" The driver giggled.

Bill gnawed on the end of the bone. *"Of course. I like the ticas and the casinos."*

"Sí, the Americans like the ticas, the casinos, and the drugs." He counted each on his fingers.

"No drugs for me. Only alcohol and cigarettes. Sometimes a cigar." Bill picked the last pieces of meat from the leg and tossed it in the box. He futilely attempted to wipe the grease from his hands, then stuffed the napkins in the box and put it on the floor. He spotted the crumbs of skin on his pants and shook them off. The driver scowled, and the Virgin Mary looked on from the dash.

"Mind if I smoke?"

The driver acquiesced, and Bill drew a pack of Camel Lights from his jacket. He pulled out a cig, placed it between his lips, and deftly lit it. He leaned back as he inhaled, then cracked the window and sighed as the smoke rolled from his mouth. Raindrops dotted his shoulder. The buildings lining the road became more numerous and grew in size. Traffic lights sprouted up, and the driver hooked a left into the heart of the city. Bill peeked under the veil—people walking under umbrellas, vendors on corners hawking lotto tickets, hobos, shoeless, wrapped in dirty blankets under two-foot roof overhangs, scores of people attempting to stay dry while waiting for buses, taxi drivers in long lines waiting for passengers, and business owners standing in doorways watching the day unfold. In the Plaza de la Cultura, he saw the Gran Hotel and National Theater, both towering neoclassical structures, built with colones from coffee barons of the late nineteenth century. Bill had heard that Truman, Kennedy, Carter, King Pelé, whoever that was, and John Wayne had all stayed at the Gran. And that it was reasonably priced, but he wasn't interested. His mouth raised into a grin, however, as they turned onto Calle 6, and a different neoclassical building came into view. It was six stories high and pink. Like the Gran Hotel and the Theater, it, too, was a National Treasure. Gunmen had been positioned on its roof during The 1948 Revolution. Casino Tropical and The Horseshoe stood at lower elevations around it. The driver pulled the car up next to the behemoth building, put it in park, and dashed into the rain. Gathering Bill's suitcase as quickly as possible, he ran up the steps of Hotel Del Rey. Bill left the chicken box behind and followed the driver to the top of the stairs.

"I'm with him," the driver told the security guards.

With the flick of a metal detecting wand, a guard waved him through. He hurried across the pink tile and handed the suitcase to a hotel employee, an older man in a worn blazer and slacks. He had slicked back hair.

The driver glanced into the smoky bar and met Bill at the door. *"Eighteen thousand colones, please."*

Bill reached in his wallet and fished out two ten thousand notes. *"Keep the change,"* he said.

"Gracias." The driver took one last look in the bar and darted out.

Bill walked to the front desk, favoring one leg. The man in the blazer and slacks smiled, his face cleanly shaven except for a well-groomed mustache. "Hello," he said. "How can I help you?"

"Bill Larimore."

"Yes, uh, Mr. Larimore." The man paged through a notebook. "We have you booked in a single room. You wanted a... Sixth floor room with a balcony, correct?"

"That's right."

"Great. It has a super view of the city."

Bill gave him a credit card.

"And, was it three days that you planned to stay for?"

"For now. I'll let you know tomorrow."

"Can you sign this, please?"

Bill grabbed the pen with his left hand.

"Great. Here is your room key, number 601. If you need anything, ask for me, Eduardo." His large smile was constant.

"Could you have someone take my bag up?" said Bill. "I feel like a drink."

"No problem, sir. You know about our facilities?"

"Oh, yeah." Bill slapped the counter and headed to the bar. The air on the other side of the doorway was hazy with smoke. Bill stopped and took out a Camel. He eyed the girls as he lit it. A few raised their eyebrows, winked, and kissed the air. There were close to twenty, and only six guys. They ranged from short to tall, light skin to dark, A cup to D. They had dusky eyes and hair except a couple bleached blonde. A whole lot of makeup. Most wore tight jeans and shirts, a few short skirts. All were flashing cleavage. Bill winked and nodded to them. 'Bold college girls out on the town,' he thought.

He stepped up to the wraparound bar. A big lacquered blue marlin was atop it, nose pointing to a television. Liquor bottles covered the shelves. *"Can I get a Jack and Coke?"*

"Of course," the bartender said with a sweet voice. *"I'll be right back."*

Bill leaned over the counter and stared at her ass. Her heels clicked as she moved. She returned with the drink, and Bill looked back and forth between her eyes and red tube top. *"What do I owe, guapa?"*

"Two thousand colones."

Bill gave her ten thousand colones. *"Just hold onto it. I'll be getting a couple more."*

He gave her one last look and walked to a table. Just as he sat his drink down and pulled out a chair, a woman in a tight red dress approached. He guessed she was in her mid-thirties. Her eyebrows were plucked and painted on. Her skin, like his own, appeared granular from years of smoking.

"You looking for a good time?" She set her hand on his thigh.

Bill pushed it away. "Not with you."

"Come on. I know how to pleasure a man better than these little girls." Her accent was thick. "I'm cheaper, too."

"Not interested." Bill sat in the chair.

"Thirty thousand colones. I'll go for as long as you want." She leaned in and cupped his balls.

Bill put his lips close to her ear. *"Get the fuck out of here before I knock your teeth out."*

The woman's makeup didn't hide her fear, and she quickly retreated. She repositioned herself against a wall, avoiding the eyes of the others.

Bill took a drink and looked about the room. The women's eyes connected with his, beckoning. He scanned the room and then devoted time to individually studying each woman. He liked the shy girls. It was innocence he was after, and he narrowed his choices to three. 'Great body, but skin a little too dark,' he thought. 'Other girl's tits are fuller, but she's a little short.' He locked on one. 'Just right. Five foot six inches. Couldn't be much over eighteen,' he figured. She had golden caramel skin complimented by dark straight hair hanging just below the shoulders. Thick juicy legs and a captivatingly round ass. Her waist was thin, C cups above, and her lower lip was copious. 'Better get her before some other gringo.' He tipped the rest of his drink back and bee lined for her.

Bill watched her as he approached, and she didn't look at his face until he was close. Her eyes had a hard look that he hadn't expected. Her skirt was frayed around its bottom. *"Hola."* He gave her a wide smile.

The smell of his drink went straight to her nose. She looked at the red skin under his thinning hair. *"Want to go to your room?"*

Bill stepped back and motioned to the bar. *"Would you like to have a drink first?"*

"Wouldn't you rather go to your room?"

She looked directly in his eyes for the first time, and Bill was reminded of the looks he got from popular girls in high school. Boredom. He searched for words, thinking of how he wanted to avoid a situation that seemed mechanical. He wanted an intimate connection, or at least the simulation of one. *"Won't you sit with me for a few minutes before going upstairs?"*

"Okay." She gave in, but her countenance didn't.

Bill arranged two bar stools and ordered another Jack and Coke. *"What would you like?"* he said.

"Solamente un Coke." She avoided his eyes.

"Just a Coke for her," he told the bartender.

The woman filled a glass and put it before her. The girl picked up the drink and sipped it through the straw, staring at the grains in the bar.

"Do you have a name?" said Bill.

"Flora."

"I'm Bill." He smiled. *"How old are you?"*

"Nineteen."

Bill huffed. *"Listen, Flora. I don't know what's going on, but the rest of the girls in here would be happy to talk to me."*

She bit her lip and stared down.

"I just want to get to know you," he said.

She looked up from the bar with glassy eyes. *"I'm a college student. I live on my own. No family."*

Bill gave a tender look. *"Life can be rough,"* he said. He felt alive in his pants and wanted to put his arms around her. "*Would you still accompany me to my room?*"

"*Sí,*" she said.

Bill took Flora's hand and led her out while a couple of girls glowered. He stopped at the front desk. "*Eduardo, Flora will be joining me.*"

She took a health card from her purse and handed it to him.

Eduardo looked between her and the card and handed it back. "*That's five thousand for us.*"

Bill pulled crinkled bills from his pocket and dug out a five thousand note. He then slipped his arm around Flora's back and walked her to the elevator.

The old man watched them. Her puffy eyes. Frayed dress. Luscious thighs. He held his grin until the elevator closed.

2001

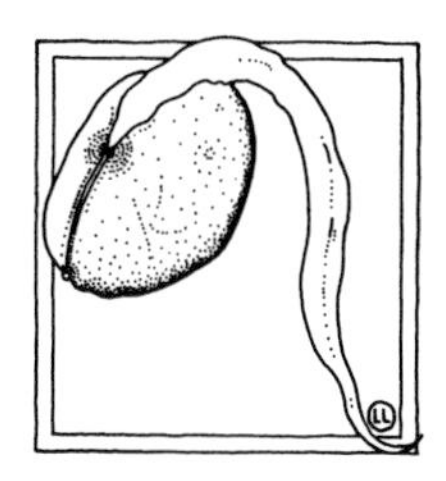

The pair walked from the forest shade to a patch of intense sun, a fairly even spot on the North side of the hill. The red clay beneath them was soft with moisture. The air was humid, and they breathed heavily. Dark pockets of perspiration stood out on their shirts.

"This water isn't going to last." Ben set two four liter bottles in the shade.

"Hopefully, long enough," said Chi Cho. He set down two more. A pool of sweat sat in the cavity at the base of his neck.

The two gathered the tools they had set out the night before, two machetes, one hatchet, and a bow saw. Ben handed a machete to Chi Cho. *"Let's clean the area."*

"All this?" Chi Cho stared at the thicket.

"All," said Ben.

They slipped on their gloves and began hacking weeds under the noise of birds. The grass fell with one swipe, and a metallic ting rang through the forest. The brambles were tougher. They required more work and produced a less harmonic sound.

Ben stared up through the opening. He noted the sun and approximated where it would be throughout the day. *"This tree has to go."* His eyes rested on a tree with smooth green and brown speckled bark. It was eight inches wide, twenty feet tall. He unsheathed the bow saw and began dragging it back and forth against the tree, keeping a rhythm. The blade went easily into the moist wood, but the task grew difficult as he worked the blade further in. The muscles in his arms and chest grew tight. His face glistened. He stopped sawing and let out a pant. *"You want to help me?"*

Chi Cho slowly turned toward him. Even a swing of the neck felt difficult in the heat. He threw his machete into the hard clay and walked over, his shoulders and head drooping.

"Pull this back as I cut. It's pinching the blade."

Chi Cho grabbed the tree and pulled hard as Ben dug the blade further in. After a dozen pulls on the saw, a crack sounded from the tree, followed by the sound of birds fleeing their perches. Then there was a crash as the tree hit the forest floor. Ben took the saw to a piece of bark that still held the tree to the stump. He cut through it with a few swipes and pushed it to the ground. His heart was beating fast. *"Looks like three more to go."*

"Which ones?" said Chi Cho.

"That, that, and that." Ben pointed at trees surrounding the sunny patch.

"Why those? They're not blocking any sun."

"They will this afternoon." Ben gulped water from one of the jugs. It made a popping sound as he withdrew it from his lips. *"In Wisconsin, I once cut down a beautiful walnut tree, a little bigger than this."* He motioned toward the fallen tree. *"I didn't want to, but it would have cost me a few thousand dollars in sun light."*

"I don't want that," said Chi Cho. *"Chop away. I just hope no one stumbles on this. The land is protected."*

"We'll know if they do. That's why we got the motion cameras."

Ben handed the jug to Chi Cho and moved to the next tree. Chi Cho chugged from the bottle and then returned to the weeds. The machete sang against them while the bow saw growled. The birds chimed in, and Chi Cho and Ben added pants and groans. A half hour in, their music was interrupted.

Chi Cho screamed.

Ben stopped the saw and looked behind him. Chi Cho was jumping around, rubbing his knee. His face was scrunched up like he'd sucked a lemon.

"Thorns?" said Ben.

"Sí, big fucking thorns."

Ben shook his head. *"That'll happen."*

"Hijo de puta," said Chi Cho. He rolled his pant leg up and inspected the damage. Blood oozed out. He rolled his pants down and allowed the blood to stain his jeans.

Once again they returned to their work, tools harmonizing and sweat dripping. They'd pause for water breaks every twenty to thirty minutes. Other than that, their music was continuous. Now and again it would be punctuated by a loud crack and a bass note from a tree hitting the forest floor. After three hours of the arduous work Ben and Chi Cho sat on the clay in the middle of the patch.

"Looks like a little field," said Chi Cho. *"Preparing it for piña."* He squeezed his shirt, and water seeped out.

"Sí." Ben looked over the patch and then the sky. *"We shouldn't have to worry about flyovers here. In the U.S. I was always worried about planes. Not here. Still, we'll cover the ground with the weeds."* He waved a weary arm as he spoke.

Chi Cho scraped up some clay in his hand. *"What do we got to do to make this good for dope?"*

Ben sucked in a long breath. *"We're going to have to come back in the night and burn this stuff. We'll have to chop the trees. Then we'll burn it slowly and mix the coals with the clay. Should provide a good growing medium."*

"You've done it before?"

"No, it's a method people used here a thousand years ago."

"Lots of hours."

"If you don't like that idea, we could always do what the California growers do, dig out big holes and replace them with potting soil."

"Expensive," said Chi Cho.

"Sí, and you can imagine hiking all those bags in."

Chi Cho shook his head. *"Gringos are crazy."*

"It's what they're taught. Buy new stuff. Throw out the old." Ben pushed himself up and gathered the tools. He walked into the woods and slid them under a pile of brush. "Ahhh!" he screamed.

Chi Cho turned quickly to his friend with images of poisonous snakes dancing in his mind.

Ben swatted at his forearm. He ripped off his shirt and smacked his body.

A great guffaw came from Chi Cho. *"Ants grandes!"* he laughed.

Ben looked over his shirt to make sure they were gone. He then inspected the two red marks where an ant had broken his skin.

Chi Cho walked over and looked at the bites. *"Leaf cutter ants,"* he said. *"Must have thought you were a plant. Tried to eat you."*

"Let's get the fuck out of here," said Ben.

"Woo, that was great, gringo. You should have seen the look on your face."

Ben slipped on his shirt, and they entered the dense forest.

"We coming back out tonight?" said Chi Cho.

"Fuck that. I'm resting tonight," said Ben. *"We'll have a full night's work tomorrow. And, I'm bringing poison out. Won't have any assholes eating our plants."*

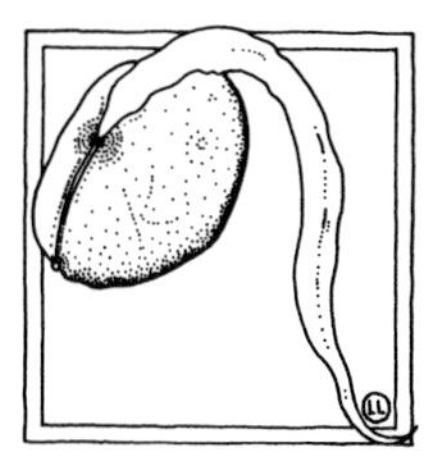

It was six o'clock, and Ron sat in a cushy chair of the Marriott lobby. He glanced at his watch, then to the door. He was too frustrated to read, and the room smelled of cleaners. Guests moved in and out the doors. A man in a crisp gray suit outlined in red greeted them. Eight gold buttons formed a rectangle on his torso, white gloves covered his hands, and a doorman's hat sat atop his head. Bellboys in crimson suits wheeled in luggage. Seven minutes later, Bill strutted in. His clothes were spotted with rain. He wiped it from his thinning hair and stamped his feet, then quickly scanned the room while walking toward Ron. "Hell of a rainstorm," he said.

Ron nodded.

"We going to the bar?" Bill looked up at the domed ceiling.

Ron stuck his files in his briefcase and followed him across the granite floor. Inside the doorway of the restaurant, a host in a cream colored suit greeted them. "Good evening. Will you be having dinner or drinks?"

"Just drinks," said Bill.

"Follow me this way, please." He led them into the tavern. Ten guys were huddled by the bar, staring at the television. World Cup matches. A man in a light gray suit let out a yelp, and a cheer broke out amongst his group. They all high-fived. The man had a nickel-sized bald spot on the crown of his head. He and his three friends wore expensive suits. They looked to be in their thirties. All were clean shaven except for one with a tuft of hair below his lip. As they tipped back their drinks, Ron noticed their teeth were as pearly as the white of their eyes.

"I apologize," said the host. "Some guests are a little excited about the football."

"Can we sit there?" Ron pointed to a table in the corner.

"Of course." The host escorted them to the secluded spot and handed them drink menus.

Ron waved them off. "Coffee for me. Cream and sugar."

"I'll have the same, black." Bill rubbed at his bloodshot eyes.

"One minute." He turned and sped off.

Another cheer came from the bar. *"¡Viva Argentina!"* The man with the hairy under lip danced with another. His light blue suit shook. Bill's eyes moved from the bar back to Ron. "What's new?"

"Not much. " He set his briefcase on the table. "We got news from Robert, though."

Another man in a cream jacket approached with their coffee.

"Could you quiet them, please?" said Ron.

"Yes, I will ask."

"You can leave the pot here," said Bill.

The man stared, then he set down the pot and walked away.

"Fuckin' idiot," said Bill.

Ron dipped sugar from a bowl. "Hey, Bill. Does 395019 ring a bell?"

Bill stared and took a swig of coffee.

"The plate on a car. Driver, five foot five. Late thirties. Short hair, none facial. Dark blue jeans. White, button down, short sleeve shirt."

"What's my taxi have to do with this?" Bill looked to the waiter talking with the men at the bar, then saw him wave his hand in their direction. The four Argentineans gawked.

"I saw you hand him your bag and walk away," said Ron.

"No one gets away with my stuff. Don't worry."

"I don't want to see it again."

Bill looked back at the group. They were quiet as they watched the tube. The bartender also watched it while slowly wiping glasses. "Let's hear the news," he said.

Ron pushed his coffee aside and cracked the briefcase. He took out a folder and handed it to Bill. "Our impostor in Peru claims he got the job through Inglés America. Story checks out. The school was expecting Starosta, but Roesing showed up." He blew on his coffee and took a sip. "The school still paid the money to Starosta. Then Starosta paid the money back through money orders. Then the school paid Roesing."

"Someone at the school knows Starosta," said Bill.

"Yeah, someone's on it."

Bill threw the files on the table. "One thing's missing. Why does his passport show he's in Peru? If he's using his along with Westby's, it would show one of them leaving a country he never went to. Only way it would work is if he made it back to the U.S. without passing through customs"

"Yeah, I'm assuming that's the case," said Ron. "Unfortunately, Roesing's no help."

"He's been thoroughly broken down?"

"Yeah, he's been broken. He'd have to be a mastermind to hold up."

Bill poured coffee in his cup and stared off. Yelling came from the bar, and he and Ron turned. Two men argued with the Argentineans. *"For fuck's sake! They're playing Serbia!"* one yelled.

"What's going on?" said Ron.

Bill chuckled. "Two Germans got sick of the Argentineans." He laughed thunderously, and his face reddened as he watched.

Two of the Argentineans looked at Bill, the one with the bald spot and one in a pinstriped suit.

Ron and Bill watched the bartender intervene between the two parties. *"There's no fighting in this bar,"* he said. *"You get along, or you leave."*

The Germans and Argentineans shook hands and called a truce with shots of Scotch. *"Hope we play,"* said one. *"We'll crush you."*

"Come to Germany. We'll watch it together." They quieted and once again fixed their eyes to the screen.

"I did some grunt work," said Ron. "Flashed his picture at the airport."

"How'd it work?"

"They knew him. Nice guy, good tipper, bit of a flirt. One girl remembered him coming through a week ago. No one's seen him leave, yet."

"Fucker could be right here," said Bill.

"All the hotels in the country have been notified. If he goes to one as himself or Ryan Westby, we got him."

"Unless he has more I.D.s." Bill stared in his cup. "I gotta use the pisser," he said. He groaned and pushed his bulky frame from the chair.

Ron watched him walk toward the bar. He saw the man in the gray suit exchange words with him.

"Why are you not watching fútbol?" The man slapped him on the back and took a big drink. Ron saw the bald spot as he tipped his head.

Bill brushed his arm away.

The man then looked him in the eyes, swaying. Beads of sweat dotted his smooth, oily skin. *"If my country's team was that bad, I wouldn't watch either."* He laughed.

Bill moved close to the man's ear. *"Your country's a banana republic."* He turned agilely on his heel and went into the bathroom. He smiled in the mirror as he passed, and his dimples blazed as he undid his belt and threw back his head.

The door creaked open. Bill looked from the corner of his eye. It was the Argentinean. He stifled his spray and pulled up his boxers. The elastic snapped against his skin. He heard the man's feet move quickly on the tile and saw a leg coming toward him. *"Hij..."*

Bill grabbed the bottom of the man's foot and yanked up, thrusting it over his head. The man did half a flip, and Bill marked the one-inch tile where his head would hit. He zipped up as the man's bald spot collided with the floor, then buckled up and stepped over him. *"Soccer's for faggots,"* he said, then smiled in the mirror as he left.

In the bar, Bill walked smoothly to the television, his limp unnoticeable. *"Argentina is winning!"* he yelled.

The men cheered and slapped his back.

"And Germany?" he said.

"They won earlier," said one of the Germans.

"Drinks on me." Bill threw thirty thousand colones on the bar. *"This should take care of ours, too,"* he told the bartender. He slapped the people's backs, high-fived them, and walked back to his table. His smile faded as he drew near. "Put your jacket on. Let's go," he whispered.

"Huh?"

Bill looked Ron in the eye. "Let's go."

Ron tossed his papers in his briefcase and followed Bill to the door.

"¡Pura Vida!" Bill yelled as they left.

"¡Pura Vida!" The people held their glasses in the air.

The sound faded as they entered the lobby, and their shoes clicked as they moved across the granite floor.

"I laid him out," said Bill.

Ron's face contorted. "What? You serious?"

"Fuckin' jumped me... While pissin'. I'd stay in your room. Relocate. The Mango across the street. Better place. Message me." Bill turned left, toward the door, and Ron right, toward the elevator. The doorman touched his white glove to his hat as he passed. Another worker opened a taxi door. *"El Radisson,"* said Bill. *"The casino."*

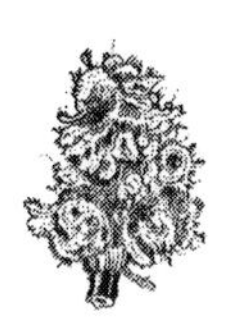

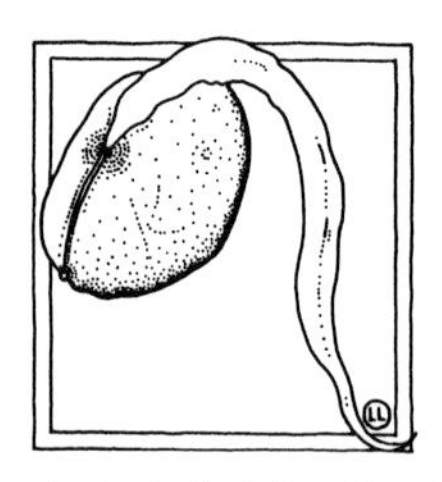

The couple let out a sigh as they entered Tamarindo. The six-hour drive over rough, narrow roads had been tiresome, but the sexual tension had made them restless. Ben stroked Daniela's thigh, and she stared into his face with narrowed eyes. They passed a small surf shop on their left. The Pacific was visible to their right. People moved about in bathing suits, some wearing sandals, others barefoot. Power lines and trees hung over the road, palms and others with big waxy leaves. Strangler figs choked at them. Ben and Daniela's windows remained up, locking the stifling heat of Guanacaste outside. The smell of synthetic air freshener permeated the car.

The buildings grew from small shops to elephantine hotels on the beach side. Bob Dylan's *Gospel Plow* howled from the radio as they hooked a left before the main street dead-ended into a hotel. The road was dirt, like all but the main street. Ben bayed along to the music, "Keep your hand on that plow, hold on."

Daniela giggled.

"You know the lines," he said. "Sing it."

Daniela joined in, a step behind. "Well I never been to heaven, but I've heard the streets up there are lined with gold. Keep your hand on that plow, hold on. Oh Lord, Oh Lord, keep your hand on that plow, hold on." They lumbered through it, Ben's voice rougher than Bob's, Daniela's smooth, but oddly accented.

"¡Ay! Perfect harmony," Ben hollered.

He drove slow to avoid bumps in the road. People on the dirt path stared at the movement and hubbub in the car. A group of small wooden buildings with shingled roofs came into view, and Ben turned right into a small lot in front of them. He left the car running, and Dylan's voice yowled inside.

"Ready to brave the heat?" he said.

"The faster we'll get to the air conditioning," said Daniela.

"And the bedroom." Ben lifted his eyebrows.

They hopped out of the car, and Ben locked the doors. His shoulders fell under the weight of the sun. The song left his tongue. They looked at the pool and walked into the building closest to the road. Ben let out an "ah" as he stepped into the cool air. *"¡Larissa, buenas tardes!"*

A thin blonde in her late forties looked up from a desk. She wore earrings of shell and a silver necklace. *"Ah, how are you?"* She hurried over and exchanged a kiss on the cheek with each of them.

"We're good," said Ben.

"It's been a while."

"A few months," he said. *"We never go longer than that."*

"And, always a weekday for that cheap price."

"You gave it to me once. Now you have to live with it."

"One of these times you'll come, and I'll be booked up." She walked to the desk and looked over a large book. *"How long you plan on staying?"*

Ben glanced at Daniela. *"Maybe a full week."*

"Okay, I'll give you the keys to cabin number five. No reservations for it this week. Just stop in on Thursday to let me know if you want it for the weekend."

"Will do."

"If you don't, I'll be knocking at your door."

"Gracias." Daniela smiled before leaving, and Ben waved.

They walked back to the car, gathered the luggage from the back seat, and carried it up a brick path to the court yard. Birds sang from the trees. A white man sat in a lounge chair by the pool. He lifted a wide-brimmed hat from his face and watched them. The outside of the building was a cinnamon colored wood. Daniela put her nose to it.

"It's been treated, love. No scent."

"Smells like chemicals," she said.

Ben threw the door open. A blue futon sat to the left, a small kitchen and dining room to the right. A bedroom with an attached bathroom lay behind the futon on a raised level. Ben dropped his luggage, turned on the air conditioning, and slammed the windows closed. *"Time to make this place a refrigerator."* A hum filled the cabin, and the linen curtains danced in front of the machine. Ben headed back out to grab the bags. He felt the man's eyes on him as he passed the pool and gave him a glance. The guy looked to be in his thirties. His ghost white skin glistened with sunscreen, contrasting with the dark black hair on his chest and abs. Ben noticed his colorful swim trunks and new flip-flops and wondered if he'd just gotten them from a beach store. The sunglasses and hat also looked to be of that quality. Ben unlocked the trunk, hoisted out two of the hockey bags, and slammed it close. As he walked up the brick path, a duffel bag over each shoulder, he nodded to a cleaning lady. Perspiration gathered on his neck and back.

"Lotta luggage there," said the guy. "Big bags."

"Yep, they're big." Ben didn't slow his pace. He opened the cabin's door, stuck the bags under the futon, and went back for the third, ignoring the man. As he pulled the last from the trunk, he peeked around the edge. The man was watching him. 'Fuck,' he thought before slamming the trunk and heading up the path.

"Another bag," said the guy. "You movin' in?"

"Bedding," said Ben. "My girlfriend's paranoid about hotel stuff."

The man chuckled, and Ben entered the cabin and locked the door. Daniela was unpacking. He walked to the kitchen for a glass of water and then went to the window, peeling back the curtain.

"What are you doing over there?" said Daniela.

"Nothing." He dropped the curtain.

"You look tense."

Ben mounted the stairs to the bedroom. *"It's just that guy at the pool. He was making me nervous."*

"How?"

"Just looking at me. Asking questions."

"If I were him, I'd be looking at you and asking questions, too." Daniela leaned in and kissed him, putting her arms around his neck. Ben grasped her butt, and she pushed him to the bed. She placed a knee on each side of his waist, bit his lip, and worked her mouth over his neck and earlobes. She took off his shirt and kissed his chest. Then she leaned back and removed her shirt while Ben unbuttoned her pants. As she moved her lips back to his, Ben squeezed her breasts and then moved his hands to the hinges of her white lacy bra. Her breasts dropped, and he cupped them. Daniela held them over his face. He moved his tongue over her small, dark nipples and around the circumference of her breasts. The foreplay lasted a half an hour, but after the long separation, the sex didn't reach ten minutes. Tears were at the edge of Daniela's eyes.

"What's the matter?" he said.

"I just missed you so much."

Ben and Daniela woke to banging at the door. The clock read eight forty, and light cut in around the curtains. The air conditioner hummed. Daniela threw on shorts and a tank top and scurried to the door. Ben rolled over, turning his back to the noise. "Wait!" He jumped up. "Look out the window. See who it is."

Daniela pulled back the curtain to see a scruffy gringo. He had greasy shoulder length hair and a long goatee. A hiking pack covered his back, and a blue-nosed pit bull stood to his right. "Just Charles," she said.

She opened the door. *"Hola, Charles."*

"Buenos días." Charles released the dog, and it ran around Daniela, excitedly throwing its body into her legs.

Daniela giggled and patted his side. *"Careful, Blue. Careful."*

Ben looked groggily up from bed. "Blue! Stop it!" he yelled.

Blue took off, leaped to the bed, and stuck his nose in Ben's face.

"Hey," said Ben. He wrapped his arms around the dog's body and bear hugged him. The dog's white belly showed. He kicked his legs and convulsed until he squirmed free. Then he stood and wiped his mouth across Ben's chest, leaving a viscous trail.

"Uhh!" yelled Ben. "Get the fuck off me." He pushed the dog, and Blue fell awkwardly from the bed. "Down! Down!" he said.

Ben slipped on a pair of shorts and walked to the bathroom. He then moistened a wash cloth and scrubbed at the drool. Red, itchy patches speckled his body where the dog had rubbed against him. He threw the wash cloth on the shower floor and walked out. "I can't believe someone would keep such a disgusting creature. A mucus machine."

"Oh, you drool, too," said Daniela.

Ben blushed. "Yeah, but mine's not like his. It's like oil. Can't be cleaned."

"Who's the guy outside?" said Charles.

"That fucker's still there?" Ben hurried to the window and looked out.

"Yeah... He was giving me a weird look. Being all friendly and petting Blue." Charles took his time with each word. "He creeped me out."

Daniela moved pans around in the kitchen.

"He can't be a cop," said Ben. "Any cop would have enough sense to stake the place out from his room."

"Cops can be pretty dumb," said Charles.

"Well, we're going to have to keep an eye on him. Wait for him to leave to get this pot out. He saw me carrying the bags."

"He asked you about 'em?"

"Could have been common curiosity," said Ben. "They are big bags."

Daniela looked over from the stove. "Why don't you ask Larissa about him?"

Ben stared at the curtain. "Good point. I'll do it after breakfast."

Daniela set items from the fridge onto the counter. "You hungry, Charles?"

"Not really... I ate a couple hours ago." He stretched, let out a groan, and took a seat on the futon.

"I'll fix you a little plate." Daniela's shirt exposed her belly as she stood on her tiptoes, pulling plates from the cupboard.

Charles reached in his pocket and took out a bag of weed and a glass pipe. He grabbed a local paper from the floor and began breaking up a bud. He looked like a surgeon as he tore the stem out and broke up the Haze.

Ben grabbed the bag from Charles's lap. He stared at the crystals on the buds. Then put the bag to his nose and smelled. "Haze, huh?"

"Yep. Quebrada Grande Haze."

Daniela laughed from the kitchen.

Charles handed Ben the pipe. It was a traditional spoon piece, made of hand blown Pyrex. It was inside out, a layer of clear glass covering swirling orange, yellow, and blue on the inside. There was a carb to the left of the bowl and a bubble of glass with an image of a gold fish inside protruding from the right.

"Where's the Volcano?" said Ben.

"Dude… I don't bring the Volcano on land."

"It's alright. I haven't smoked for awhile." Ben put the pipe to his lips and touched the lighter to the side for no more than two seconds, being careful not to roast the whole top. He passed it to Charles and exhaled, already feeling a lightness in his head. Charles lit the pipe and hit it voraciously. No sooner had Ben taken it from him then Charles started to cough furiously.

Daniela stared from the kitchen as he hunched over his knees, red faced. *"Are you okay,"* she asked.

"Sí. Pura Vida." His voice was hoarse.

Ben slapped his knee. "He always hits it that way. Back before I moved down here, I was at his place one time, and we were hitting his bong."

Daniela rolled her eyes.

"One of the double bubbles. And, he tells me, 'I'm going to stand up... So I can hit my lower lungs.' You see, when you're bent over..." Ben leaned forward and pantomimed hitting a bong. "Smoke can't get to the lower part of your lungs because they're compressed. This man wants to blacken every square inch."

Daniela shook her head as she stirred the cilantro and onions into the rice and beans. Ben hit the pipe and passed it on, and, again, Charles hit it till he choked. He inhaled deeply through his nose, and it sounded like distortion from a speaker.

"Food's ready, guys."

"Just a sec, hon. Charles will have this bowl finished in another couple hits." Ben took another puff and passed it. "I'm good," he said, getting up and taking a seat at the table. He peeled the white curtain back and looked out the window. The man was still there with his chair angled at their cabin. Plastic sunglasses covered his eyes. 'Fucker,' thought Ben.

Charles took a couple more hits, coughed, and then tapped the pipe out over the trashcan. He slid it in his pocket and walked to the table, sniffling as he took a seat. He looked at a plate filled with rice and beans, fried plantains, and sliced pineapple, watermelon, and mango. *"Gallo pinto, always the tico breakfast,"* he said.

"You probably eat it a lot on the trip down here, huh?" said Daniela.

"I mostly eat on the boat, but I get it when I go to port. Nicaragua uses the pinto beans, though."

Ben pulled on the curtain. "Guy's gone. Hopefully he went to the beach. Up, guess not. There's still a bottle of sunscreen there."

"How many days do you spend on the water before coming in?" said Daniela.

"I go wherever the weather will let me. Sometimes I spend only a few days without a stop, sometimes I spend weeks."

"How's your dog like it when you're out so long?"

"Doesn't seem to mind. He doesn't have quite the energy as when he was a puppy, but he still swims for exercise every day. I throw a toy way out, and he fetches it."

"Shark bait," said Ben.

"I pity the shark that does get him, because you know he'll go right for that nose."

Ben again pulled back the curtain. The poolside was still empty, but he thought he saw the curtain shake in the cabin across from his, maybe a white hand. "This guy's destroying my mind."

"What's he doing?" said Charles.

"I don't know." Ben opened the curtain narrowly and put his eye to the glass.

"Your Spanish is better," said Daniela.

"Gracias. I've been practicing a lot. I need to anytime I go to port. How do you think my accent is, though?"

"It's good. I have no problems understanding you. You still have a little gringo accent, but it's cute."

Ben dropped the curtain. *"You don't ever want to lose the gringo accent all together."* He accentuated his speech to sound like a novice. *"It helps get the girls."*

"You lost most your gringo accent," said Daniela. *"Except you still have trouble saying Pura Vida."*

"You wish I was a little more gringo, don't you?"

She reached over and pinched his cheek. *"You'll always be my little gringo."*

Charles looked at the wall and back. "Anyway, what are the plans?"

"The plan is you bust out some dollars," said Ben.

"It's all in the bag." He motioned to the hiking pack by the futon.

"Four hundred thousand?"

"Three hundred ninety, at least."

Ben paused to swallow. "Must be all twenties again, huh?"

"Mostly. Weighs about forty pounds."

"Get hundreds and you can bring it in a briefcase." Ben glanced out the window.

"I wish."

"Then you'd look like someone in a movie," said Daniela. "You'd need to wear a suit, though. And, you'd have to shave."

"But the people in the movies will have a briefcase full of hundreds and say it's anywhere from a hundred thousand to a million," said Charles. "The average briefcase would hold three hundred fifty grand in hundreds, tops."

"Can't expect poor screenwriters to know what large sums of cash look like." Ben ate a piece of pineapple and blinked at the bitterness. "I got a batch of a hundred twenty pounds for you." Strings of the fruit hung from his teeth.

"You gonna run it back with me?"

Daniela stared at Ben.

"I just went on a run with you. I need to spend some time with my lady." He looked into Daniela's eyes.

"It's all good," said Charles. "We can fit you, too. Maybe another girl."

Daniela set her knife and fork on her empty plate. "Maybe sometime, Charles."

"I definitely will," said Ben, "but not on this trip." He looked out the window to the pool. The man was back lounging in his chair, his belly protruding slightly over the waistband of his shorts. "Fucker's back again," he said. "I don't know if we can move it today. You stayin' around here?"

"I could."

Ben glanced at the window. "I'll talk to Larissa, and then we'll head out to the cat. I don't want to keep this money here with that guy around."

Ben carried their plate to the sink and washed them. "One of the advantages to running this dank, you get to spend time at the beach. It's just too bad this guy's fuckin' it up."

Daniela got up and carried over the rest of the dirty dishes. "Charles, you have tea over here," she said.

"Oh, didn't see it."

She set it on the table, and he stared at the golden water before taking a gulp. *"Ahh, tea of coca leaf,"* he said.

"Sí," said Ben.

"Looks like someone was in South America."

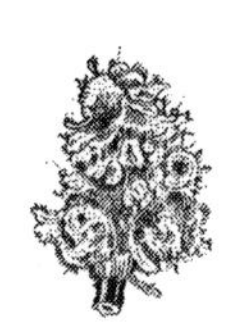

Ron stood outside The Mango, glancing at his watch. The sun had just climbed over the buildings behind him. His suitcase sat on the ground, and he held his briefcase. Taxi drivers waiting for fares watched him from their cars. He flapped the bottom of his navy blue jacket. He was hot. He let out a deep breath and shook his head, then spotted a midsize silver car enter the lot. Bill was behind the wheel. He drove around the outer edge and then came to a smooth stop by the curb. The trunk opened, and the window buzzed down. Bill's sleeves were rolled up, and he rested a meaty forearm on the wheel. Wide sunglasses covered his face. "Hop in," he said.

Ron set his suitcase in the trunk and walked to the door, shoes tapping. He slammed it and clicked on his seat belt. "What's going on?"

"We're going to get Starosta." Bill's tie was loosened and collar undone. A few brown chest hairs snuck out his shirt.

"Where?" said Ron.

The taxi drivers stared as they passed.

"Quebrada Grande."

"Quebrama what?"

"Quebrada Grande, village, a little over two hours."

"How do we know he's there?" said Ron.

"We don't. Just a hunch."

"Whose?"

"Mine," said Bill.

Ron looked out the window at a tin strip mall. There were two restaurants and a couple of tourist shops. The fronts were open, as was a side wall on one of the restaurants. Vegetation crowded the building, threatening to swallow it. Dark green leaves hung over the roof, and a type of orange fruit dotted the ground. "Let's hear this hunch," said Ron.

Bill repositioned himself in his seat and drove with one hand on the wheel. "Well, I was going over the case yesterday." He scratched his crotch. "It seems obvious that Starosta's staying with someone. Records show he's been in Costa Rica a lot, but give no whereabouts. First time was summer of 2000. I then noticed he'd earned college credits that summer from a school in California. I called the school, and they said the credits were through a volunteer program, International Student Volunteers. You know Fred Baxtley?"

"Yeah, I know him."

"Well, they sent Fred over to ISV's office and got us the details. Starosta did community development work in Quebrada Grande."

"Good work. You got info on the town?"

"Folder's in the backseat. Just a little farm town. The land was given to the people if they work it for so long. Bunch of protected rainforest around it."

Ron reached back and grabbed the folder. "Where'd you get the car?"

"Rented it. Robert signed off."

"What the hell is it?"

"Octavia. Skoda Octavia. Czech car."

Ron ran his hand over the leather seats and inhaled the smell of air freshener. "Not bad," he said.

Bill turned off the Pan-American Highway to a slightly narrower road. He pulled his cigarettes from his pocket, slid one in his mouth, and lit it. Ron gave him a look, and Bill cracked the window, tossing his pack on the dash. The engine whinnied as the road ascended. The humid air grew cool. Bill rolled his window down further and hung his arm out. Fog draped the valleys below, and Bill watched the wind burn up his cigarette. He took one last drag and flicked it into the cloud forest. "If I were Starosta," he said. "This is where I'd be. Feels like seventy."

"Says here it's hot in Quebrada Grande. Hotter than San Jose."

"Yeah, pineapple farms."

The tires screeched as Bill took a corner too fast.

"Careful," said Ron. "I'm already queasy."

Bill looked in his face. He did look pale. He swung his eyes back to see a long train of vehicles in the distance. "Fuck," he said. "This two-hour trip could turn to four."

Ron looked up at the line of cars and then over the bank. He couldn't see the bottom of the valley. "This road doesn't seem safe," he said.

Bill punched the gas as they went over a hump. Ron let out a groan, and the papers fell to his lap. Bill slowed as they approached the back of a yellow Nissan.

They followed the train for an hour before the leading semi reached a bridge and pulled over. The cars took turns crossing the one lane bridge. A motorcycle flew by the line of cars, went over the bridge, and was quickly out of sight.

"That's the way to travel here," said Bill.

Eventually, they made it over the bridge and got up to forty miles per hour. Ron still let out an occasional groan at bumps and corners. Bill held his arm straight out the window. "Beautiful up here, ain't it?"

"Peachy," said Ron.

Another hour and a half down the spiraling mountain roads, and they were descending to Ciudad Quesada. Bill rolled up the windows and blasted the air conditioning as the cool mountain air receded.

"Pretty big town," said Ron.

"Yeah, for way out here." Bill navigated them through the one way streets that made up the downtown. Palm trees grew in the central plaza. Businesses were everywhere, including a Pizza Hut. They passed an enormous church with towering white walls and a reddish orange tin roof. Black mold stained it. They wound their way out from the center and left town, descending into the San Carlos region. Tracts of land separated the houses as they got further out. Cows grazed in fields. They were on the road for twenty minutes before a sign popped up for Pital.

"Alright," said Bill. "Pital. We're close." He pulled out a colorful road map as they entered.

Ron noted the businesses they passed, fruit stand, butcher, shoe store, stationary store, pizza joint. When they circled around the soccer field and came back to the fruit stand, he turned to Bill. "Lost?"

Bill parked the car in front of the church. "Fuck it. I'm going to ask those cab drivers for directions." He shut off the car and stepped out.

Ron watched heads turn toward Bill as he walked through the plaza. He wasn't just the only white man there but also the only person in a suit and tie. Ron turned the car back on to feel the A/C as Bill approached a taxi.

"Perdon, Señor."

A man in the driver's seat of a small red SUV looked back. His arm rested on the window sill above a yellow triangular taxi sign.

"Do you know how to get to Quebrada Grande?"

"Sí, I can take you."

"No, I only need directions."

"Very cheap, only five thousand colones."

Bill stared him down like he was searching for a poker read. *"No, only directions."*

"Four thousand. I'll cut you a deal on the ride back."

Bill wiped sweat from his forehead. *"No, I have a car."* He motioned to the Skoda. *"I only need directions."*

"Nice car," said the driver. *"Too nice for the road. You'll destroy it."*

"Not important. It's a rental."

The driver laughed. *"Okay. Take that street and follow it for twenty kilometers."* He pointed to a street next to the church. *"You'll pass through a town, Veracruz. After the town, you'll see a big metal building, pineapple factory."* Bill nodded as he spoke. *"Take a right after it. Ugly road. Big rocks. Might hurt the car. Goes straight to Quebrada Grande."*

"Muchas gracias," said Bill. He pulled a thousand note from his wallet and handed it to him.

"No, no," said the driver. *"Directions are free."*

"Take it." Bill pushed it closer.

The driver shook his head, and, finally, Bill stuck it back in his pocket and turned to the car. *"Gracias,"* he said.

"¡Pura Vida!" said the driver.

Bill got in the car and turned the A/C up all the way. He loosened the laces on his shoes and pulled on his shirt.

"Know how to get there?" said Ron.

"Yeah, we just take this road here." Bill waved to the road leaving north from the plaza. As he turned onto the street the sky grew dim.

"More rain," said Ron. "Can't go a day without it."

The rain beat down. Bill turned his wipers to maximum, but they failed to clear the window. He slowed down fifteen kilometers per hour, leaned his head close to the windshield, and squinted. The car bounced, and his head hit the window. It shook like they were on railroad tracks. The sound of water hitting the car's sides and bottom echoed inside. Bill laid on the brakes and brought the car to a crawl till they made it past the busted pavement.

"Fuck," said Bill. "Good thing this is insured."

Ron let out a deep breath and wiped his forehead. He felt a warm sensation over his arms and back and a drip of sweat run down from his armpit.

The pair drove on at a slower pace while the water streamed down the windows. Outside of Veracruz it slowed, and the pineapple plants became visible. Bill pushed on the accelerator and rolled down the windows. Moist air poured over them. A large soccer field came into view on their left and a pulpería to their right. Bill looked at a couple teenage girls under the bus stop and turned back to see a white speed bump in the road. He tapped the brakes, but a little too late. The Octavia's front wheels rose off the ground, and the underbody scraped the pavement. Everyone stared. An old man in front of the pulpería pointed, and Ron covered his face.

"Hoo," said Bill. "Again, good thing it's insured."

"Yeah. Good thing," said Ron.

They were soon rounding the sharp corner at the edge of town, and the tin pineapple building was growing large. Bill stopped the car next to it. "That must be it." He pointed at the jagged road.

"What?" said Ron.

"That. The guy said the road next to the big tin building runs to Quebrada Grande."

"That thing?" Ron stared at the mess of rocks and puddles.

"Yep."

"It looks just for tractors."

"We'll see." Bill turned onto the road and proceeded cautiously, no faster than ten kilometers per hour. The car shook like an old roller coaster, and Ron felt like a Champagne bottle ready to burst. The sun peeked out again, and Bill stared at the mountains to his left. Fog hung around the tops of the lush green trees.

"This road's hell," said Ron.

"Could be better. View's good, though." Bill nodded to the hills.

"If you're into Jurassic Park," said Ron. "I crave civilization."

A few small homes came into view, and children outside waved. Bill waved back. "There's your civilization," he said.

"If you call it that," said Ron. "Look at that house. I don't even think it has a door."

Bill stared at the vegetation in the yard, hibiscus bushes six feet high, covered with red trumpeted flowers. He looked ahead as music blasted from a home. They could hear it clear a hundred feet away.

"No rules against disturbing the peace?" said Ron.,

Bill stared at the home, still fifty feet off, obscured by a coconut tree. "No, music is more important to them. More latinos sing and dance. They believe in a right to play music loud during daytime hours."

"Right to a headache," said Ron.

As they passed the coconut tree, a crowd of young people dancing came into view. Bill's eyes fell on a girl of fourteen dancing in the center. Her hips swung. Her exposed midsection twisted. He thought he could hear the jingle of her bracelets and fantasized that she motioned to him, luring him from the vehicle.

"That's certainly not civilized," said Ron. "I guess now we know where all this rain comes from."

"Savage and superb," said Bill. "I think the one in the middle looks stately."

"The girl?"

The right front tire plunged into a puddle, causing an enormous splash. Water flew in the passenger window, dousing Ron, and the youngsters stopped their dancing to laugh. Ron squeezed his face tight with anger and wiped his clothes. "Watch where you're driving," he said.

"This road's hard to maneuver on." Bill looked back to the girl, and she smiled. He hoped it was for him.

"Well, quit checkin' out teenagers. You got water on my shirt. Probably seething with parasites." Ron put his window up and reached for the air conditioner. "The air's soupy, anyway."

They drove on, listening to the car's vibrations and the occasional rock scraping against the car's underbody. After ten minutes, they came upon a row of houses, then a church, then a soccer field, a school, and some community buildings. Bill parked the car in the grass across from a pulpería.

"Who we going to talk to?" said Ron.

"Them." Bill bobbed his head toward the pulpería. It looked like a concession stand at a ball game. There were a few teenagers and one adult sitting outside. "Just act stern."

They got out, and Ron followed behind, rubbing at his clothes.

"¡Hola! ¿Como están?" yelled the man behind the counter. He appeared to be in his fifties. His hair and mustache were black with streaks of gray, and his skin was slightly rough. His smile, however, made him look as young as the teenagers outside.

"Bien. Bien," said Bill. *"We'd like two Pepsis."* He slapped a five thousand note on the counter.

"Dos Pepsis," said the man, reaching into a cooler.

The other customers stared at the agents.

"What brings you businessmen here today?" The man popped off the caps and set them on the counter.

"We're looking for a friend. Maybe you know him. His name's Benjamin Starosta, Ben."

The man's eyebrows rose. *"I've never heard of him,"* he said.

Ron eyed the other patrons. They looked away when he met their eyes.

"He visited with a group a few years back, International Student Volunteers."

"Many volunteers come here," said the man. *"I'm not good with names."* He looked up to the sky and appeared to think. *"I recall... A Molly... A Stephanie... A Lisa... A Katie..."*

Bill and Ron exchanged looks.

"A Rebecca... A Darlene... A... A... A Jackie, but no, no Benjamin Starostro. I'm sorry. I tend to remember ladies much more than men." He grinned widely.

Bill slipped a picture onto the counter. *"This face doesn't look familiar to you?"*

The man stared at the photo and then looked into Bill's eyes.

"How about you guys?" said Bill. *"Do you know this guy?"* He held the picture before their faces.

"No, no." They shook their heads.

"We don't know no gringos," said one.

"Okay," said Bill. *"Thanks for your time."* He slipped the picture in his pocket and tipped back the soda. He winked at Ron and walked around the corner. "We're going to have to try houses," he said. "Start here." He pointed to a small house hidden behind a thick mass of vegetation.

Ron nodded and followed Bill around the bush and up the thin sidewalk. There was a child playing with a doll in the doorway of the small home. She looked up and stared at Bill, her mouth hanging open.

Bill put on a large smile. *"Perdon, niña. Tu mamá o papá está aquí?"*

The girl didn't move a muscle, then turned and ran through the house.

"Hopefully, she'll get her mother," said Bill.

"Hopefully, she'll get Benjamin Starosta," said Ron.

A short woman with dark, curly hair walked out. She smiled wide, exposing her crooked teeth.

"Good afternoon, miss. I was hoping we could ask you a couple questions."

"Yes, of course. Have a seat." She motioned to a faded pink and gray sofa on the porch. Foam busted out from broken seams.

Bill sat down, and Ron followed, setting his hands in his lap. The woman held her paisley dress against her legs as she lowered herself into a matching chair across from them. The little girl stared from the doorway.

"My name is Bill, and this is Ron."

Ron waved.

"My name is Elicia. It's nice to meet you."

"Doña Elicia, we are looking for a friend of ours. We're supposed to be meeting him here, but can't seem to find him. His name is Ben, Ben Starosta."

The little girl's eyes grew as wide as full moons, and the woman looked the pair over. *"I have never heard that name before."*

"Perhaps you know him by face." Bill handed her the picture.

She took it and handed it back. *"No, I don't know this man."*

"He was definitely here," said Bill. *"He came here with a group doing volunteer work."*

"Maybe he was one of the shy ones," she said. *"Many know no Spanish, and we never get to talk with them."*

"I don't understand," said Bill. *"He told us to meet him here."*

"I don't know him."

Bill shook his head. *"Well, we appreciate your help."*

"No problem."

Bill and Ron got up, waved, and left. The young girl watched them walk down the narrow sidewalk. When they were gone, she walked to her mother. *"Who were they?"* she said.

"Dangerous men. Never trust men in suits."

Candles lit the cabin, and the white satin curtain fell against the window. Ben jumped up the stairs to the bedroom. "Watch him," he whispered.

Daniela drew back the curtain and put her eye to the window. The middle aged gringo was in his lounge chair. He wore shorts and a Hawaiian shirt. Head phone wires ran below his straw hat, his flip flops lay on the ground, and a book was open on his belly. To his right flickered a tiki torch. The moon was waning gibbous, and the stars shone down from above.

The bedroom window screeched as Ben tugged it open and leaned out. Charles stared up. "You ready?" Ben whispered.

"Yeah."

Ben glanced at Daniela who was still watching the front window. He picked up one of the duffels and slowly lowered it out. Charles laid it softly on the ground while Ben reached for another.

"¡Psst!"

Ben turned to Daniela who was wide-eyed and waving frantically. *"He's up! He's up!"*

Ben leaned out the window. "Hand it up! Hand it up!" he said.

Charles heaved up the bag, then looked around and crouched against the building. Ben ran to Daniela, put his eye to the window, and looked to the lounge chair. It was empty save for an open book on the seat. His eyes went to a faint light coming from the guy's cabin.

Again, he thought the curtain moved. "Fuck, we gotta get this outta here."

Ben ran to the back window. "Look out," he said. He tossed the bags one after another, and each hit the soil with a thud. Then Ben hoisted himself into the window and jumped out, bending his knees upon landing. He grabbed a bag in each hand and ran toward the car, struggling to hold them above his waist. Charles picked up the other and trailed behind. Ben popped the car's trunk with his key chain and threw in the bags. He hopped in the car and started it as Charles threw in the last bag and slammed the trunk. The seat belt sign beeped as they pulled out and sped away.

"What happened?" said Charles.

"The guy got up."

"Was he walking around the cabin?"

Ben felt his chest pounding. "No, in his cabin. Door was open."

They hit uneven spots in the road, and the car shook. Ben looked in the rear view mirror and then from side to side. There were flashing lights from a bar, and he thought of cops.

"I think we're safe," said Charles.

Ben rubbed his eyes. "I know. I'm paranoid." He looked in his mirrors and glanced around. "We have to get the dinghy from the surf shop, right?"

"No, it's still on the water."

"You crazy? It could be gone."

"No. Someone's watching it."

"Don't joke," said Ben.

"It's fine. It's a girl I met last night."

"A girl from the bar? Fuckin' idiot. They're prostitutes." Ben stared out the windshield. "We're just gonna carry these three mammoth bags onto your boat with some whore watching. Fuckin' brilliant."

"It's fine. She's cool," said Charles.

Ben turned onto the paved road and passed a towering hotel. "Should I park at the surf shop?"

"Yeah, that's fine."

Ben pulled into a small, dark lot and scanned the area. There weren't any other cars. He locked the doors and walked to the street, then looked in both directions. People hung outside a loud reggae bar a block away. Waves crashed in the background. He walked to the trunk, grabbed two of the bags, and crisscrossed the straps around his neck. Charles took the other. "You lead the way," said Ben.

The duffel brushed Charles's knee while crossing the street. He lifted it in front of him as he entered a narrow path cutting through the weeds. The moon and stars illuminated their way. Sea shells dotted the sand, long conical spirals. Ben could smell the ocean.

"It's up here." Charles pointed north up the beach line. "Maybe two hundred yards."

The beach appeared empty. 'Safe,' thought Ben. Their feet felt heavy as they sank in the sand and labored to pull them out. The straps on the bags dug into their skin. Charles rotated his bag from one shoulder to the other. Ben flexed his upper body and marched at a steady pace till his foot fell in a hole, and he tumbled. The plastic bags inside the duffel crinkled as they hit the sand. "Fuck!"

"You alright?" Charles stood over him and glanced toward Tamarindo. Sweat dripped from his brow.

"Yeah." Ben pushed himself up and repositioned the bags. "Almost rolled my ankle, though." He hustled on, and Charles lagged behind. Laughter broke the air to their left, and both turned. 'A drunk couple finding love,' thought Ben. A smile almost broke his lips. He turned back to Charles who was staring at the seas of the moon, then looked ahead to a dark shadow in the distance. "That it?" he said.

"Yeah."

'At least it's there,' he thought. 'What's it worth? Six hundred dollars. A thousand. At least a couple hundred on the black market.'

As they drew near, Ben noticed the outline of a person in the raft. He was surprised Blue wasn't there with her. Charles rarely left the dog alone. His eyes then went back to the silhouette of the girl. He wondered who she was and looked at Charles. 'Was he sniffing coke off her tits last night?'

Ben's mind drifted to his first time in Costa Rica. He was at a bar with a friend from Pital. The guy had once lived in the States, St. Louis. He'd worked construction there, and his wife and child were still there. He couldn't get a green card. The man raved about the U.S. "You can go to Wal-Mart, buy anything you need. Nice stuff, little money." He had fond memories of barbeques. He told other ticos, *"You don't understand. We can't barbeque like them. It's all about the sauces. Mmm... The sauces."* He licked his lips, then remembered how cold it got in winter, his boss telling him, "Mateus, you need to wear gloves." Ben was back at the bar with him, Pital. They'd both drunk too much Scotch. Costa Rica consumed more of it than any country outside its homeland. Mateus walked up to him, swaying with bags under his eyes. "Do you want to get some more marijuana? This guy can get it." He pointed to a sleazy looking man, scrawny with a bony face.

The green quality there was horrible, certainly not sinsemilla. Ben had a little in his luggage. "Sure," he said.

Ben followed Mateus and the emaciated man through the streets, finally following a dark, dusty one out of town. His head felt light, his stomach heavy. His feet moved unsteadily like a cartoon character with one foot stuck in a bucket. A pang of fear hung over him. 'Mateus is my friend,' he thought. 'He wouldn't let something bad happen to me, but why is he so intent on hiking all this way for pot?'

Not too far outside of town they came upon a gravel driveway with trees hanging over it. It was too dark to see where it led, but it looked like a farm. Ben followed the two, tripping over uneven spots. Finally, after what seemed like twenty minutes, they came to a small shack. Ben knew the routine. He gave the stranger his money. He was being taxed five, ten, maybe fifteen dollars. The sleazy man banged on the side of the tin house. A man inside yelled groggily. There was a woman's voice, too. The deal was done through a window, no screen or glass, not even a curtain.

Shortly after, Ben figured out where his tax had gone, crack for the sleazy man and his friend. Mateus would tell him later, "If I were in the States, I wouldn't do it."

The stranger asked Ben for some of his weed to mix with the crack. Reluctantly, Ben acquiesced, and they moved along slowly with the ticos pausing to hit the crack, seemingly, every couple seconds. Five minutes passed since they last hit it, and the man made the same request, though it sounded like a command. Ben flexed all his muscle and looked into his ghoul like eyes. The guy's face appeared skeletal. "No," he said.

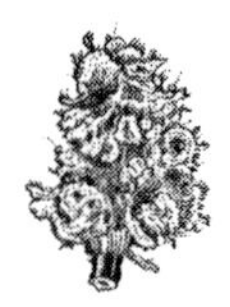

Ben hoped Charles wasn't using cocaine. He couldn't deal with losing half a million dollars and his method of transport. He had a revolution to fund.

"Carmela, mi hermano, Ben. Ben, Carmela."

"Pleased to meet you." The girl's smile seemed to cover her whole face. She looked barely twenty and, in tight pants and a little shirt, wasn't dressed unlike Daniela.

"Equally," said Ben. He sounded like a man whose local sports

team had just pissed away a Super Bowl. He set his duffel bags in the front of the raft and sat on the bow. Charles exchanged a long kiss with Carmela and tossed in his duffel. Then he dug his hands into the dinghy and pushed it from the sand. He hopped in, dropped the motor, and with a few tugs of the cord, they were off.

"You live here in Costa Rica, your brother tells me," Carmela yelled over the buzz of the engine and the wind's clamor.

Ben was staring over the water and turned to her dumbly.

"Your brother says you live here," she said.

"Not here, Pital de San Carlos, near Ciudad Quesada."

"¿San Carlos?" Laughter intermingled her words. *"Why there?"*

"I'm a farmer."

Again Carmela laughed. *"Let me see your hands."*

Ben held them out, and she inspected them, feeling them with her own soft hands. *"Clean fingers. No dirt under the nails. You do have calluses, though. More than Charles."*

Ben looked at the moon, which, in a role reversal, was being pulled by the waves of Aquarius. Carmela dropped his hands and turned to Charles. They giggled and gave each other googly eyes. Ben watched her run her nails over Charles's thigh, then turned and was happy to notice a white mast fast approaching. It glowed from the moon, and the catamaran's two hulls jutted toward them.

Charles cut the engine, and Ben grabbed a rail as the raft hit the boat. The stickers on the hull looked faded in the moonlight, but the fiberglass was smooth. Ben could hear Blue's muffled bark as he tied up the raft. He picked up his two duffels, threw them onto the deck, and climbed up. Noticing Carmela struggling, he leaned over and held out a hand.

Charles handed up the third bag, and Ben stacked it on the other two. "Where we going with these?" he said.

"We'll put 'em in the saloon."

"Gonna keep her out here?" Ben nodded toward Carmela.

"Why?"

"Why do you think?"

Charles glared. "I gotta new place for it. Carry it to the saloon." He picked up one of the bags and placed a hand on Carmela's back. *"To the saloon, beautiful."*

Ben picked up the bags and followed. The whole top of the boat was flat, except the center, where the living quarters stuck out. A garden with tomatoes, peppers, cucumbers, and beans was planted in two troughs at the front of the boat. The mast stood behind it. A solar panel lay above the living quarters, and windows encircled it. The three moved to the back and down a couple stairs where Charles took keys from his pocket and fumbled with the lock on a large steel door. They heard Blue whining and scratching on the other side. As Charles threw open the door, the dog came tearing out. He took short, quick steps and stuck his snout into Charles and Carmela's legs. His body quivered with excitement. Charles and Carmela edged past him and into the saloon. Then the dog ran for Ben. Ben watched the animal's body shake as he danced around. He wiped slobber on Ben's knee and shin. Then Ben groaned and walked in. He set his bags by Charles's and walked out, calling to the dog, "Come on Blue."

Ben rubbed Blue's head and body. "Now stop," he said. He pointed at him and walked to the end of the hull. Blue walked close and slapped him with his bony tail.

"Back." Ben shoved him across the fiberglass. "Stay," he said.

He washed his hands and leg in the sea as the dog stared and then returned to the saloon. The beastly smell of dog inside hit him, and he kinked his neck. Charles and the bags were gone. Carmela sat to the left on a small worn wraparound sofa. Quarters were cramped as there was barely enough room for a six by nine throw rug between the sofa and wall. Carmela played with the stereo remote, and Toots and the Maytals played from the speakers. "*Where'd he go?*" said Ben.

"His bedroom." She pointed through the small kitchen to Ben's right.

Ben walked over the linoleum floor of the kitchen, past the

bathroom, and into the bedroom. There was an unmade queen size bed, a nightstand with a digital alarm clock, two tall dressers against a wall, and a dog bed on the floor. Charles stood by an open closet with shirts dangling inside. Ben shut the door and locked it, and the reggae music turned to a hum.

"You haven't seen my latest addition." Charles smiled and moved one of the dressers away from the wall. Ben's eyes widened as he slid open a plastic cover exposing a switch. He flipped it up, and the floor of the closet rose at an angle, showing a large stainless steel trunk. Charles took his keys from his pocket and unlocked the trunk. He stuffed the bags inside, closed it, and flicked the switch behind the dresser. With a drone, the floor closed.

"Cool," said Ben. "Some James Bond shit."

"Yeah, check out this switch, too." Charles pulled open another plastic cover. "If I hit this switch, the box gets dropped to the sea."

"Hopefully, you never have to do that. A lot of cash gone."

"There's a tracking device in the box," said Charles.

"Better stay in shallow water."

"I don't go out far."

Ben stared at a print of *Swans Reflecting Elephants* on the wall. "This isn't going to protect you from her, though." He nodded toward the door.

"She's just a fuckin' woman," said Charles. "Not a cop. Clean."

"She's got eyes and a mouth. Studied my face and yours."

"She's not gonna say anything."

"No? She's not gonna tell her friends about the gringo she met? His nice boat? His brother and him moving duffel bags in the middle of the night?"

Charles stared in his eyes. His nostrils flared. "We can always do pickups somewhere else."

"No, we can't. It's all set up here. I don't know anywhere else."

Charles shrugged. "Well, she'll be coming with me and won't have time to tell anyone."

Ben turned back to the Dalí print. "That's the only choice you have now."

Charles pushed the dresser back and unlocked the door. "I expect you can at least throw off your suspicion for a moment and have a bag with us."

Ben stared at the floor as Charles walked out. He thought about the operation, Quebrada Grande, the projects in South America, the U.S., and Mexico. His life. He worried it could come crashing down. A couple minutes passed before he walked out. Charles sat at the near end of the couch, Carmela in the middle. He walked past them and took a seat next to her.

"Volcano's warm," said Charles. He stuck a popcorn size bud in a thin metal grinder, turned it a couple times, then pulled it apart, and tapped the pieces together. The weed fell onto a magazine in his lap, High Times. He then folded the magazine and poured the green into a tiny French press. He set the press atop a small conical machine sitting on the end table to his right. It had a brushed metal exterior. Charles pressed a button, and it hummed as warm air flowed out the top and through the press. He snapped a hard plastic piece with a bag on it to the top. The bag slowly rose as it filled with THC vapor. Ben stared at it. He had once looked at the rising bag as a symbol of the expansion of his revolution. He had thought of Anarchist Catalonia, hoping he could help anarchism flower as it once had there. He turned to Carmela and studied her visage, hoping she wasn't a Franco.

"Well, what the fuck are we supposed to do?" Bill leaned across the top of the payphone, his armpits wedged tight against it, and stared at the soccer field across the street. He swore he could see rain falling lightly over it, but none fell on his side.

"It isn't possible for you to get information in a friendly way?" The man's voice was tinny through the receiver.

"Up to this point we've been unable." Bill stared at the soccer goal. Just bars, no net. His eyes went out of focus, and it waved back and forth, like lines on a distorted television screen.

"You're not convinced you'll be able to if you keep working at it?"

Bill gripped the back of the payphone. The polished steel was warm on his fingers. "I'm not sure." He pushed himself up and stretched. His face was red and moist. He raised an arm and exposed a large pit stain. "The point I'm trying to make is if you were to send a small team down from Benning, we'd get everything we need, two days, tops. Drag him out and hand 'em right to us."

"Bill, we know the situation." The man's tone was stern, like a teacher reprimanding a troublemaker. "You have to understand that we've already looked into it. It's a last option. We don't want to catch a news story. Especially, if we don't get our man."

"Commie guerrillas," said Bill.

"As I said, last course of action. Your job is to find him. We're not going to send a team in for the hell of it."

"I apologize, sir. Just wanted to let you know we could get information this way."

"I appreciate your input, but it's not the best course of action. Let us know when you find out more."

"Alright, thanks, Robert." He stared at the wispy clouds barely diluting the sun's rays.

"Keep doin' what you do, Bill."

"Goodbye," he said.

"Bye."

Bill hung up and took an acute left angle across the street. His head hung down. He shook it and mumbled, then walked in the open door of the town's pizza joint. A fan stood by the door. Next to it a couple kids watched fútbol on television. Their eyes glowed with excitement. Bill walked over the old tile floor to a turquoise booth where Ron sat. Colorful advertisements were plastered above.

"How is it?" said Bill.

Ron brought the slice down from his mouth and pulled on the strings of cheese that refused to break. "Not bad," he said.

Bill watched the saucy crust rotate around in Ron's mouth as he chewed.

"What's up with Robert?"

Bill stared beyond him, appearing in a trance. "Continue doing what we're doin'."

"You let him know about the difficulties."

"Of course, I did."

"What?" said Ron, "Robert mad or something?"

"No, I'm mad," he whispered. "Every fucker in that village is lying to us."

"We'll get him," said Ron.

Bill stared at a Pepsi ad on the wall. "I suggested sending a team in."

"Rebuffed?"

"Yeah."

Ron leaned forward. The beads of sweat on Bill's head grew to puddles. "I have an idea," he said.

Bill looked at him.

"Roadblock. My contact could get a couple officers for it, maybe even soldiers."

"Costa Rica doesn't have soldiers," said Bill.

"They're the same."

"Yeah." Bill nodded.

Ron picked up his slice of pizza. "We could have the block set up by morning."

Ben pulled up next to a bus stop, and a girl in a little shirt with spaghetti straps, skin tight capris, and sneakers lowered her thumb. Ten people were scattered around the benches behind her. There wasn't a cloud in the sky. The rainy season didn't reach Guanacaste. Ben turned down his radio, rolled down the window, and leaned over Daniela's lap. *"Where you headed?"*

"Palmira." Sun glistened off her metal rings.

"We're going," said Ben.

She flicked her neck and looked back at the bus stop. Her yellow star-shaped plastic earrings shook. Two boys in shorts and t-shirts hopped off the bench and ran to the car. They kicked up dust. One of the boys was small and awkward, just hitting puberty. They made him sit in the middle.

Ben stole a glance at them as he pulled out. The girl looked barely out of high school, and the older of the boys seemed to be balanced between the two in age.

"What's in Palmira?" said Ben.

The girl brushed hair from her face. *"Home. We're from Palmira. We work out here."* Her eyebrows were plucked thin.

"What do you do?"

"We work for a resort. I clean rooms, and they take care of horses."

Ben looked at the boys in the rear view mirror. *"You guys like horses?"*

"I hate them," said the oldest. His eyes were tough.

"What do you have against horses?"

"Their shit."

Daniela and Ben chuckled. *"Fair enough,"* he said. *"So, you guys do horse tours there?"*

"Sí." The younger boy nodded with the older.

"Aren't there jaguars around here? You see them on tours?"

"No, no. The jaguar's a night hunter."

"Have you seen one?" said Ben.

"No. There aren't a lot of them around."

Ben noticed the boy's eyes light up in the mirror.

"The Osa Peninsula, though. They have them there. They sneak out to the beaches at night to eat sea turtles. A few years back, at Carate beach, a jaguar was out looking for a turtle when he found something else. A gringo, also waiting for turtles. They watch for them to come in and lay their eggs, then they collect them to make sure all the eggs become turtles. He had fallen asleep on the beach, and the jaguar spotted him. The gringo must have looked too easy to pass up. The jaguar moved in and stood over him, breathing warm air on his face." The boy put his mouth close to the back of Ben's neck and breathed on it loudly. *"Then the jaguar opened his mouth and bit into the man's temple, piercing his brain. This, I believe, is when he would have awakened, but it was too late. His neck was snapped in a second. Easier than having to crack open a turtle's shell."* He knocked on the younger boy's skull, then turned to the girl.

"Uhh." She turned away.

Daniela gave a shake.

"Wow," said Ben. *"I know people who've collected turtle eggs. I could have done it with a volunteer program."*

"Volunteer program!" said the boy. *"They got gringos working for free, and they don't even teach 'em about the dangers?"*

"Not only that, but I paid to do volunteer work, about a million colones."

"¡Jesus Cristo!" The kid's eyes bulged. *"Where can I get a gringo to*

pay me to do my work?"

"I might be able to find you one."

The boy's visage folded into a mess of confusion.

Daniela shook her head and held her legs back while Ben fumbled through the glove box. He pulled out a pen and note card and handed it back. *"Put your name and address on that, phone number if you have one, and I'll try to find someone."*

The boy took the card and stared at it. He looked in the rear view mirror. *"You serious, or you just fucking with me for lying?"* He grinned widely.

"*You made that story up!"* Daniela turned and glared. *"What's wrong with you?"*

The boy giggled.

"He's always making up lies," said the younger boy. His voice squeaked like an old screen door.

"He's a dick face," said the girl.

The younger boy watched the older one scribble down a name and address on the card.

"Alright," said Ben. *"You told your story, now it's time to tell mine. I'm from..."*

"We're already in Palmira." The kid smiled. *"You can drop us here."*

"But I want to tell my story," said Ben.

"Aww." Daniela rubbed his thigh.

Ben slowed the car and parked by the curb.

"Here's your card." The boy tossed it in his lap and stepped out the car. The other two followed.

"Gracias for the ride," said the girl.

"Gracias," said the young boy.

"You're welcome," Daniela said.

Ben rolled down his window. *"Just wait."* He reached in the glove box and pulled out a sheet of paper, then surreptitiously wrapped something inside. *"Here, take this."* As the boy grabbed it, Ben sped off and waved out the window.

The girl and the young boy watched him unfold the paper. He slowly drew it back to expose a rectangular piece of paper with a puma on it jumping out from a blue background. There was a jaguar's face next to it. The kids' eyes bulged as he slid it back, and there were more behind it with the same image.

"Ten thousand notes. How many are there?" The younger boy asked. He watched him count five. *"I bet you wish you would have given him your real name now."*

The boy stared at the bills in his hands.

"You're such a dick face," said the girl.

2001

The moon shone waxing crescent. A surprisingly clear night. Insects buzzed in the trees. Diurnal creatures slept. Chi Cho and Ben walked along the rock road, each carrying a shovel and toolbox. They talked in whispers.

"You runnin' me back to Ciudad Quesada tomorrow?" said Ben.

"Of course not."

"Amigo," he pleaded.

"I have no reason to go into town."

The clouds had parted from above. Ursa Major and Minor were out, along with Draco, a few of the circumpolar constellations Ben always saw in Wisconsin.

"Halfway? ¿Pital?" he said.

Chi Cho's smirk was hidden in the darkness. *"No, I don't think so."* He stopped before a gate of barbed wire and pulled the wood pole aside. Ben walked through, and Chi Cho closed it.

"I have to get back to Daniela."

Laughter cut through Chi Cho's lips.

"It's not funny. I haven't seen her in three days. I can't think straight."

"And once you see her, you won't think straight for another three days," said Chi Cho.

They hiked past Alfredo's livestock, two milking cows and a pen with several pigs. Ben noticed a cow staring at him, ellipsis shining.

There was constant movement in its jaw as it chewed its cud.

"Listen, I know you don't know what it's like going without sex. I heard you and Isabel last night. You're giving me a ride, or I'm stealing your vehicle."

"I think there's a bicycle. David's."

"Asshole."

The stars vanished as they walked under the cover of trees and ascended the hills. Chi Cho occasionally flicked on a flashlight to check the trail.

"Worry about stepping on snakes," said Chi Cho. *"It'll get that pussy off your mind."*

A rustling came from their right. Chi Cho and Ben froze and glanced about, then heard a stamping on the hard clay. They turned and darted down the hill to their left. Brambles caught their clothes and skin, grabbed at their shovels, and scraped loudly against the plastic toolboxes. Thin pointed branches slapped and cut them. Ben hit a tree, and it knocked him back. It dazed him, but he ran on, stumbling as his shoulder throbbed.

"Psst. Gringo."

Ben stopped and looked around. He saw a shadow pull at his pant leg.

"Let's wait here."

Ben handed Chi Cho the shovel and toolbox, and he slid them under some weeds. He then knelt down and listened, quietly rubbing the cuts on his arms and massaging his shoulder. Their heavy breathing was all they could hear over the buzz of insects. Mosquitoes preyed on Ben, and he brushed them from his arms, neck, and face. He used his finger to feel a lump on his forehead.

"What was it?" whispered Chi Cho.

"Don't know," Ben panted. *"Thought I heard someone... Running... When we first took off."* Ben brushed at a mosquito in his ear, then rested his hand on the cool ground to steady himself.

"I'm not sure there was anyone," said Chi Cho.

"What was it then?"

"I don't know. People would have shined flashlights."

"True." Ben's thighs began to ache from the kneeling. *"That's what sucks about this. Makes you paranoid."*

"Paranoia can be good," said Chi Cho.

"Doesn't feel good."

"You wanna walk up and check?"

Ben groaned and got to his feet. Chi Cho picked up a long, spongy stick and leaned it against a tree. *"That's our marker."*

The pair tiptoed back the way they'd come, like Indians on a hunt. All the muscles in their bodies were tight. Every four steps, they'd stop and listen. Nothing was audible over the buzzing insects.

"Are we going the right way?" said Ben.

"I don't know."

They held their arms in front, feeling ahead. Chi Cho tripped over a rotting tree and hit the ground hard. The dense clay let out a bass note, and Chi Cho groaned.

"You alright?" Ben whispered.

"Sí," he moaned. He pushed himself to his knees, then his feet. *"This is stupid. I'm turning the light on."* He flicked on the flashlight and shined it across the ground. *"We're lucky we didn't get bit by a snake, running through here blind."*

"Only mosquitoes," said Ben. He itched his arms.

"They didn't get me."

"Of course."

The pair followed the flashlight, Ben staring at the light and moving his feet quickly to stay close. Chi Cho stopped. *"We went through there."* He shined the light into a patch of brambles. *"My arms can attest to it."*

"Not just yours." Ben followed Chi Cho into the briars. *"I hit a tree here, too. Almost broke my shoulder."*

The buzz of the insects was piercing. The pair's eyes were huge, and their breathing heavy. Sweat dotted their brows, backs, and chests. *"Okay. This is where we walked up."* Chi Cho stopped and shined the flashlight down the hill. *"We were a little farther up."* He studied the ground as they slowly mounted the hill. *"Okay. This is where we ran."* He held the light on a patch of clay mangled by their sharp turns. *"Lucky it wasn't wet,"* he said.

Ben rubbed his shoulder. "*Would have been better than running through there.*"

Chi Cho turned to his right. He drew back a couple branches and walked in while Ben followed. They scanned the ground, like basset hounds. Fifteen feet in they came upon a spot where the vegetation was matted down. Chi Cho shined the light on it.

"Deer bed," said Ben. He looked over the ground as Chi Cho stared at him.

"What?"

Ben pointed to some small hoof prints in the clay. "Deer," he said. He put his hands to his head like antlers.

"Ciervo," said Chi Cho.

"Sí, ciervo. I thought you didn't have them here."

"They're in the country, but I didn't think they were here."

"Better they're not. They can fuck with plants." Ben crouched down and studied the tracks. *"Tiny. Wouldn't be much meat on it."* He stood up while Chi Cho stared blankly at the ground. *"All that for a baby deer,"* he said.

Chi Cho turned to walk out, giving one last glance at the deer bed. He retraced their path to the shovels and toolboxes. Ben stayed on his heels, though at one point he had to stop and ask Chi Cho for light, so he could pull a briar tentacle from his shirt.

"This is dangerous," said Chi Cho. *"If one of us were to step on a snake, we'd never make it to the hospital. A leg would be lost... If not more."* He dug out the shovels and handed one to Ben. Ben felt the grains in the wood handle as he grabbed it, then took his toolbox and followed on Chi Cho's heels. His shirt was clinging to him, and his calves felt hot. A little farther, Chi Cho stopped and leaned over his

knee. *"With all your sexual tension, you should have walked these out yourself."*

"You shouldn't complain. I used to run plants out in dirt. Picture making three trips up here, a tray in front of you filled with cups of dirt, forty pounds."

Chi Cho scoffed. *"We would have lost half of them."*

"That's the importance of the clone machine."

Chi Cho stood back up and led them up the hill. The sound of their feet hitting the hard clay was faintly audible over the buzzing insects. Howler monkeys could be heard in the distance. The pair crossed over the top of the hill and dropped into their clearing on the south side. The stars came back into view.

"Alright, let's stash 'em," said Ben. *"We'll be back in the morning to plant."*

"All this way just to drop them off. It's a shame we can't plant them now."

"Maybe if there was a full moon. You're too tired anyway."

"I just hope I can get out here in the morning."

"You'll do it. You love the work."

"What are we doing for dinner?"

"I don't know." Daniela yawned. "There's nothing in the house."

"La campesina?"

"That's fine."

The sun faded as Ben drove slowly into town. Concrete homes with tin roofs lined the street, many surrounded by short metal picket fences. Ben pulled the car to the curb in front of a light pink house. Vegetation hid the fence, separating it from the neighbor's yard. Puddles gathered on the uneven sidewalk. It was close to five o'clock and would soon be dark. Both of them yawned, exited the car, and stretched before beginning to unload. Ben grabbed the backpack of cash from the trunk and strapped it on. He then took a small duffel bag with one arm, a couple plastic bags of clothes in the other, and wedged a box between his hands. Daniela grabbed all she could and followed him to the house. On the way, Ben accidentally dropped his MP3 player in the coarse grass and stooped to get it. Daniela stepped around him and moved up the stone walkway. She noticed an envelope taped to the door, then set down some of her luggage and tore it off. She ripped the edge open to find a piece of yellow paper inside. She pulled it out and read it, her eyes jutting back and forth. They grew wider. Her mouth dropped, and the bags from under her arms fell.

Ben tromped up from behind.

"They're looking for you?" said Daniela. She didn't turn from the door.

Ben grunted and shifted the load in his arms. "Who's looking for me?"

"The imperialists. This is what happens when you defy them." Tears welled in her eyes.

"Let me see that." Ben scrunched his face, then turned and dropped his luggage on the grass. Daniela handed the note without looking his way. The paper crinkled, and she stooped to gather her things. Her muscles were tense as she walked in.

"So there were two guys in suits looking for me in Quebrada." His eyes stayed on the note as he spoke loudly from outside. "That's unfortunate. No worry, though. They can't trace me here." Ben folded the note and stuck it in his pocket. He then gathered his things from the lawn and dropped them in a pile on the living room floor. The hiking bag thumped as it hit. He plopped onto the sofa and listened to Daniela unpacking in the bedroom.

"You ready, hon?" he yelled.

"Sí." Her voice wasn't as loud as the drawers opening and closing.

He heard her feet drawing near and looked up from the couch. "Restaurant?"

"Sí." Her eyes were vacant.

Ben groaned as he heaved himself up. He picked up his MP3 player and walked tiredly out while Daniela shut off the lights and locked the door. The sun had set, and the town's lights gave the sky a violet hue. A couple of stars could be seen. Daniela didn't notice as she walked quickly down the stone path. She didn't even look at Ben thumbing through his player when she got in. She fastened her seat belt and stared out the windshield. The hibiscus flowers in her neighbor's yard looked like birds in the darkness, a slight breeze giving them movement. Ben set down the player, and Ramblin' Jack's voice rang out over the strumming of an acoustic guitar. He laid his arm across Daniela's seat and mumbled the words to *Roving Gambler.*

Daniela turned to the side window. She saw houses with people on the porches. Each one faded into the next. The blocks passed, and Ben eased the car to a stop before an intersection. His head bobbed to the rhythm as he looked both ways. Daniela looked at a cat picking through garbage. Its fur was long and poofy but stained with dirt. It moved with extreme caution.

Ben turned left, and they climbed a hill toward downtown, eventually approaching a large cement plaza. Trees, a species similar to box elder, stood high above the people who sat on concrete benches. Yellow light gleamed down from lampposts, and children played soccer on a small concrete court at one end. Netless basketball hoops hung limply over the goals.

Ben watched the children play. *"I don't know how they can see the ball,"* he said.

Daniela glanced over and then turned back to her window. She caught a reflection of herself in the mirror. *'What are you going to do?'* she thought. She blinked, and the businesses outside passed in a blur.

They turned left, and Ben eyed a parking spot behind a red hatchback at the end of the street. Fluorescent light emanated from a restaurant on the corner across from it. Its two outer walls were open with only a wood railing separating the dining area from the sidewalk. He pulled in behind the little car, then sang the last lines of another Jack tune before shutting the player down. Daniela was already outside and walking toward the restaurant. It annoyed Ben, but not enough to keep him from staring at her tight pants. As he drew closer Ben could see tables with Formica tops and flimsy metal chairs. Only half of them were occupied, but most hadn't been cleared. Flies picked at the crumbs. A counter for those who preferred to stand was bolted to the far wall. Daniela was staring at the chalkboard menus. A middle-aged man in a white collared shirt stood behind the main counter. At the griddle farther back, a guy in a white t-shirt cooked. The grease hung thick in the air. A small woman walked from the kitchen struggling under the weight of a large tray of food. *"Move your big farmer body,"* she said.

The man in the white collared shirt stepped aside in an exaggerated manner. Ben stepped onto the dirty tile floor. It was slick beneath his shoes. The man turned back to spot him. *"Ah, my favorite North American,"* he said.

Ben smiled, and Daniela continued to stare blankly at the menus.

"Why have you been away so long?" The man's belly touched the counter.

"Traveling," said Ben.

"Always running like a criminal."

Daniela's eyes grew. She glanced around the restaurant. Over half the patrons were staring at Ben.

"A rolling stone gathers no moss," he said.

The man chuckled. *"What can I get you two tonight?"*

"Chicken soup, please," said Daniela.

"El casado for me."

"Un casado y una sopa de pollo," he said to the cook.

"Drinks?"

"Café," said Daniela.

"Tamarindo."

"A coffee and a beach town. We'll have them right out."

Ben followed Daniela to a table on the edge of the dining room. The other diners' eyes followed them. He winked at a child and smiled at the family, then slid into a chair opposite Daniela. He looked in her hardened face, which stared out at the plaza. "What's up?" he said.

"Nothing." Her eyes remained distant.

Ben stared at her for a moment longer, frowned, and then looked to the plaza. The children were gone from the soccer court, but other people still hung around on benches. Older people congregated in one area, teenagers in another. He watched a couple boys shove each other in initiatory fashion and then checked out the people in the restaurant. There were three different families with children, a table with two middle-aged men, and another with a teenage couple. The parents of two of the families were younger than he and Daniela. He looked at the teenage couple and watched them fumble over words, their conversation split up by awkward pauses. Then he turned to see an old man eating alone. He brought spoonfuls of soup slowly to his mouth. Ben watched him fish a piece of chicken from the bowl and eat it off the bone. He moved it back and forth, like he was hitting notes on a harmonica. Ben gave a glance behind to notice a baby's large brown eyes staring at him. The child's bronze face was chubby and smooth, and his hair stood straight up. Ben winked and waved his fingers, but the baby didn't move, just stared back intently. Movement from the kitchen caught his attention, and Ben turned to see the short woman bringing their drinks. She smiled as she set them on the table.

"Gracias," said Ben.

"Gracias," Daniela mumbled. She picked up her coffee and blew on it. Steam rolled off. She took the smallest of sips and stared at the plaza. Ben took a drink of his juice and watched the tiny particles of tamarind spinning in his glass.

The waitress hurried back, carefully set down Daniela's soup, and then went for Ben's. A large chunk of chicken protruded from the golden broth, and a soothing aroma wafted from it. The waitress returned with a plate of rice and beans, steak, onions, a small salad, and a fried plantain. "*Enjoy,*" she said.

Ben tore into his meal while Daniela slowly ate hers, blowing on each spoonful. She cut into a piece of yuca, and steam poured out.

"Steak's good," said Ben. "A little tough but good flavor."

Daniela glanced at his plate, then went back to her soup.

Ben shoveled his food until two thirds of it was gone. Then he leaned back and rubbed his stomach. *"I'm getting full."*

Daniela slurped from her spoon. *"I'm about done, too."*

"You still have half a bowl of soup."

"I'm not hungry."

"Is there something wrong with it?"

"No, I'm just not hungry." She set her spoon down and looked out at the plaza.

Ben cut up the last bits of steak and shoveled in another few mouthfuls. He began to groan after every bite, then set down his fork. *"I don't think I can eat anymore."* He leaned back and breathed heavily, then pushed himself up, walked to the counter, and pulled out a wad of cash. *"What do I owe you?"*

"Well, these prices are just for ticos." The man waved his hand toward one of the chalkboards. *"For North Americans we double them."*

A couple people at a table laughed. Daniela turned to watch.

"For Nicaraguans we lower the price," the man whispered.

"I'm a tingo," said Ben. *"Does that count for anything?"*

The man laughed. *"Tingos, they only have to pay one and a half times the menu price. Should be more, though... Stealing our beautiful ticas."* He smiled to Daniela, and Ben looked her way. Her eyes betrayed her false grin.

"Sopa, casado, café y tamarindo. Five thousand colones."

Ben handed him the money.

"Thanks for coming," said the man.

"Thank you." Ben noticed the waitress's eyes on him as he went to turn. They sparkled, and he grinned wider.

"And don't go leaving money on the table for my waitress," said the man. *"She makes enough. You give her anymore, and she'll leave me."*

Ben threw a ten thousand note on the table and stuffed the wad in his pocket. Daniela got up and walked out, waving quickly to the man behind the counter. Ben waved to everyone.

"¡Pura Vida!" yelled the vocal man.

"¡Pura Vida!" said Ben. He trotted out to catch up with Daniela. *"Hon, wait up. You're going too fast."*

She didn't slow her pace.

"Honey, what's the matter?" He laid his hand on her shoulder.

Daniela turned fiercely. "You're the problem." Her eyes were narrow. "You get a letter telling you people are after you, and you do nothing. Your skin doesn't attract enough attention? You need to throw money around, wink and wave, talk loudly with everyone? *¡Pura Vida! ¡Pura Vida!"* she mocked.

Older people in the plaza stared.

"Don't you care what happens to you?" Tears welled in her eyes. "You can't parade around like you're Pancho Villa. They're going to find you."

Ben stared at her, his mouth hanging. "Daniela, the letter said everyone in Quebrada Grande said they didn't know me."

"How can you be so sure?" Her voice cracked, and a couple tears rolled down her cheeks.

"If the people of Quebrada Grande say something, I'm going to believe them." Ben's eyes were resolute. "The letter's a couple days old. It says Chi Cho's coming tomorrow. So, I'm going to stay until then."

"Something has to be done. What happened in Tamarindo... It was too much. Now this. I can't take it." She grabbed the top of her head and held her palms against her temples.

Ben put his arms around her. "It's scary. I know, honey. But we have to wait until we get word." He rocked her from side to side. "I'll probably have to go into hiding, and I hope you'll come with me. It won't be bad. We can go somewhere, settle down, and relax. Just you and me living a quiet life in the country." He squeezed her, and her tears slowed. "For now you don't have to worry. If they knew about you, they'd already be here."

A drizzle fell, and as Ron banged at the motel room door, water dripped into the collar of his clear yellow poncho. He paused and knocked again. The metal door echoed. He saw finger tips brush aside the red curtain in the window at his left. Finally, Bill pulled open the door and stood lifelessly in a pair of red and white boxer shorts. The television played loudly in the background. "We have to go," said Ron.

"You catch word?"

"Roadblock. They got someone."

Bill grabbed his charcoal suit pants from a chair and slipped them on. Then he took a white button up shirt from a hanger, put it on without buttoning it, and took a seat on the bed. "You got a extra one of those things." He looked up from his shoe laces, staring at the poncho.

"Yeah, one in the car."

"Great, let's move." Bill sprung up but paused to lock the door. Two girls with umbrellas stared as he jogged to the car. They watched him slide across the grass, like a silent film star, shirt tails flapping. He maneuvered into the driver's seat of the Octavia, and the tires spun as they sped off.

"Is it him?" said Bill.

"Someone that fits the description. There was a whole group of Americans heading in."

"What for?"

"Volunteer work."

Bill slowed the car as they navigated the small town streets. The windshield wipers moved quickly, exposing a few umbrellas bobbing up and down on the sidewalk. Teenagers, shivering under the bus stop, clasped their arms over their chests. The temperature had dropped to the low seventies. Bill spotted a young girl with a shapely body walking under an umbrella. 'Wow. Just like Flora,' he thought.

As they turned left past the church, Bill hit the gas and watched the town fade away in his mirror. He turned his wipers up all the way where they screeched on the windshield. He pictured Flora sitting next to him as he played cards at the casino. She wore dark lipstick and rested her hand on his thigh. He felt the car descending, snapped to it, and punched the brakes. Ron grasped at the handle above his door. Bill then let off the brakes, turned into the other lane, and crept around the potholes. He hit the gas as they bounced over the final obstacle. The car hesitated. "Jesus, let's go," he said, and the car wheezed up the hill.

Bill gripped the steering wheel with both hands. "Alright, straight road rest of the way."

Ron watched the speedometer push one hundred twenty kilometers. He could feel every crack in the road. "Just remember the speed bump," he said.

Bill glanced his way, shirt still open and no seat belt across his chest. "I got this road down," he said.

Ron looked at the fields to his right, spotting workers moving through the rows. He wondered if they had to acclimate their bodies to work in the rain or if they were genetically programmed.

They entered Veracruz, and Bill slowed the car. People were gathered under the roof of the pulpería with their backs to the road. The soccer field across the street was empty as it had been each time they'd passed. The car dipped softly over the speed bump, and Ron eyed the half dozen people under the bus stop. They watched the silver car pass, faces indifferent. Bill kept it slow until they approached the corner at the edge of town, where he gunned it. The pineapple processing plant grew from a dot to an imposing structure. Its old tin walls speckled with rust. One large truck sat outside.

"That thing's seen better days." Bill stared at the letters on its walls, which were barely visible.

"A lot of people from Quebrada Grande used to pick pineapple for them," said Ron. "Now they have their own land."

"They find silver or something?"

"Who knows?" said Ron.

Bill squinted and slowly drove onto the rock road. Their bodies shook as the car bounced over the rough surface. Ron grimaced at the hills beyond. He imagined the vicious food chain with jaguars, pumas, and leopards ruling the forest. They rambled farther, and the road block came into view. There was a black SUV in the center of the road with the word "POLICÍA" unit in big white letters. A red shuttle bus was stopped on the right, and an officer spoke with someone in a truck on the left. Bill parked the silver car behind the bus. He shut it off and began to button his shirt. Ron tossed him a small plastic bag. "Here's your poncho," he said.

Bill ripped the package open as he got out. An officer met him there. *"What do we got here?"* said Bill. The poncho crinkled as he shook it and slipped the blue transparent plastic over his head.

"Americans trying to enter. One of them is named Ben." The officer wore a navy blue raincoat and pants, combat boots on his feet. There was a yellow emblem on the jacket, and a pistol grip stuck out from his waist. *"Here's his passport."*

Bill took the small blue book and flipped through it. It was one of the newer types with a thick paper cover. Patriotic pictures and quotes on each page. A bald eagle stared at him as he looked over the kid's background. 'Glassbury, Benjamin Frank, 17 April 1980. Place of birth, Ohio, U.S.A.' There was only one stamp. It covered George Washington's head on Mount Rushmore. It was from the day before.

"Bring him out," said Bill. *"Bring out the leader, too."*

He leaned against the car and handed the passport to Ron. The raindrops snapped as they hit his poncho.

"Looks legit," said Ron.

"Sure does. Can't be certain without scanning it, though."

"I'll call it in." Ron pulled out a cell phone and dialed. He put it to his ear, then hung up and shook his head. "No service."

"It's sketchy here. Try twenty feet that way." Bill pointed down the road.

The officer returned with a tall, skinny man at his right. Light blond hair hung to his shoulders. A short gray haired man was on the left. Both wore shorts, but the college kid had on a t-shirt, and the older man a short sleeve button up. His socks went half way to his knees.

Bill got up from the car. "You Glassbury?"

The older man stepped forward. "What does this pertain to, sir? We've been traveling for a long time." Irritation showed in his face.

"Who are you?" said Bill.

"Brian Hathway. I'm responsible for this group."

"Give your passport to him, Brian." Bill pointed to Ron, but the man stared indignantly.

Bill tightened his face. "We're with the U.S. Government. An American has put a lot of people in danger in this area."

The older man's eyes expanded. His lips fell open, and he slowly reached for his passport.

"Thank you," said Ron. He looked it over and jotted down information in a notebook.

"Ben, you have another form of I.D. on ya?" said Bill.

"Yeah, driver's license."

"Hand it to my partner."

He reached in his cargo pocket and took out a thin Velcro wallet. It was blue like the cops' uniforms. The tiny plastic strands wailed as he ripped it open.

"How old are you?" said Bill.

The kid looked to the sky. "Twenty six."

"Ever been to Wisconsin?"

"No. Never."

"Where do you, did you, go to school?" said Bill.

"Penn State."

"And, what's the name of their stadium there?"

Again, his eyes went up. "Beaver Stadium."

"You from Pennsylvania originally?"

"Yeah, Mount Pleasant, just outside of Bloomsburg... East of the Appalachians."

"It's what his license says," said Ron.

"What's the capital there, Ben?"

"Harrisburg."

Bill turned to the group leader. "Okay, Brian, you want to have your kids line up outside the bus? Just want to take a peak. Take down passport numbers."

"Okay." The short man turned to the bus.

"You can have your passport," said Ron.

The guy swung back, then took the booklet and stuck it in his shorts.

Bill looked at Ben. "You can go line up with 'em."

The kid stared at Ron. "Do I get my passport back?"

"I suppose."

The kid grabbed the little blue book and driver's license and walked to the bus.

"What do ya think?" said Bill.

"Waste of time."

"Same here." He let out a puff of air and kicked a small rock. "Let's write down some numbers," he said.

"I'll look over the bus."

The older man stepped off and moved to the side as the kids filed out. Nine girls and four boys stood along the length of the bus. Only two wore ponchos, and the others' clothes quickly became dotted with rain. Vexation shot from each eye. A couple looked confused and fearful, but most stared at the agents with contempt.

"Okay," said Bill. "I just need to take down your passport numbers. Then you're free to go. I'm sorry about the inconvenience, but it will be over shortly. As far as the weather..." He held his arms out and looked up. "I got no control."

Ron entered the bus. He noticed the driver's dark features, nodded to him, and then proceeded to look in the seats. Stuff was strewn about—jackets, magazines, books, and food. He bent down and looked under the seats. Then he walked to the back and lifted up bags to make sure nobody was stashed underneath. He noticed MP3 players, cameras, and a couple of Spanish phrase books. A copy of *The Electric Kool-Aid Acid Test* lay open on a seat. He nodded to the driver and stepped off.

Ron walked around the front of the bus. He took his time glancing underneath the muddy vehicle and tapping at the side panels. An aluminum ladder on the back caught his eye, and he grabbed ahold and climbed up. The rungs were slippery beneath his dress shoes, but he held tight and loosened a tarp covering luggage. He raised it up to reveal shiny hiking packs, then secured it and climbed down, walking slowly back around. The clothes of the kids in line looked soaked. One of the boys ran his hand through his hair, flicking water on the girl next to him. Bill was at the end of the line in front of a thin blonde in an orange poncho. Her hair was soaked, and the poncho hung just below her tiny shorts, giving the appearance that there was nothing underneath it.

"Is this right?" said Bill. "Your name is Candice Barr."

"I'm a sweet one." She had a smile that could end wars.

Bill looked her over and grinned. "We better get you back on the bus. Might melt." He bit his lip as he turned to the group leader. "We're done here."

The kids hurried on the bus.

"Brian," said Ron. "A quick word with you, please."

"Of course," he said.

"I know you don't have phones out here. At least there's no lines, and cells rarely work, but I want to give you our card. Maybe you could call if you hear anything regarding a Ben Starosta." He said the name slowly. "White guy, twenty eight. He's a criminal who could bring trouble to the entire area."

"Should I be concerned about my group?"

Ron took a photo from his notebook and held it out. "This is the man we're looking for. We don't believe him to be dangerous. It's more the people he knows. He's deep in some shit. If anyone in your group hears of him, call us." Ron handed him a card with his phone number scrawled in pen.

"I'll call you." The man looked directly in Ron's eyes before turning.

Ron walked over to Bill who was talking with the two cops. *"Okay. We're going to let this bus through,"* said Bill.

"But you wanted a North American, Ben," said the officer.

"It's not him," said Bill.

"Looks like him to us."

"It's not. Let them through."

Expletives shot from the man's mouth as he walked to the SUV, got in, and moved it. From the driver's seat he rudely gesticulated for the driver to go. The bus's engine grumbled as it turned over, and the other officer waved it on.

"Thanks for the call," said Bill to the calmer tico.

"No problem."

"Maybe next time."

The other officer slammed the door on his SUV, and Ron and Bill heard him as they left. *"Fuckin' gringos. Come into our country. Boss us around. I paid over a hundred thousand colones and filed forms. They wouldn't let me on their land."*

There was a slight rattling on Daniela's tin roof as the rain fell. Ben lay on the couch with his feet crossed at the ankles, reading a book. His shirt was bunched up, exposing his lightly tanned belly, and he fiddled with the string of his shorts. He jumped at the sound of a vehicle stopping outside. 'Chi Cho's truck,' he thought as he got up to peek out the window. The lights flickered off on the faded old truck, and Ben dropped the curtain. He opened the door a crack and walked back to the couch, picking up his book. He heard Chi Cho kick his boots off on the porch, and left O'Brien's war stories behind as the door swung open.

"Goddamn, gringo, I thought I was going to have to take a rubber glove for you."

Ben sat up and set the book aside. *"What's going on?"* he said.

Chi Cho walked over and slapped Ben's hand, then sat next to him. *"The fuckers got a roadblock set up outside Quebrada. Off the main road so you can't see it."*

Ben's eyes swelled. *"When did they do it?"*

"Two days ago." Chi Cho wiped rain from his face and neck and looked into Ben's eyes. *"They were tico cops today, but yesterday the gringos were there."*

"Back up here. Who are these gringos?"

"Two guys in suits. Look like businessmen. They hassled the volunteers."

"They're looking for me?"

"Oh yeah. I'm going to the yuca plant to fill the back of my truck. Want it to look like I had a reason to go."

"Alright," Ben said slowly. *"Let's go over the whole story."*

"Okay. A few days ago..."

"Wait, these gringos have shiny shoes?"

"Could see your reflection," said Chi Cho. *"They've been going around asking about a Benjamin Starosta. They mentioned that you did volunteer work there five years ago. At first they claimed they were your friend. That you told them to meet you there. Now the story's worn thin."*

There was a loud thud outside, and the pair jumped from the couch. Ben peeled back the curtain. *"Just a branch,"* he said.

They eased back into the couch. *"Yesterday, a group came in. The pigs stopped them thinking you were aboard. Then they got the gringo agents out there and really hassled them."*

"Jesus Christ."

"I was freakin' out about the patches," said Chi Cho, *"but the cameras show no one's been around. They're not hot."*

"That's good. But if they tracked me here, they must know something. Know I had someone else posing as me in Peru."

"Fuck! They think you're a gangster."

"They must, to come all the way here." Ben got up and looked out the window, then paced across the floor. *"I'm gonna get the hell out of here. It's not safe."*

Chi Cho stared into Ben's strained eyes, which fell to the hiking pack resting against the coach.

"What are you going to do with this money?" Ben kicked the bag.

"I don't know," said Chi Cho. *"But I'm not going to bring it back there."*

"I don't want to leave it here, just in case they find out about Daniela. And, I don't want to take it with me."

"I'm sure we can leave it somewhere."

"Yeah."

"How about Victor's."

"Ha ha," said Ben.

"He'd be willing to help. He loves you." Chi Cho smiled.

"No, he loves all white people. He'd just a soon turn me in if he could trade one gringo pal for two." Ben stared at the floor, and Chi Cho scratched his head.

"Benigno," said Ben. *"We can leave it with him. He won't steal it."*

"Yeah, Benigno's good." Chi Cho again looked into Ben's face, then scrunched his eyebrows. *"So where you going to go?"*

"I got a place," he said. *"I'll leave tomorrow. Can you meet me in a month?"*

"A month? Sí."

"Volcán Poás, the crater. Eleven am, last day of July. If you need to get ahold of me, you can send a message to one of my emails. I should occasionally be able to check it." He ran his hand through his hair.

Chi Cho felt the thigh of his jeans. He reached in his pocket and brought out a Ziploc full of sticky green buds. Ben raised his eyebrows as the pungent aroma hit his nostrils. Chi Cho threw the bag up, and Ben clapped his hands around it.

"Damn, Chi Cho, you're a savior." He put the bag to his nose and inhaled deeply. *"How'd ya sneak it past the pigs?"*

"I just snapped the plastic casing up from around the stick shift. They weren't looking for weed, just you."

"Surprised they didn't smell it."

"It was in six bags."

Ben smelled the pot again, and Chi Cho smiled. He looked at photographs on the wall of Ben and Daniela in a water fight. Isabel had taken them five years ago outside their home. It was new then. Paid for with the crop. *"So, is Daniela going with you?"* he said.

"Sí, I'm sure she will." He threw the bag on the couch and took a seat. The distant look returned to his eyes. *"She's going to talk to the school today. They won't be happy about it."*

"She's going to miss those kids, too."

"I know. She's not taking it well."

"Hopefully the time away will help." Chi Cho's tone was subdued.

"We'll see."

"Well, I better get going if I'm going to pick up that yuca." Chi Cho pushed himself to his feet, and Ben followed. The two hugged, squeezing tightly.

"I hope nothing happens to anyone in Quebrada Grande," said Ben. *"I love those people."*

"I know you do."

They withdrew, and Ben wiped at tears in his eyes. *"It was good seeing you."*

"You, too," said Chi Cho. He moved for the door.

"Just wait," said Ben. *"Don't forget the money."*

Chi Cho gave a chuckle. *"Silly me."* He smiled, then walked to the bag and heaved it on his back. He stood and looked in Ben's eyes. *"We'll miss you, gringo."*

"I'll miss you. Miss you all."

Chi Cho turned and walked out the door. Ben went to the window and watched him pull away, then remained, staring at the rain dotting the puddles. Eventually, he returned to the couch and picked up his book.

Bill stomped his feet and shook his jacket as he stepped under the roof of an open air restaurant. He pulled out a chair, and its wodden legs squeaked against the tile floor. Then he threw his jacket over the back. The temperature was eighty four. The rain fell unremittingly while the bartender and two groups watched telenovelas on a large TV in the corner. Bill walked to the bar. *"Hola,"* he said.

"¡Pura Vida!"

The bartender was young. 'Couldn't be more than a year past eighteen,' thought Bill. He was clean shaven. Hair slicked back. Staunch cologne.

"I need a drink, the workingman's drink, vodka tonic in a water glass."

The bartender squinted. *"Why's that a workingman's drink?"*

"No one can smell it on your breath," Bill said gruffly.

The bartender grinned and grabbed a glass.

"I'm going to be in town for a little while. There isn't anywhere for some fun, is there?" Bill winked at him.

"There's a bar outside of town that throws big parties on weekends."

"A little more vodka, amigo." Bill pointed to the glass, and the bartender obliged, then poured in the tonic water.

"I'm looking for gambling," said Bill. *"And, girls for money,"* he whispered.

The bartender looked up at the tin roof. *"There's a place in town where people play cards."*

"What type of cards?" Bill sipped from the glass.

"Blackjack."

"No poker?"

"No, only blackjack." He glanced at the other tables and leaned in close. *"If you really want, I can get you in a cockfight."*

Bill looked at the roof and sipped on his drink. *"That sounds interesting, but I could really go for a girl."*

The boy worked a towel over in his hands. *"There's a town two hours from here with a bunch of whore houses. Or, you could always try La Fortuna."*

"La Fortuna, that's where Volcán Arenal is, right?"

"Sí."

"Hmm. Big tourist town." Bill rubbed his chin. *"There's bound to be girls."*

Bill's head snapped around to the thud of feet on the wet ground. He saw the shadow of a man with an umbrella. As it drew closer, Ron's face emerged from the darkness. Bill slipped a ten thousand note on the counter and looked into the bartender's pupils. *"Gracias."* He nodded slowly and walked to a table.

Ron shook his umbrella out and leaned it against a pole. His galoshes chirped against the tile. *"Café,"* he told to the bartender as he walked by.

The slick faced boy grabbed a pot of coffee and a mug and followed. As Ron took a seat, he set down the mug and filled it. *"Nata o azúcar?"* he asked.

"Tell him I want both," said Ron.

"Ambos, por favor."

The bartender returned with a steel creamer and a saucer with several packs of sugar and a spoon laid neatly on it. He set them down, nodded, and returned to the bar.

"So, how long we gonna have to hang out here?" said Bill

Ron spilled a couple drops of cream and wiped them up with

a thin napkin. "Week and a half. Two. We're supposed to keep the roadblock up till we determine if he's there."

"We might not ever determine that… Without a team."

"Not our call." He stirred in the sugar.

Bill glanced at the bar. The kid with the slicked hair was back to watching television. "I was thinking. I have an old friend here. He might have some ideas on how to get through to these people. If I could meet with him, would you be able to do the check-ins for a day?"

Ron blew on his coffee. "It'd be possible. Where is this guy? Would you even be able to get to him in a day?"

"*La Fortuna.* Half hour away." He took a large gulp from his water glass and breathed out his nose.

"Isn't that a tourist spot?" Ron's eyes narrowed as he scrutinized him.

Bill leaned back with his drink in hand. "Yeah, it's where he's living. He does a job every month or so. Other than that, he hangs at the spas, picking up tourists."

"Delightful." Ron rolled his eyes and took a sip. "So, did you get ahold of him?"

"I shot him an email."

"I don't want you sitting around at the spas."

"I'll try, but you know..."

Ron shook his head and looked into the darkness outside. The pounding on the roof was methodic. He sipped his coffee, set it on the table, and wiped the dampness from below his lip. "I spoke with one of the teachers. Asked if we could come in and talk to the kids."

"And?"

"Didn't want to frighten the children. I think he was upset about the volunteer group."

"I don't think any of 'em would talk, anyway. Their parents got 'em scared. I can see it in their eyes."

Ron's looked at the shadow of a soccer goal outside, then his coffee. "I guess we should be gettin' out to the roadblock."

"Probably," said Bill. He tipped back his drink and downed it, then wiped his forehead.

Ron pushed aside his mug. "How much is a coffee?" he said.

"Just leave two thousand." Bill got up and slipped on his jacket. Ron threw the money on the table and went for his umbrella. His galoshes squawked.

"Hasta luego." Bill waived to the bartender.

The kid looked from the TV and waved back. *"¡Chau!"* he yelled.

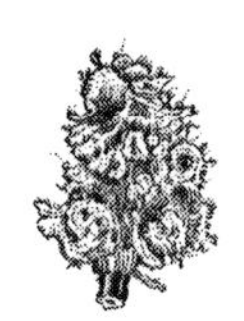

Bill stood before the counter in Pital's lone book store. He scratched his ankle, then looked at the foam bottom of his sandal. He wore royal blue swim trunks, a beige cotton, button down shirt, and brown aviator sunglasses. The trunks went halfway to his knees, exposing legs as white as a dead earthworm. Like a Northerner on his winter vacation, he was ready to expose his pallid flesh to the sun.

A plump tico behind the counter waved a road map. *"Just a map?"* he said.

"Sí."

"We have books in English here." The man grabbed a few from a stack behind him. "Emma Goldman, Noam Chomsky, Howard Zinn."

"I don't want any of that shit," said Bill. *"Just the map."*

"Okay. Okay. Two thousand colones."

Bill threw a couple thousand notes on the counter and walked out.

"¡Pura Vida!" the man yelled.

Bill envisioned himself saying, "Pura this," and grabbing his crotch, but he quietly walked out to the silver Skoda. The rain had parted and made way for the sun. And though rain was still a possibility, the day appeared pleasant as Bill hopped in and hit the accelerator till the engine whined. The temperature and humidity were both above ninety. Mirages appeared and disappeared on the road. Bill glanced around, espied workers slowly planting pineapple, then tossed out his cigarette butt, and rolled up the window. The air conditioning was pumping, and a smile graced his face.

Bill reached over and unfolded the map. He studied the road, then grabbed a brochure he'd printed from the internet. 'La Fortuna, pop. 6,000,' he read. 'At times it draws as many tourists in a week. In 1968, it was just a mountain. Before the massive eruption, which lasted several days. Eighty seven people killed. Three small villages buried.' Bill looked out the windshield and thought of Quebrada Grande. 'While the eruptions destroyed the lives of many, down the road it would enhance the lives of many more. The eruptions formed three active craters, which continue to erupt daily. Because of these active craters, Volcán Arenal would never pose a threat again.' Bill turned the page of the National Park brochure. He saw information on hikes and horseback riding, adventure activities. He threw it aside and picked up the hot springs pages. The first was for Baldí Termael. It had a photo of several white women sitting at a swim up bar. He stared at it, then turned back to the road. He wondered at the possibilities of picking up a tourist. Then his mind drifted to Flora. He thought of her on top of him, head tipped back, her breasts bouncing as he clutched her ass. Bill's mouth hung down, then he saw a corner fast approaching and punched the brakes.

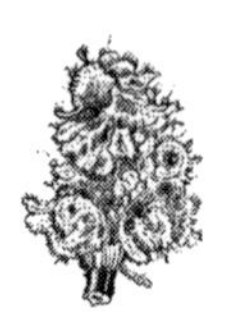

Daniela and Ben were driving up narrow mountain roads into the cloud forest, leaving behind the steamy rainforest. The temperature had dropped to the low seventies. Unfortunately for them, the change in weather outside hadn't led to a change in atmosphere inside. At times Ben felt nearly as light as the fog, but Daniela looked caught in yesterday's downpour. Her body sunk into the seat. Uncertainty preyed on her. 'If the agents go to my home, I can never return. People will always stare. Whisper.' The dirge playing lightly from the car's radio was fitting. Ben cracked his window, hoping the clean, cool air would blow away the dark clouds.

Ben pulled off the road in front of a small, white concrete building. A sign out front read, "Mirador de la Catarata San Fernando." He turned down the music and got out, then bent an ear toward a deep noise echoing in the distance. He listened as he waited for Daniela to slowly walk around the car, then took her hand before entering the open doorway. The old, wooden floor was soft beneath their feet. Ben stared at the dusty surface, thinking about the last time he'd stepped on a wooden floor, back in the States. The place was filled with colorful tourist souvenirs, racks of postcards, small watercolors on a shelf, and cheap jewelry. A woman in jogging pants and a sweatshirt played with her child on the floor. The father smiled as he watched from a chair. *"Buenos días."* They greeted Daniela and Ben while the baby stared, wide-eyed.

"¡Pura Vida!" Ben smiled, then waved at the child, like he was cupping a ball in his hand.

Daniela gave an *"hola"* but refused to smile.

The pair walked straight through to the metal deck at the rear. A few small tables sat along the wall, and humming bird feeders hung all around. Twenty of the fluttering creatures buzzed through the air. They varied in size from butterfly to barn swallow. Some were iridescent blue, others a mix of black and emerald green, some deep violet, and, yet, others scarlet red. They were like polished gemstones with wings. Even Daniela's melancholy couldn't hold up against them. She smiled as they whizzed by her head and chased each other from the feeders. She even let out a laugh and pointed.

The birds, however, weren't the only thing raising her spirits. Beyond them, across the lush valley lay the waterfall of San Fernando, the largest in the country. It had a height of nearly three hundred feet, though the upper portion was veiled with fog. The deep sound of the water crashing faded into a soothing tone at the deck. Ben turned to Daniela, noticed the bliss in her eyes, and grinned wider than he had in days. His plan had worked. Her dour mood couldn't last in the magical environment.

Ben rubbed her back as she leaned her forearms on the railing. The tension was receding. He kissed her on the back of the neck and led her to one of the small tables. As they sat across from one another, Daniela grasped Ben's hand and gazed into his eyes. "I'm sorry," she said.

His pupils expanded to take in hers. "It's okay," he said, then leaned in and kissed her. Their lips had been together for three seconds when the woman in sweats stepped onto the deck. She grinned and walked softly over. *"Are you ready for drinks?"*

"Sí." Ben picked up the menu, a sheet of yellow laminated paper, and scanned the drinks. *"I'd like a strawberry juice,"* he said.

The woman nodded, and Daniela looked up from her menu. *"Pineapple juice, por favor."*

The woman again nodded, then gave a quick glance to Ben.

"I think we're ready to order food, too," he said. *"Rice and beans, plantains?"* He looked at Daniela.

"Sí, that's fine."

"For both of us, please." He slid his menu back into its holder on the edge of the table.

"Okay. One moment." The woman smiled and went back inside.

Ben looked to the waterfall that held Daniela's gaze.

"I've been in such a bad mood," she said.

"It's fine. I understand how difficult this is." Ben rubbed her hand.

Daniela watched a bird flutter by. "I'm good now," she said. "I've been worrying about the future too much." She again looked in his eyes. "You have to be more careful, though. Sometimes you make the present scary. No more being the center of attention. It makes me nervous."

Ben smirked. "I'll try."

Daniela lifted his hands and slammed them on the table. *"You'll do it. I'll make sure of it."*

The woman returned with their drinks. *"One strawberry juice and one pineapple."*

"Gracias." The couple nodded, then Ben picked up his drink.

Daniela turned back to the waterfall. "There's no point in me being here if I'm unhappy. If stuff ever gets to be too much, there's waterfalls by the cabin. Humming bird gardens, too." She watched Ben swill his drink. "Maybe we could even have our own humming bird garden."

"Maybe, hon." Ben set down his glass, felt the rush of sugar, and then picked it back up. A bird flew inches from his head, and he turned quickly.

Daniela giggled, and the woman stepped back out carrying two plates. She laid one before each of them. *"Anything else I can get you?"*

"No." Daniela shook her head.

Ben raised his empty glass. *"More strawberry juice, please."*

The woman's smile popped like fireworks. *"Thirsty, huh?"*

"He's crazy for that juice," said Daniela.

The woman laughed as she walked away. Daniela and Ben looked at their golden yellow plantains, black beans and rice, then at the scenery as they ate. They'd barely touched their food when the woman returned with Ben's juice. *"You're not going to want another one right now are you?"*

"No, this should hold me." Ben thought about how he'd actually like one more, then chopped off a piece of the mushy plantain and ate it. His tongue tingled from the sweetness.

"You know," said Daniela. "I think we didn't bring enough books."

Ben wiped his mouth. "Yeah, about twenty just came in to Pital. We can pr'y call Tiago and have him ship them if we want. Order more, too." He used his tongue to pick a piece of rice from his teeth.

Daniela nodded.

The two finished the rest of their food and took in their last views of the landscape. "This is going to be good," said Ben. "I always dreamed of living here."

Daniela sighed. Then her eyes followed the birds. Ben glanced at the check and tossed down several thousand colones. Daniela narrowed her eyes and stared.

"What?" said Ben.

"This is what I'm talking about." She picked up the money and shook it. "People don't tip in this country."

"Honey, we're in a tourist shop. Gringos tip. It won't arise suspicion."

"You're insufferable."

The couple rose and left. Ben hooked his arm around Daniela's waist, and she played with his hair. Outside, Ben laid soft kisses behind her ear, and she giggled and pushed him away. As they got back in their car and left the waterfall lookout behind, Bill was coasting into La Fortuna.

He passed a couple of cheap hotels and tourist shops with beach towels outside before an open air bar came into view. No cars were parked along the street. Bill put on his blinker and steered in. He squinted under the palm frond roof into the dim bar. No one was around, just a bartender organizing glasses. Bill reached in the back seat and grabbed a panama hat. It had a hat ring with a red and white flower pattern on it. He lowered his head and pushed it on, then stooped out and sprung to his feet. He seemed to move fluidly, like it was the suit that had been holding him back all this time. His new clothes and found enthusiasm didn't stop a cringe from passing through his lips, though. He reached down and rearranged the front of his swim trunks before ambling to the bar in the smoothest gait he could muster.

'Why the fuck do they have Goldman and Chomsky there?' he thought.

A white woman in her mid-thirties passed on the sidewalk with two children. She wore a large brimmed hat, a light cotton shirt, and polyester shorts. Bill touched his hat and nodded before entering the bar.

Inside, he peeled off his shades, stood in place, and waited for his eyes to adjust. Most of the place was constructed of bamboo, the bar top and floor the only exceptions. Dull orange light came from conch shells mounted around the bar. Unlit candles sat on tables beside clean ash trays. Bill walked to the bar, pulled out a bamboo stool, and plopped down. He dropped his hat next to him as the bartender casually walked over. The man wore black work pants and a lime green shirt. His clothes accentuated his slim frame. "*Buenos días.* What can I get you?"

"Hola, amigo." It was the most cheerful voice to come from Bill since San Jose. "Give me a piña colada."

"No problem." The bartender scooped ice into a cocktail shaker and poured in white rum and coconut cream. "Going to the Volcano?" he asked.

Bill stared at a calendar behind the bar with a photo of a girl in a bikini on it. "No, I think I'd rather see the volcano from a distance, while sitting in a hot pool of water."

The bartender laughed. "No canopy tours either, eh?" He poured in pineapple juice and gave it a vigorous shake.

Bill bent over the bar. "You talkin' zip line?"

"There are bridges for those not so adventurous." The man reached in the cooler and grabbed a cup made from a pineapple rind. Water vapor hung around the vessel as he set it on the counter and poured in the drink.

Bill laughed. "My life is adventurous enough. That's why I'm here." He reached in his shirt pocket and took out his Camels. He knocked the pack against his wrist and pulled one out with his lips. "Today, I want to be on my feet as little as possible."

The bartender tossed a straw and miniature umbrella in the drink and planted it in front of him. "Off to the hot springs, then?"

Bill lit his cigarette. "*Sí,* I'm not sure which one, though." He dropped his lighter in his pocket and picked up his drink. He sipped it through the pink straw while holding back the umbrella.

The bartender leaned against the counter behind him and crossed his arms. "Tabacón is supposed to be the best, but you have to stay at their hotel. Baldí Termael is the next."

"Yeah, I looked at a flier for that one." Bill blew smoke out his nose.

"I go there a few times a year. It has sixteen pools, a couple with swim up bars, long chairs in the water, and, of course, the volcano." The man gestured with his arms. "Beautiful," he said. "It's wise to get your drinks here, though."

Bill glanced at the calendar. It was a latina beauty in an orange thong and a yellow and orange striped top. "I'm looking for a different type of tourist attraction. You might be able to help."

"What is it?" The man leaned in.

"Ladies."

The bartender laughed. "You're looking for some real exercise. You want El Cuba Libre. Place is full of them."

"Cuba Libre? Is it a bar?" Bill puffed on the diminishing butt.

"That and more. They have rooms upstairs."

"Is it close?"

"You leave like you're going to Baldí." The bartender turned and swung his arm over his shoulder. "About a mile outside of town you will see a purple building off to your right. It's a ways off the road. Calle de Aguadulce."

"Lots of girls?" Bill poked the cigarette out in the ash tray.

"Definitely, at night. I don't know about now. There's bound to be some, though."

"Thank you. You've been really helpful." Bill took a long sip from the pink straw. He felt the texture of the rind in his hand.

"No problem." The bartender slapped the counter and walked to a cooler where he took out a bag of limes. He grabbed a knife and cutting board from a shelf and started slicing. Bill could smell the strong citric aroma. He stared at the calendar as he slurped the rest of his drink. The girl's eyes seemed to beckon him. He hoped there'd be a girl at El Cuba Libre to rival her. 'Couldn't have teeth that white,' he thought. He blew pulp from the straw and drug it across the bottom of the hull, drawing out the last drops of liquid. He then pushed on his hat and tossed a ten thousand note on the bar.

"Another?" said the bartender.

"No, I'm off to the springs." Bill gave a wink and slid on his sunglasses. He let out a huff as he got to his feet.

"Enjoy it," said the man.

"Adios, amigo." Bill waved as he left.

The bartender's eyes fell on the ten thousand note. Then he looked up to see Bill on the sidewalk. *"¡Pura Vida!"* he yelled.

Bill raised his hand without turning. Then he tossed his panama hat in the back of the car, got in, and pulled away.

From the Mirador Ben and Daniela continued further up the mountains. The windows were cracked, and the cool moist air enveloped them. They sang along to music and laughed when one sung the wrong lines. They held hands and stared into the forest, but as they dipped down into a valley, their singing stopped. Another waterfall, La Paz, came into view. It was only a third the height of San Fernando, but the road crossed over the valley less than a hundred feet away. Ben parked the car, and the two got out. The sound of the fall was overpowering. Mist hung in the air and dotted them as they walked across the bridge. Birds chirped in the background. Ben stared to the stream below where the water crashed. On the other side of the bridge there were two stands, one for snacks, one for trinkets. *"I'm going to get a bottle of water,"* said Daniela. *"You want anything?"*

"No," yelled Ben, running up the dirt path that led to the waterfall. As he drew closer the mist grew thicker. He looked toward Daniela who appeared to be conversing with the people below. He then walked behind the fall and sat on the cold, hard dirt, crossing his legs. The cataract was as wide as Daniela's car was long. Ben controlled his breathing and stared into it, ignoring the mist that ran down his face. His eyes went out of focus, and the water grew blurry. He continued rhythmically breathing deeply, and the fall disappeared. The sound of the water crashing faded. He pictured himself in a concrete room. It was bright, and there was an electrical hum in the background. He felt cold, but his throat was hot, and there was a burning in his chest. Ben panicked and tried to flail his limbs but couldn't. Someone squeezed his shoulder, and he thrust his eyes open to Daniela.

"Are you alright?"

Ben moved his tongue around his mouth. *"I don't know. I feel dehydrated."*

"Here." Daniela handed him a bottle of water, and Ben unscrewed the cap and gulped it. *"How do you get dehydrated sitting under a waterfall?"* she said.

Ben looked himself over. His wet shirt clung to his body, and small beads covered his skin. *"I don't know."*

Daniela reached into the fall and flicked water in his face.

He tipped the rest of the bottle back and stood up. *"Seen enough?"*

"For today." She leaned back and smiled. Ben wrapped his arms around her and kissed her. When he brought his lips away, he saw a couple of children racing up the path.

"We better get out of here. I think I'm being too conspicuous."

"You can be as conspicuous as you want when you're loving me." She kissed him and grabbed his lower lip between hers, then slowly released. Ben held Daniela's hand while she cautiously checked her footing. They then hugged the mountainside as the children

scampered by.

"Oh, you have to go to the stand. There's something I want to show you."

Ben followed Daniela down the path and across the street. The stand consisted of a table under a vinyl tent with sunglasses and jewelry scattered about. Ben noticed pipes of cheap porcelain, rock, and wood. He stared at one with a statuette of an indigenous person on the shaft. The man had a large erect penis half his height.

Daniela giggled. "Do you see it?"

Ben turned from the table. "Oh, I saw it. Looked like an American Priapus."

The two walked back to the car and buckled up. Daniela took hold of the MP3 player and selected *Renegades of Funk*. Morello created a squealing with his pedal board, the drums banged, and the guitar wailed. She waved to the workers at the refreshment stand as they started to climb the hill, and the waterfall faded away. As they ascended, the engine whinnied along with the sound produced by the pedal board. A little ways up they passed a tourist resort to their right. Buses sat in the lot.

"I want to visit there," said Daniela. "The butterfly gardens."

"If we go there, we'll sneak in from the trail by La Paz. Thirty two dollars to hike trails," he scoffed.

Further on, they passed out of the deep forest region into an area cleared long ago for agriculture. Small, bushy trees with waxy green leaves covered one hillside, coffee plants. Some were speckled with red, ripe berries, looking similar to cranberries and ready to be picked. The cool temperature and nutrient rich volcanic soil were ideal. Greenhouses for strawberries and ferns lay on the other hillside.

The road came to a T, and Ben hooked left. The coffee fields vanished while greenhouses and cattle remained. One cow stretched its neck through the fence, preferring grass outside its domain. Not far along, they came upon a boy standing by the side of the road. He held a gallon bag in each hand. One was white, the other red. Ben pulled the car over and rolled down his window. There were five of the white bags, tied shut at the top, sitting on the ground. *"How much for the strawberries?"* said Ben.

"One thousand colones." The boy's t-shirt was tight around his skinny arms. Peach fuzz dusted his upper lip.

Ben handed him the money, and the kid gave back a sack of berries. *"What's in the other bags?"*

"Sour cream," he said.

"Maybe later this week."

"I'll be here," said the boy.

"Gracias." Ben slid the transmission into drive. *"¡Pura Vida!"* he said.

"¡Pura Vida!" yelled the boy.

Ben and Daniela continued up the slope. The grass in the pastures was verdant as it ran down to the forest line. Small patches of woods were scattered there amongst the greenhouses. Ben ate the berries, one after another, and threw the tops out his window. Daniela ate them at a slower pace. Not more than two miles up the road, a series of A-frame cabins appeared. They had faded, red tin roofs, spotted with moss, and blue cinder block walls. There were white borders around the windows and doors. A large brown building resembling a barn stood next to the road, and Ben turned left into a driveway behind it.

Ben drove up to a large A-frame at the end of the row, the only one with a second floor. It towered above the rest and sat at an angle to them. Across the driveway lay a typical tico home, one story with a rectangular frame of concrete blocks. Ben gave a light stretch as he got out and set the strawberries on the seat. *"Might as well try the restaurant,"* he said. *"Guy's probably up there. What's his name?"*

"Fermín," said Daniela.

"Fermín? That's a new one for me."

"The festival in Pamplona," said Daniela. *"With the running of the bulls, it's for Saint Fermín."*

They walked up the gravel driveway. *"Almost chilly enough for a jacket,"* said Ben.

"More than cold enough." Daniela pulled the strings of her hood and held her arms against her chest.

Ben took in a huge breath of the cool mountain air. *"Seems cold now, but you'll be used to it in a week. Chilly at night, though."*

Daniela pulled her jacket tighter, and they walked to the front of the building. She tugged open the large wooden door to reveal hardwood tables and chairs. There were old metal light fixtures and large windows overlooking the valley below. A young girl in jeans and a sweater approached from the side. *"Two?"* she said.

"We're looking for Fermín," said Ben.

"I'll get him." The girl walked to their right and through a wooden swivel door. A moment later she followed out a short, stocky man. He wore jeans and a t-shirt. A mustache brushed his pudgy cheeks as he smiled.

"Hola. Hola. How are you?" The short man shook Ben's hand and nodded quickly to Daniela.

"We're good. I'm Ben, and this is Daniela."

He looked at her. *"Sí. I spoke with you on the phone."*

"Sí. It's nice to meet you," she said.

"You, too."

"Cabin still available?" said Ben.

"Of course. Of course. I have the key. Let's go look." Ben and Daniela followed the man. He threw his arms back and forth, and they had to hustle along the gravel drive to keep up. *"We only have three of the little cabins rented today."* Fermín motioned to the A-frames. They were spaced ten feet away from each other, and their tile floors stretched from inside onto the porch. There was a chair sitting at each side of the red doors, a wooden railing before it, and a small flower garden in front. *"People don't go for the big one. A family would just as soon rent a couple of the others and eat at the restaurant than have a kitchen."* He looked at Ben. *"I don't think you North Americans like to cook."*

"Not on vacation," said Ben.

"Sí. Sí."

They stepped onto the smooth tile porch, slick beneath their shoes, and Fermín's keys jingled as he unlocked the door. He left them in and swung it open. *"You have a living room."* He motioned to the right where a couch, chair, and coffee table sat before a television on a low stand. *"A kitchen and dining room."* He waved to a small, round dinner table to their left and pointed at the kitchen.

"There's a stove." Fermín opened the door of a small black wood burner in the corner. *"It gets a little cold at night. You may want a fire. I keep wood stocked up outside. If you're using this every night we'll have to make some sort of deal."* Ben nodded, and Fermín walked to a heavy wooden ladder leading upstairs. Ben and Daniela followed, ducking as they made it up.

Fermín smiled at Ben. *"You'll only be able to stand up in the middle. Plenty of room, though. Dressers, closet."*

Ben stared at the old bureaus and wondered how Fermín had gotten them up stairs. The hole they'd climbed through looked smaller than both of the dressers.

Daniela felt the quilt on the bed. The bright colors reminded her of humming birds and the flowers out front. She glanced out the octagonal window above it. Cows grazed in the valley below. Fermín stepped onto the ladder, and they followed him down. *"It's not anything big, but enough for two people."* He walked to the couch and leaned against the back of it.

"*Sí, it should be enough."* Ben reached in his pocket and took out an envelope fat with bills. *"A million two hundred thousand, three months."*

Fermín grabbed it like change from a salesclerk. *"Sí, sounds good."*

"You'll make a lot more off us from the restaurant," said Ben.

Fermín chuckled and took his keys from the door. He worked a key off the ring and held it out. *"Here you go. It's all yours. If you need anything, Luna or I are usually in the restaurant or bar. If not, we're over there."* He pointed to the house apart from the cabins.

"Gracias," said Ben.

"Sí, gracias," said Daniela.

"¡Pura Vida!" Fermín turned and walked to his house with short quick steps, arms swinging.

"¡Pura Vida!" said Ben and Daniela.

Ben tossed the key on the dining room table. *"This is it. Our new home."*

"It's wonderful." Daniela smiled and grabbed Ben at the waist. *"I love you,"* she said.

Ben leaned in and kissed her. *"I love you, too."*

Bill passed the bars and restaurants, Internet cafes, tourists shops, and hotels that made up La Fortuna. Wooden sculptures covered a parking lot at the end of town. Bill stared, wondering if tourists purchased them and how they got them home. A couple of miles out, he spotted a large magenta building in the distance. There were a few cars in front. The names Emma Goldman, Noam Chomsky, and Howard Zinn echoed in his head. 'Fuckin' commies,' he thought. He put on his blinker and turned down the gravel road. The car shook, and papers fell from the visor. As Bill drew nearer, he counted six vehicles in the lot. Four as new as his. Two SUVs. There was a painting of a cowgirl on the side of the building staring toward a horizon. The moon rose as the sun descended. A horse appeared to whinny in the background. "El Cuba Libre" was inscribed in Old English typeface. He turned into the lot and pulled up next to a tan Jeep, then shut off the car and looked about. There was no movement. The cowgirl's eyes stared at him in the rear view mirror. He left the panama hat in the backseat and ducked out. Faint music could be heard from inside. Deep bass notes. He felt the gravel poking through the bottoms of his sandals, and as he drew closer, he noticed paint chipping from the mural. He spat, grabbed the large steel door, and pulled. Music and the smell of cigarettes and stale beer flowed out. He inhaled deeply and entered. The place was dim. Bill took off his shades and saw two men, one white, and one latino, talking with girls on a dance floor to his right. Purple and green light moved over them. Another white man flirted with a girl by the wall. His hand was in the back of her pants. Bill walked to the bar and took a seat. There were two ticos drinking Imperial beer at the far end and four girls on stools. They chatted amongst themselves but looked up as Bill sat down. He noticed one with an innocent face and one who looked dangerous, like she wanted to rip his clothes off, tie him, and beat him. Her eyes seemed to glow as she pulled a cigarette from her mouth.

"*¡Pura Vida!*" said the bartender. He was Bill's age and size. A tico equivalent without the receding hair.

"*¡Pura Vida!*" said Bill.

"*What can I get you?*" He strained to be heard over the music.

"*How about a Cuba Libre?*"

"*Of course.*" The man grabbed a glass from above and scooped in ice. He picked up a bottle of Ron Marques, poured in two finger lengths, and shot cola in from a nozzle. He let off when the bubbles hit the top of the glass, then slid two slices of lime on the edge and set it in front of him.

"*Bueno,*" said Bill. "*This is the only place that doesn't serve them in a can.*"

"*Everything here is high quality.*" The bartender looked at the girls, and they smiled.

"*I see that.*" Bill looked to the girls, and two of them stood to display the whole package. One was skinny with dyed blonde hair. Bill looked past her to the other. She wore tight low-rise jeans and heels. A small red button down shirt was tied off below her breasts. Her ass wasn't as shapely as Flora's, but it protruded farther than the other girls', at least as far as he could tell.

"*How's this operation work?*" Bill took the limes off the glass, set them on a napkin, and sipped from the straw.

"*What do you mean?*"

"*Do you have rooms here, or are we expected to take the girls back to our hotel?*" Bill wiped the condensation from his glass with a napkin.

"*There are rooms upstairs for your convenience.*"

Bill glanced at the balcony. "*What's the charge?*"

"*Twenty five thousand colones for a quick lay. Forty thousand for an hour.*"

"*Go through you or the girl?*"

"*Whichever.*"

Bill tossed out the straw and swigged from his drink. "*How about that little one?*" He pointed to the girl in the red top.

"*¡Jessica! ¡Venga!*" He pronounced her name Yessica.

The girl casually walked to Bill, shaking her hips extravagantly. She laid her hand on his thigh and looked him in the eyes. "You would like go upstairs?"

Bill grabbed a handful of her ass. "Yes, I would." He stared into her cleavage.

The girl took his hand and led him away. The floor felt sticky beneath his shoes. He reached back for his drink and noticed the bartender smile. Bill then watched the girl's butt as he followed and nodded to another as they passed. The girl clutched the railing with one hand as she walked up the concrete stairs. Bill looked down to avoid catching his sandals. At the top step he bent down and bit her butt cheek. The girl turned with a shocked look. "You bad." She grinned.

Bill squeezed on her tush with his left hand and tipped his glass back with his right. He watched the lights whirling over the dance floor as she opened the door. She tugged on his arm and pulled him in. Bill followed with wide eyes, set his drink on a shelf, and started to undo her shirt. The girl then brushed his hands aside. "First money."

He reached for his wallet. *"How much?"*

"What do you want?" she said.

"I want it all. Full hour."

"Fifty thousand colones."

Bill smiled. *"The man out there said forty."*

"I'll do anything for fifty." She slipped her hands up Bill's shirt and ran her nails down his chest. Then she slipped them down his shorts and drug them over his thighs.

Bill took a wad of cash from his wallet. *"Here's sixty."*

"Set it on the shelf." She dropped his shorts to the floor and began massaging him. Her perfume filled his nostrils, and he undid her shirt and fondled her before she fell to her knees. The woman then rose, grabbed a condom and a bottle of massage oil, and led him to bed.

An hour later, Bill stumbled down the stairs. His legs were like Jello, his head light, and eyes narrow. His mouth formed a grin as he pulled a cigarette from his mouth. Smoke curled to the ceiling, and chest hair hung out under an extra undone button. As his sandals hit the floor, Bill released the railing and glanced around. He winked and pouted his lips to the other girls. *"¡Pura Vida!"* he told a tico by the bar.

"How was it?" said the bartender.

"Spectacular." Bill blew a smoke trail over the man's shoulder, then leaned over the bar. *"Can you hear her down here?"* he said.

"That's what the music's for." The bartender laughed. *"You owe me two thousand for the drink."*

Bill reached in his pocket and pulled out a ten thousand note. *"Two shots of whiskey before I go."* Smoke poured out his nostrils.

"What kind?"

"You got Jack Daniels?"

"Sí." The bartender laid a shot glass down and filled it with Old No. 7. Bill picked it up, threw it back, and then slammed it down. A quiver went through his body. He hit his cigarette hard as the man refilled

the glass. Bill took another puff, exhaled, and gulped the second shot. His body quivered less than before. *"Gracias,"* he said. *"Gracias for everything."* He leaned over the bar and slapped the man's shoulder. The bartender stared at his large hand. *"I'll be back again,"* said Bill.

"We hope to have you back. ¡Pura Vida!"

Bill opened the door and squinted into the sun. *"¡Pura Vida!"* he yelled. *"¡Pura Vida!"*

He flicked his cigarette and pulled out his sunglasses, then slipped them on as he walked to the car. The gravel felt good under his sandals, like mild reflexology. He hit a button on his key chain, and the door locks clicked open. Bill then fell into the seat and inhaled deeply, smelling her perfume, but instead thinking of Flora. He started the car and pulled out. The image of the cowgirl followed him in the rear view mirror. Her eyes looked distant and wild. Her hair blew in the breeze. "Goodbye, Yessica." He saluted the image.

The car vibrated up the gravel drive, tall grass waved at the sides, and vehicles whizzed by ahead. Bill, expecting rain, skeptically inspected the clear sky. He pulled to a stop and watched a small green car fly by before turning out toward the springs. Black steel fences lined the road. Inside them, hotels scraped the sky. Bill crooked his neck to check out the resorts and then sized up the security guards outside. He noticed one with an automatic rifle. 'Just a scared man with a gun,' he thought. 'I would make him shit his pants.'

Bill passed a set of open gates and turned his head just in time to see a Baldí Termael sign. He looked up at the road, then in his mirror. There were no cars. He hit the brakes and yanked the wheel. The tires screeched, followed by the stench of burnt rubber. A thin white man in a Hawaiian shirt stared as Bill drove in the lot. He waved and backed the car between two new rental cars. They sparkled in the sun. Bill grabbed his towel from the back and slid on the panama hat. The car's headlights flashed as he hit the lock on the keychain. Then his left foot slipped out of his sandal and touched the hot blacktop. He yelped and slid it back in, then hopped toward the entrance. Two men in polo shirts were stationed at a desk just inside the open doorway. "Hello, would you like dinner with your admission?" said one.

Bill studied the young man's face. "No, I wouldn't."

"Okay. It's twelve thousand colones."

Bill handed him fifteen and took the change.

"Enjoy your time," he said.

Bill turned to see a pool not more than twenty feet away. It was curvy, like an amoeba. A bar stretched into it. To Bill there might as well have been beams of light radiating from it, cherubs hovering in the air. He slid his shoes under a beach chair and unbuttoned his shirt. His white paunch dropped. He then stretched back his arms and slipped off the shirt as he walked to the water, eyes big, like planets. The cement felt like dense pumice on his feet. He held the railing tight in one hand, his shirt wrapped around his smokes and wallet in the other, and cringed as he stepped into the fiery water. He held his jaw tight as he moved in farther, then pushed through it to the bar.

"Hey, buddy, would you watch this for me." Bill held out his shirt to a bartender in slacks and a Hawaiian shirt. He was tall and handsome, a light beard dotting his face. "I'll be gettin' drinks in a second."

"No problem." said the man.

Bill turned and moved toward a submerged lounge chair. It was covered with brightly colored tiles arranged in labyrinthine patterns. He held onto the seat as he submerged the rest of his body, letting out a sigh. Immediately, the heat began working away any leftover tension. He closed his eyes and moved into a state somewhere between sleep and wakefulness. The names Emma Goldman, Noam Chomsky, and Howard Zinn, again, echoed in his head. 'Who buys English books there?' he thought. 'And who buys that shit?'

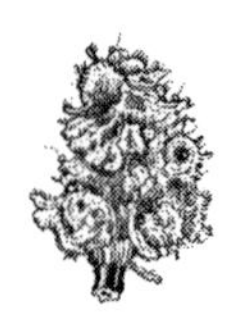

"I want to thank everyone for coming out tonight, though I apologize for it having to be under these circumstances." A middle-aged tica stood on a narrow foot-high platform before a crowd of a hundred. She was slim and wore a thin cotton dress. Wrinkles showed in her face. *"Everyone knows why this meeting has been called—the roadblock."*

Some people in the crowd nodded while others stared resolutely. They filled long benches placed side by side in seven rows. The crowd had overflowed onto the tops of tables in back of the shelter. More stood around the perimeter, hands across their chests, leaning against support poles. Most women wore dresses like the speaker, and the men wore jeans and t-shirts, the older males button down shirts. There were kids as young as twelve present while younger children played outside. Voices hung in the air, and the moon reflected off tilapia ponds nearby.

"Two white men who work for the U.S. have been nosing around, looking for Amigo. They began by going door to door, posing as friends. Then they brought in police to harass everyone coming and going from town. Yesterday, they stopped the bus of volunteers, holding them for two hours. Still, today the roadblock remains.

"We need to come to a decision. How will we deal with this? The floor is open."

An elderly man raised his hand and stood in the fourth row. He wore tall rubber boots, and his sleeves were rolled to his elbows. He smelled of sweat.

"Don Bazulto," said the speaker. She motioned to him, and the people in the crowd craned their necks.

"Gracias, Martina." He nodded, then turned from side to side, looking at his neighbors. *"Amigo has helped us,"* he said. *"Every person here. A library, improved our schools, given us jobs. These two gringos, though. They seem to be fools, but they're dangerous fools with no respect. And I am afraid more will come."* Don Bazulto nodded to Martina and sat.

A gust of wind blew, and the tin roof creaked overhead.

"Don Baz..." Martina didn't finish before a man in his late twenties spoke in the back. He donned a black t-shirt, jeans, and beat-up Nikes. *"I agree with Bazulto,"* he said. *"We should give the gringos what they want. Amigo's helped us. I can't lie."* His eyes widened as he said it. *"However, we didn't ask for help. He held out money, and we took it, like anyone would. He didn't tell us danger would come with it. Do we owe him our safety? I don't think so."* He looked around the room before sitting.

Two hands shot up, one from a middle-aged woman in the third row, and another from a skinny young man in the second. The woman had a weathered face and kind eyes

Martina nodded to them and then addressed the crowd. *"Leandro, thank you for giving your opinion. If someone has something they feel should be said, let it out. We want to hear from everyone. And on that note, I'll go to Gabriela, then Alonzo."*

The woman in the third row stood, then turned and waved to those behind her. *"I only have a question."* She stared at Martina with wrinkled brow. *"Why are these white men here? What has Amigo done wrong?"*

Martina looked around the shelter as the woman sat. *"Thank you for bringing this up, Gabriela. I understand this may be confusing for some, and it needs to be addressed. Amigo has given us money..."*

Shushes went through the crowd, and heads turned toward the driveway at their right. Footsteps were heard on the gravel.

"It's Brian!" said someone.

A woman got up from the crowd and hustled to the driveway. She stopped the short, gray-haired white man fifteen feet from the shelter. Everyone stared.

"We came back of town, and no one is here." The crowd strained to hear his broken Spanish.

"We're in a meeting," the woman said slowly. *"We will all be back soon."*

"Can I stay until finished?"

"I'm sorry. The meeting's for community members only."

"What?"

"No, I am sorry," the woman slowly enunciated the words. *"Only community members can be here, people of Quebrada Grande."*

The man looked in the shelter, and the people stared back unwelcoming.

"¡Alita! ¡Maite! ¡Venga!" the woman yelled. *"¡Alita! ¡Maite!"*

Two young girls ran over. Their faces smeared with dirt.

"Walk Brian to the house," she said. *"Your papa and I will be back soon."* She turned to the white man, who looked confused. *"We can't spoil any surprises we might have for your group. We'll all be back soon."*

The girls took the man's hands and pulled him along the path. He stared back as they left, and the crowd watched.

"Where was I?" said Martina. *"Yes, why are they after our friend? Amigo doesn't believe in government, or, rather, that people can govern themselves. Because of his aversion, he's never paid taxes. All the money he brought here, in the eyes of the gringo government, was stolen. They didn't get their part. Though it's unlikely they know about his work here, as I understand it, Amigo did it in other places, too. Colombia and Mexico, countries the U.S. watches closely. Hopefully, this answers the question. Is there anything anyone would like to add to that topic?"*

A woman with a stern visage stood in the fourth row. Her coarse, graying hair stood high. *"How do we know the money wasn't stolen? If he's so anti-government, so anti-capitalist, what would stop him from stealing from their system? Robbing a bank?"* The woman looked directly in Martina's eyes.

"Alejandra, it is important to bring this up," said Martina. *"The only answer is that we don't know. Whether he legitimately stole from the imperialists or not, they are here for him. I don't believe this..."*

"If he stole from them, and we took from him, we're just as guilty," she said.

Martina looked past the woman to a short sinewy man nodding to her in the back. *"Rodrigo."*

"Listen," he said *"The gringos don't know he gave us money. If they did, they wouldn't be in suits. They'd be wearing the green they're infamous for."*

Heads shook throughout the crowd, and Alejandra took her seat.

"Alejandra, is that answer sufficient?" said Martina.

"I hope he doesn't get us all hung," she said.

A boy next to her covered his eyes.

"Okay," said Martina. *"Alonzo, I believe you had something to say."*

The skinny young man in the second row stood, and the people in front turned. *"Gracias, Martina."* He moved to face the audience. *"I understand that people are scared. It's natural. But I beg you not to turn your backs on Amigo."* Alonzo looked to Alejandra, then around the shelter until his eyes met Leandro's. *"I understand where Leandro's speech came from. He has a wife and two children, and he, like Don Bazulto, like all of us, is scared. However, I know that behind this fear, Leandro knows he should stand up for Amigo. You see, a couple years back, I was with Leandro at a bar in Chaparrón. A stranger befriended us and bought us drinks. We talked with him, shared tales. Then later that night, someone tried to pick a fight with him. But, because of Leandro, the fight never happened. He stood between the two and told the provoker that he would have to fight both of them if he wanted to fight one. Why'd he do it? Friendship. And, it can't be denied that we're all friends with Amigo.*

"Now I understand the situation's different from that of the bar in

Chaparrón. Leandro was only standing up to some jerk, not an army. However, we can't be governed by fear. If we continue to deny knowing him, the gringos will leave. Thank you." The young man took his seat, and the crowd members' eyes appeared to look inward.

Martina waited a moment, then spoke, *"Thank you, Alonzo. You have provided the other half of the question. Do we turn him in, or do we continue with the current plan, claiming ignorance?"* She looked into the people's eyes. *"Does anyone have anything they'd like to add?"*

No one stirred. Some of the children watched from outside the shelter. Their bodies swayed from weariness. Others still ran in the grass, their voices carrying through the valley.

"Okay, then. The question we're voting on is whether we should change our course of action with Amigo. Will we remain loyal or will we decide it's too risky? Before voting, I want everyone to know that, as usual, the community will not look down on anyone for how they vote. Both options are rational decisions, and we can all understand why one would choose either. So... We will begin with the new option. By a show of hands, who feels we should turn him in?"

People stretched their necks to look around, but nobody moved an arm. Leandro held his tight on his chest and glanced at Alonzo. Alonzo nodded. Some heads turned toward Don Bazulto. His eyes were fixed on Martina. After half a minute, she spoke, *"Okay. Apparently, everybody is comfortable with the way we're dealing with this. But, remember."* Her eyes moved over the crowd. *"If anything changes, we'll call another meeting and discuss it. Please remember, our strength comes from sticking together."* Her shoulders dropped as her muscles relaxed. *"Unless someone has something to say, this meeting is adjourned. Everyone, have a nice night."*

She remained in the center of the plywood platform and watched the crowd slowly rise. Children entered the shelter and sought their parents, grandparents, cousins, and uncles. Then Martina stepped down and joined her husband. Her young daughter ran up and threw her arms around her leg. Martina smiled and turned to those waiting to speak with her.

People walked toward their homes. Youngsters bounced on their fathers' shoulders. A few members of the women's organization walked around inside the shelter, sliding around the tables and benches. Eventually, none remained but Martina and her family, Chi Cho's family, and a couple of others.

"You can tell him," said Martina.

"I will," said Chi Cho. *"I just hope the gringos leave. Every day they're here, he loses friends."*

"Don't worry about Leandro or Alejandra. They're fine."

"There could be others."

"There could be a lot if they step up their tactics," she said.

Chi Cho hung his head. *"Only time will tell."*

"It'll be okay. ¡Pura Vida!" Martina turned and hit the lights. The place went dark.

"Pura Vida," said Chi Cho.

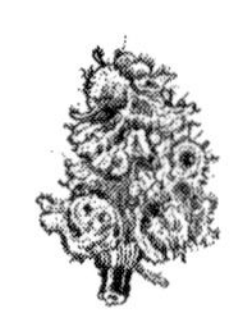

Bill puffed a cigarette as he stepped out his hotel room and squinted in the sun. He threw his arms in circles and stretched his chest, then walked down the narrow cement walk. On the other side of the lawn, he saw a woman hanging laundry. She was shoeless, dressed in shorts and a faded t-shirt. Her breasts bounced as she threw a blanket over the line. Bill felt perspiration break on his neck. He flicked his cigarette and pounded on Ron's door. Bed springs screeched inside. The rush of cool air came out as the door swung open, and Ron stood in a pair of dress slacks, an undershirt, and an unbuttoned dress shirt.

"My, aren't we casual?" said Bill.

"You came back."

"Can I come in?

"Suit yourself."

Ron stepped back while Bill entered. Clothes hung on a line tied across the room, a small television sat dark in the corner, and the air conditioner hummed. Ron sat on the twin size bed. "How was La Fortuna?" he said.

"Not bad." Bill looked about, then leaned against the wall.

"Did you learn anything besides how many beers you can consume in a hundred degree pool?"

"You have tropical drinks at the springs," said Bill.

Ron shook his head.

"So, I assume you didn't find our boy yesterday?" said Bill.

"If he's there, he's not coming out."

"Oh, he's there," said Bill. "Or somewhere close by."

Ron squinted, and Bill ran his hand over his thin hair. "Before I visited my friend yesterday, I took it upon myself to scour the town. Figured if he hangs out in Quebrada Grande, people should know him in the closest town—bus service, a gas station, toilet, etcetera. After an hour and a half of snooping around, I checked out a bookstore and asked about books in English. It just so happened he had a stack on the shelf behind him." Bill drew a small notepad from his shirt pocket. "Emma Goldman, Noam Chomsky, Howard Zinn."

Ron leaned forward on the bed.

"Jack London, George Orwell, Rudolph Rocker, Bernard Shaw, Mark T…"

"Special order?" said Ron.

"Yep, and placed by someone fitting our boy's description."

"Got an address?"

"No, he usually picks 'em up. The guy said he was expecting him any day."

"Going to call us or stake out?"

"He'll call us. I slipped him two hundred. All we do is sit and wait. Soon we'll have the prick in bracelets."

"How was your run?" Daniela sat in a metal chair on the porch. She wore jeans and a bright orange fleece and leaned forward, holding a hand up to block the sun.

"Great," said Ben. Sweat dripped from his body to the walkway. He wore blue shorts, three white stripes down the sides. The tops of his socks were just visible above his battered running shoes. He held his hands behind his back and arched his chest, watching a large black and violet humming bird chase away a green one from the feeder

"Aren't you cold with no shirt on?" Daniela squeezed her hands together.

"Do I look cold?"

She watched perspiration run down his forehead, and Ben stared at the book in her lap. There was a red flower on its cover. *"Just feel like poetry or did you finish your book?"*

"I finished it."

Ben took a seat on the porch and undid his shoes. *"What'd you think?"*

"Excellent." Daniela looked up to the cirrus clouds above. *"Was funny for most, then very somber in the end."*

He pulled off his shoes and set them on the porch. *"You can only joke about some things so long."*

"Bet you loved Milo's character." She pronounced his name Meelo.

He laid his damp socks next to his shoes and spread his toes. *"His society created him."* He sighed and leaned back to stretch. *"Awesome book."*

"Sí, very gringo."

Ben grunted as he grabbed his toe.

"It taught me a new phrase, too," she said.

He laughed. *"Now you can fit in with the English speaking intelligentsia."*

"And now you can get in the shower." She slapped his back. *"Eww,"* she said, wiping her hand on her jeans.

Ben pushed himself up with a groan and leaned in for a kiss. His body formed a rigid frame, and his legs trembled as he held it. She smacked his butt as he walked stiffly in. Sweaty prints followed on the tile.

After washing up, the pair descended the mountains to Heredia, leaving behind the humming birds, waterfalls, and hazy cloud forests. With every hundred feet they dropped in elevation, the temperature rose half a degree. A full ten for the trip. Halfway down, Daniela peeled off her orange fleece and tossed it in back. The sun seemed to cook her legs through her jeans. Ben wore shorts and sandals but still felt hot.

The city streets were noisy and crowded. Ben weaved through the narrow lanes to a thruway. They passed by KFC, Papa John's, McDonald's, and Burger King, followed by the university. Dozens of people waited at myriad bus stops along the street. The entire next block was lined with red cabs. Ben chuckled at a pimped out taxi with rims and a stereo system. A giant Eminem sticker covered its back window. The driver leaned against its trunk, an invisible crown atop his gelled hair. They hooked left into some back streets, quiet barrios. Daniela looked at the fences around the homes. They were higher than those in her hometown. Barbed wire circled their tops, razors glistening in the sun.

Daniela's eyes widened as they rounded a corner, and the large

Café Britt logo came into view. It was painted high on the side of the tall roasting and packaging building, thirty feet up. The corrugated tin was painted tan, and the letters of "Café Britt" were dark brown, like the drink itself. Rough green leaves and red berries hung over them. She waved at a security guard in a booth as they entered.

"I'm so excited," she said. *"Coffee is my culture, and I know too little about it."*

"Except that your country makes a mean cup," said Ben.

Her eyes narrowed. "Coffee here is good," she said.

"Slang, honey. I meant good." He pulled into a space before a colorful mural. It portrayed a shirtless tico in jeans, arched back, shovel in hand, planting tiny coffee plants in rows on the side of a hill. The sun was bright white, looking more like the moon as it stuck out through the clouds. Trees stood tall above the field, representing the traditional shade-grown method. The plants grew into large bushes toward the bottom, red coffee berries bursting to the size of apples. To the right, three ticos hunched to pick them. Two women and a man, dressed in white. They held large hand-woven baskets at their waists and reached to the sky, where the fruit seemed to descend from the heavens. Further on, a shirtless tico spread the seeds for drying in the sun. There were tico homes in the background. The final portion showed a close up of a tica in a white dress pouring a cup. Steam rose from the mug, drifting off toward a steel roasting machine in the background. Enormous smooth, red berries bounced across the woman's table and out of the frame.

"I thought you meant bitter." Daniela glanced up. "I remember my *mamá* telling me, *'When you first started drinking coffee, you would put in so much sugar.'"* She deepened her voice slightly. *"By the time you started school, you were drinking it as black as your father."*

"I didn't try coffee until I was twenty one," said Ben. *"Here."* He undid his seat belt and opened the door.

"Not so many smoke weed at age twelve." The door clicked behind Daniela.

"Thirteen," said Ben. *"All the pretty girls were doing it."* He pulled on his door to make sure it was locked, then looked up to the mural. *"That painting is missing something,"* he said. *"The white man that collects all the money. We could have one of these in Quebrada Grande about piña, and it would actually be true. Worker owned."*

Daniela pointed at the top left corner. *"And maybe you and Chi Cho could be on that hill with your cannabis."*

They laughed as they walked through the parking lot toward an open patch of grass. A small tree stood at the center, a wooden booth to one side. A corpulent man sold tickets there to an old couple from the States. "We'll see you back here in twenty minutes," he said, glancing at his watch. The man's skin was light, but he seemed latino. His grin couldn't get any bigger. *"¡Pura Vida!"* he hollered after them.

The man turned to Ben and Daniela. "*¡Hola!* Are you going on the tour?"

"Yes, two." Ben held up two fingers in a peace sign.

"Let me guess." He rubbed his chin. "You're a tica, and you're from the States?"

"Canada," said Ben. "I'm from Canada."

The man stared in his face. One of his front teeth was crooked. "I was close. It's thirteen thousand colones each, and it comes with a gourmet lunch buffet afterward."

"Cool." Ben gave him the cash.

"You have twenty minutes until it starts. You're welcome to follow the red trail to our restaurant for free coffee samples." He waved his hand over a brick path next to the booth.

"Thank you," said Ben.

The man made a point of making eye contact with each of them as he held his large smile. *"¡Pura Vida!"* he yelled.

"¡Pura Vida!" they repeated. Ben said it slowly, wondering why the guy cared where he was from. A zipper on his cargo shorts jingled as they moved up the path, admiring the small groomed trees and groups of flowers. Ben looked back to make sure the man wasn't watching.

A pungent coffee aroma hung in the air between the smooth tile floor and the bamboo-covered ceiling. T-shirts, jewelry, and stuffed animals were propped on shelves with other tourist chachka, but a display of twelve-ounce bags of coffee dominated the room. They covered the shelves of a large, octagonal structure in the center. Foreigners circled, like old folks at a farmers' market. "We have to get ten to get the discount," said a woman. She shoved coffee bags into a burlap tote.

Ben's eyes followed the colorful paintings around the top of the walls, which portrayed coffee fields scattered amongst tropical forests full of quetzals, toucans, flowers, and homes. A woman in a flowery dress with a soft white apron greeted them. She looked like she belonged to the nineteenth century. "*Buenos días.* Would you like to try a mocha?" She held out a round tray covered with small paper cups.

"Please," said Daniela. They could both feel the warmth through the cups. Daniela put it to her nose and smelled. It was mellow compared to the sharp aromas in the air, creamy and sweet on their tongues.

"I want to grab a normal coffee, too," said Ben. He walked to the center stand where dark wood shelves were stocked with coffee and chocolate-covered beans, nuts, and guavas. Airpots had been filled with coffee, bowls with sweets, all free. Ben tried a cup of Tres Rios Valdivia, while Daniela got a cup of Shade Grown Organic.

A pudgy white man stepped next to Ben. His face showed him to be every bit of fifty. "You're trying the Bordeaux of Costa Rican coffee," he said.

Ben eyed him. "Is that what they call it?"

"Yeah. I've tried them all and have to agree."

"Hmm," said Ben. He grabbed a handful of chocolate-covered Macadamia nuts and turned to Daniela. *"You want to go outside? We'll have plenty of time to look in here afterwards."*

"Sure." She grabbed some white chocolate-coated coffee beans before leaving.

The pair walked slowly down the red stone path, careful not to spill their drinks. Ben popped the Macadamia nuts in his mouth, one after another. He could already feel the caffeine.

"How many of those are you going to eat?" asked Daniela.

"Whole bag. Eight dollar value."

They walked past the bathrooms to the open grass where a crowd of two dozen had gathered. Some chatted while others looked at a display on the history of the area. They drank from small paper cups. Ben noticed a thin white man glancing his way. He wore a light blue polo shirt tucked into khakis and looked to be in his early thirties. Ben and Daniela sat underneath a small tree near the center. The grass was coarse and poked at Ben's legs. *"Looks like you're the only tica here,"* he said, examining the crowd.

"No, there's three ticos over there." She pointed to two ladies and a man by the display. The white man in khakis was looking back.

"Sí, we'll have to hear that barbaric tongue then." He tried to hold back a grin, giving an uneasy look. Daniela plucked a handful of grass and dropped it on his head. Ben's eyes went back to the man. He looked to be reading the display.

Ben whispered, *"There's a guy who keeps staring at me. The thin gringo by the ticos."*

Daniela stretched and turned his way. She made eye contact with him before looking off in the distance. *"Why would they be here?"* she said.

"I don't know. Fat guy tipped them off."

"What?"

"He was guessing my nationality and looking at me funny."

Daniela glared at him.

"I'm sorry. It's just, being this far from the cabin," he said.

The husky man came from the booth and walked straight toward Ben and Daniela. Ben's eyes grew. The man stopped five feet from them, smiled wide, then turned to address the crowd. He wore olive green shorts and a half apron below a white button down shirt, sleeves rolled to his elbows. His calves were huge. "If I can have everyone's attention," he said. "The tour is about to start." The man repeated the lines in Spanish.

Daniela and Ben pushed themselves up, Ben feeling tightness in his legs. They walked to the side. *"Away from the skinny gringo,"* he whispered.

"We have speakers of Spanish and English here today," the large man said. "Any French?" He looked at Ben, and Ben looked to the ground. "Okay. Only Spanish and English today. Did everyone get to try the mocha?" He motioned to the woman in the flowery dress, and a few people walked over.

Ben watched the man in khakis.

"Costa Rica is one of the best places in all the world for coffee." The man's voice was deep and powerful. "Does anyone know why?" He looked around the crowd. Ben avoided his eyes.

"It's because of all the volcanoes we have. Over time the volcanoes covered the area with lava, rich in minerals necessary for producing good coffee. Volcán Arenal lies to the East, Volcán Poás to the South, and Irazú to the West." He pointed each way as he spoke, turning like a compass.

Ben jumped as a skinny tico marched up in high rubber boots, a half apron, and bucket hat. "No, no, no. Arenal is to the West, Poás to the North, and Irazú to the East." The man repeated the lines in Spanish the same way the other had. "You'll never get them right. I'll take your tour." His voice was high, and his emotions exaggerated.

"Oops. Sorry." The bulky man gave an embarrassed look, threw up his hands, and walked quickly off. Ben watched him go, as did the man in khakis.

The skinny tico spoke quickly as he lead the group along a stone trail into the miniature coffee field. The coffee plants were as tall as Ben and immensely bushy, double the size of the plants near Daniela and Ben's cabin. Large trees stretched above them, shading the area.

A middle-aged couple turned to Ben and Daniela, "You folks from here or the States?"

"Canada," said Ben. "We live in Toronto. You?"

"The States," said the wife. She had tall, curly red hair. It held in place as she swung her head about. "Tacoma, Washington."

"Why all the shade?" said the guide. "The shade causes the beans to ripen more slowly, giving them better flavor." He pointed to a tree. "This particular tree adds beneficial nutrients to the soil for coffee. This one produces a natural chemical to keep harmful insects away." He pointed to a large tree that branched at the top like fingers from a hand.

"Slow down," Ben whispered. *"I don't want to talk to them."*

"You hear that," said the guide. The group was silent. "Birds chirping. You notice it is very thick in here. This organic shade method creates a habitat for many animals and insects."

The woman in the flowery dress, the one who had distributed mocha earlier, waited at a bend in the trail. She held a large basket at her waist and wore a bucket hat. "Paco, where have you been? You always leave me alone to pick the beans," she announced theatrically.

"I'm sorry, Lucia, but I have a group here."

"Always excuses."

The pair exhibited great chemistry and continued to slip in jokes while explaining the process of coffee cultivation. The germination of the seeds, the harvesting, the drying. They even had a building on site where the roasting and packaging were done. From there the guides ushered the group into a theatre where the hefty men returned to show the audience the best method for brewing coffee, the French press, and the proper way to sample, which involved slurping. Crowd volunteers added to the humor. The only one appearing ill at ease during the tour was Ben, and he grew more tense as the lights dropped, and Paco wheeled out a screen. "Now we will show you a video to review the whole process," he said.

Ben turned in his seat. He lost sight of his stalker. "I gotta pee," he whispered. "I'll meet you by the gift shop."

"What? You'll miss it."

"I've seen it." He stared into Daniela's eyes and kissed her on the forehead. "Remember the story."

Finally, the tour guides acted out a comedic play about the history of coffee. The corpulent man played such characters as Pope Clement VIII and Louis XIV. Daniela jumped as sound effects crashed, colorful lights flickered, and fog machines hummed. She laughed with the crowd but also searched their faces for irregular expressions.

The group was all smiles as they were escorted to the gift shop and restaurant. Daniela donned a bucket hat with a Café Britt logo. Ben stood leaning against a pole outside, a small paper cup in hand.

"Enjoy the wedding?"

"I was maid of honor." She tipped her hat. "Wish you could have been there."

"Me too. Was the skinny gringo there?"

"Yes, he was the best man. I talked with him afterward. I think he was gay. Probably why he was staring at you." She pinched his cheek.

"Shut up."

"He had a strong lisp. Nice guy."

"Let's just get some food," said Ben.

"I want to grab another coffee first."

Ben followed her into the gift shop, eying the others. The place was packed as people bought coffee bags by the box full. Ben and Daniela bought a couple of bags and headed to the open air dining room, wide-eyed and talking fast. A bar separated it from the gift shop, and a tico in a short sleeve shirt fiddled with a large stainless espresso machine. Shiny lacquered poles supported the roof. Daniela stepped outside to check out the tropical flowers and sniff the herb garden. They set their stuff on a table, and a waiter approached to take their drink orders. "You can go up to the buffet anytime," he said.

The buffet consisted of four tables in a U shape with two ticos in thick chefs' uniforms manning it. They pulled back stainless steel lids to uncover the specialty dishes. Carrots, tomatoes, seasonings, and greens mixed with meats. Cilantro speckled the rice, and garlic was swirled in the mashed potatoes. Ripe fruits were stacked high on the salad bar. Ben and Daniela piled their plates and walked back to the table. They had just taken their seats when two middle-aged women walked up. "Could we eat with you?" one asked.

"Sure," said Daniela.

The women set down their straw hats and sunglasses, and a box of Café Britt merchandise on the floor. "Ooo, that food looks good," said one. They stared at Ben and Daniela's plates before going to the buffet.

"This should be fun," said Ben.

The women returned with plates half full. "This country's so much cleaner than Asia," said one. Her cheeks were covered with freckles.

"Everywhere we went," said the other, "we saw plastic bottles on the ground." Ben stared at her arms. They were bigger than his own.

"Mmm. This food's good," said the freckled one. "It might be better than our hotel food."

"Much better than the food on the tour yesterday."

"Remember the food in Puerto Rico?" The woman had a mouthful of chicken and rice.

"Mmm. The sushi bar was to die for." Ben kept looking at her arms, dotted with cellulite.

"Have you two been doing any other traveling?" asked the freckled one.

"I just got back from Venezuela," said Ben.

"Venezuela, that's the country with the guy you always see in the news," she said.

"Hugo Chavez," said Ben. "Their president."

"Yeah, the communist."

Ben set down his fork. "Socialist," he said.

"Oh, socialist," she said sarcastically, grinning at her friend.

"You know. He's one of the few leaders who actually cares about his people. Built homes for the poor, redistributed land that was stolen from the people. His revolution seems to have good intentions."

"Ah, to be young and naive." The woman looked to the ceiling.

"Naive to what?" said Ben.

The woman's face grew sober. She looked in Ben's eyes. "Communism doesn't work. Been tried. Failed."

The big armed woman nodded, then took a fork full of food.

Ben leaned in. "The Soviet Union wasn't Communist. It was fascist. It only hid behind the guise of Communism."

"You can put lipstick on a pig," the woman said haughtily.

Her friend laughed.

"What does that mean?" said Ben.

Daniela narrowed her eyes and stared off.

"It means... You can dress Communism up however you want. It won't make it right."

"Do you know what Communism is?" he said. " The negation of capitalism. The belief that one person shouldn't possess all wealth. That all people should have health care, education. That people shouldn't starve in the street."

The woman stared blankly. "Well, we talked about politics. What religion are you?" She laughed heartily, and her friend joined in, arms shaking.

Ben looked down at his food. He ate a mouthful of chicken, rice, and vegetables. Chewed it slowly. *"I should expect that type of reaction,"* he said. *"There's no hope for that country."*

Daniela bit through the husk of a red lychee and set it on her oversized plate. She put the seed in her mouth and sucked away the aril.

"We should hurry," said Ben. *"Eyes everywhere."*

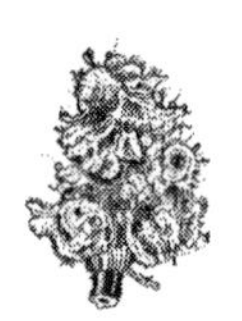

Bill jogged down the concrete path to Ron's room and banged on the door. His shirt clung to him in the humid air, and he grew sticky with sweat. The door flung open. Ron stood with his undershirt exposed.

"Got the address," said Bill. "Pack your bags. Meet me in the car." He ran back down the walkway to his room. A salamander darted up the wall as he grabbed his clothes and shoved them in his suitcase. He then picked up a pair of shoes and threw them on top before snatching his bathroom items. He took one last look before going out.

Bill tossed his bag in the trunk, then started the car, cranked the A/C, and ran to Ron's room. Ron was folding his shirts and laying them in the open suitcase on his bed. "You ready?" said Bill.

"One minute. I don't think he's leaving the country."

"Give me your key. I'll drop it off."

Bill ran back out the door and down the cement path. He turned left in front of the car and jogged up the dark gravel driveway. He could hear people inside, but threw the keys in the mailbox and ran back to the car. He hopped in the driver's seat and turned the vents toward his face, then sighed and undid the top two buttons of his shirt. Ron walked up carrying his suitcase in one hand, his briefcase in the other. He knocked on the window. "You want to pop the trunk, please?"

"Just throw them in back."

Ron complied, then got in and straightened his tie.

Bill peeled out.

"Why are you in such a hurry? Do you think Ben's leaving?"

"I want to get this taken care of. Get back to San Jose. I got business there."

The air was cool, but the sun felt warm on Ben's back. He leaned over the railing and stared into the world's second largest crater. At the bottom, nine hundred feet down, lay an azure lagoon. Sulfur gas rose from the center and the bright green fissures in the lower walls of the crater. The air smelled like rotten eggs. Ben watched a bank of fog move in.

"You enjoy the smell of that, gringo?"

Ben smiled and turned. *"Ah, Chi Cho, I knew you'd be here. A gadfly can't resist the smell of livestock."*

"Can you see the lake?" asked Chi Cho.

"If you come quick. Fog's moving in."

Chi Cho walked over and rested his arms on the railing. *"Wow. I wish I could have brought the boys."*

"Always next time," said Ben. He looked at the dozens of tourists snapping photos. *"We should probably walk."*

Chi Cho nodded, and they ambled toward a trail entering the dwarf forest. The gravel on the path was sparse, and the dirt was hard packed. Trees resembling shrubs crowded the trail and brushed their arms. They were no taller than Ben.

"I feel like I've been shrunk and placed in a bonsai forest," said Ben.

"It's different," said Chi Cho.

The weeds rustled as a small animal ran through.

"Where's Daniela?" said Chi Cho.

"At the house."

"She okay?"

"She's fine." Ben held a branch back for Chi Cho.

"Good."

"The community?" said Ben.

"Agents haven't been around. Apparently, they're not even in Pital anymore."

Ben swatted another branch. *"When's the last time you saw them?"*

"Week, week and a half."

"Not bad."

"I've been cleaning up, though."

Ben turned and squinted. *"The woods?"*

"No, just the house. I stopped cloning and put everything away. Figured I'd wait until the cycle's done." He plucked at a leaf. *"No reason to worry, though. They obviously know nothing. Just being safe."*

"That's smart." Ben reached in his pocket and brought out a folded piece of paper. *"Speaking of, I made a list of my email addresses and passwords."* He held it out to Chi Cho. *"My brother and I communicate through them. The bottom two are his. He still owes a few hundred grand."*

"You don't have to worry." said Chi Cho *"The imperialists don't have a clue. Might have given up. I stopped by Ciudad Quesada, too. Saw Daniela's brother. It's all good there. Could have been staying there the whole time."*

"Precautionary measure."

"Of course." Chi Cho slipped the note in his pocket. *"So, you see the World Cup Final?"*

"Sí, Daniela and I saw it."

"The Frenchman head-butting that guy in the chest?"

"Sí, saw it."

"It was awesome. The guy's second red card of the Cup. In extra time."

They walked from the woods to a blacktop road that led to their vehicles.

"Daniela and I will just hang low for another month," said Ben. *"Then we'll work back into our routine."*

"Sounds good," said Chi Cho.

"Want to plan another meeting? Month from today, here?"

"No problem."

"Daniela and I will plan on following you back."

"We'll be happy to have you."

"¡Pura Vida!" said Ben.

"¡Pura Vida!"

The two embraced, then went their separate ways, Ben to the little, green car, Chi Cho to his truck. There was a smile at Ben's lips, and he tapped the roof of the car before entering. 'Daniela will be so happy,' he thought.

He followed Chi Cho out of the park and blew by him on the road. Chi Cho shook his head and waved a finger as Ben coasted by. The clouds were coming out, obscuring the sun, but Ben was all sunshine. He rolled the windows down as the distance grew between him and the sulfurous crater. He honked and waved at a herd of cows in a pasture. The closest one stared dumbly. Ben then put on an upbeat Peter Mulvey song and sang along, tapping the steering wheel. "Oh, once I was standing on a Dublin street corner. I heard a fiddler pierce the veil of illusion. Once I got plastered at my best friend's bar mitzvah. Once I lived in perfect confusion. Once I was eleven. Once I was just atoms. Once I was a hilltop up in Rome. And I'm sad, sad, sad, sad, and I'm far away from home."

Ben slowed the car as he rounded the corner before the cabin, then pulled gently in. He watched clothes blowing on the line and looked to the open door as he hopped out, jacket in hand. He hummed a tune as he sprung up the steps. A large fist hit him in the gut as he crossed the threshold. He bent over, struggling for breath, as a man grabbed him by the waist. Ben could feel the man's gut against his lower back. He threw his elbows into it and tried to shake free, gasping for air. Fists swung down on his head, like hammers. Snot flew from his nose. The room became blurry. The man hit him in the head two more times, knocking him to the floor. Ben saw shiny, black shoes inches from his face. He could hear the attacker also panting, then turned to see Daniela across the room, tied to a chair with a cloth in her mouth. Her eyes were wild as she shook. Muffled screams came from her. A man stood behind the chair, holding her down. Ben tried to push himself up, but the stout man laid his large shoes into his ribs. Ben fell flat on the floor, but the kicks kept coming. He moved slower after each blow. He looked at Daniela and thought he could make out the word "killing" through the cloth in her mouth. Tears streamed down her cheeks.

Bill kept kicking. He focused on the ribs but sometimes strayed to the chest, back, and rump as Ben rolled. Two even hit him in the face, drawing blood from his nose and lips. Eventually, Ben ceased moving. Bill gave him two more kicks and leaned back, panting. Sweat dripped from his face to the floor. Ron stared at the lifeless body. In front of him, Daniela's eyes were closed, and tears squeezed through.

Bill reached in his pocket and took out a number of white cable ties. He lifted Ben's arms, but Ben flailed, and he dropped them. Bill stomped on him. "Dumb fucker!" he said. Bill tried again. He pulled the now limp arms behind Ben's back and fastened a plastic tie. It clicked as he tightened it. He wrapped around a second tie and then did the same for his lower legs. "I'm gonna get the car," he said.

Bill walked out as Ron paced the room. He fingered books on shelves, Vonnegut, Heller, Robbins, and Kerouac. He opened drawers and cupboards and walked back to the living room, eying

Ben's blood-stained face and Daniela's quivering body. Suppressed howls escaped the gag. He walked to the open door and stared out. A dim outline of the sun shined through the clouds. He watched the silver car wrap around the corner and listened to the gravel crack under the car's tires. Bill shut it off and stepped out. A cloud of dust hung behind him.

"You want me to grab his feet?"

"I can handle him," said Bill. "Get the girl."

Ron watched Bill stoop and yank Ben up by the waist. "Gonna throw your back out like that," he said.

Bill puffed out his chest and huffed as he lugged the captive toward the car. The prisoner's feet left trails in the gravel. Bill held him with one arm, swung the rear door open, and heaved him inside, leaving Ben splayed across the seat like a pile of dirty laundry.

Ron walked over to Daniela, who was still sobbing, and cut the straps that held her to the chair. Only two cable ties at her wrists and the cloth in her mouth remained. "We shouldn't need this gag anymore," he said. "But if you get loud, it goes back on." He untied it and held it in his hand. "Let's go."

Ron nudged Daniela, and she moved over the smooth floor. She shook and wailed as they passed puddles of saliva and drops of blood. He led her to the porch. Bill walked up. His shirt was stained with blood, and there were pit stains below the arms.

"What about this one?" said Ron.

"His whore"

"I'm not a whore!" Daniela yelled.

Bill brought back his hand and slapped her. He moved out of the way as she fell, hitting the ground. She bawled there loudly, clutching her face.

"We'll take her in," he said.

Ron's eyes were huge.

Bill turned back to Daniela. "Ya rude bitch. I was talking," he said. "Now get up." He rolled her over, grabbed the cable tie, and jerked her up. The plastic cut into her wrists, and she kicked at him as he yanked her forward. Bill flung her to the ground. "You better fuckin' stop. You don't want what your boyfriend got." He pulled her up again, and she passively followed. Bits of gravel and dust stuck to her skin. He walked her to the other side of the car and pushed her in the back.

Daniela threw her bound hands around Ben's neck. "I love you," she said. "I love you." Her tears fell on his face, and she kissed his cheek and forehead, wiping away the blood.

Ron took his briefcase from the passenger seat, set it on the hood, and popped it. He took out a syringe and removed its plastic cap. "Hold her."

Bill squinted. "What do you got?"

"Ketamine."

"Good idea." Bill stepped to the car, grabbed Daniela's arms, and pushed her against the seat. Ron held up the syringe and squeezed some out. He then jabbed it in her arm and gently pressed down. "Good girl," he said.

Bill cringed. "Ooo. Can't feel good with a flexed arm."

Ron walked to the other side of the car with a second syringe and pulled off the cap. He looked in at Ben, whose back moved up and down as he wheezed. "He's getting blood on the seat," said Ron.

"I'm not wiping his face." Bill reached in his pocket and took out his Camel Lights. From across the car, he watched Ron thrust the needle into Ben's bicep. Ron pushed the drug in quickly, not taking the care he had with Daniela. "There's a safe trip," he said.

Bill looked at Daniela. Her eyes were open, and she was mumbling, but she didn't move. He nudged her arm, and she still didn't move. He reached out and felt her breast, then pulled his hand away as Ron walked around.

"Works great," said Ron.

Bill again nudged Daniela. "They're good while we round up their stuff?"

"They're going nowhere," said Ron.

Bill walked to the house, and Ron followed. They opened up all the drawers and cupboards, searching for clues. Bill carried out a computer and set it in the trunk. Ron carried a stack of books and dumped them in the trunk, too. "I saw notebooks in the bedroom," he said.

"I'll get 'em," said Bill.

The pair carried out a few more loads, then glanced around the house. Daniela and Ben's few possessions were scattered in the kitchen and living room. They closed the door and walked back to the car. Bill slammed the trunk and leaned across the vehicle. "Congratulations," he said.

Ron smiled. "I'll feel better when he's locked up." He opened his door.

The car shook as Bill climbed in. He looked at the bodies in the backseat, then started the car as he took out another cig. "Where would the world be if it weren't for people like us?" he said.

Ron looked in his face. "Our country wouldn't exist," he said.

Bill watched the blue and white cabins fade in his rear view mirror. 'Mission one complete,' he thought. 'On to mission two.'

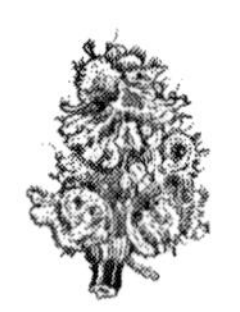

Ben walked across a dim plane with dark, blotchy objects in the distance. The ground appeared an intricate quilt of interwoven fabrics, many colors. Suddenly, his body was sucked into the quilt, and he was in a room of all green, floating. He was naked, clutching his knees to his chest, and spinning slowly through the air. There was only wide-open space, no ground or boundaries in sight. A place of nothingness except green. Eventually, he noticed he was spinning toward a wall, which expanded infinitely into the world. It was yellow and smooth, like glass. He felt no fear. It seemed natural and exhilarating as he crashed through it, entering a new plane of reality. This world was no different than the last, except the green had been replaced with orange. Ben, however, understood he was progressing as he spun through it, moving on to something greater. He became excited as he saw a red wall drawing near. It collapsed, and he felt submerged in a thick liquid of indigo. He saw both violet and blue simultaneously and moved slower than in the previous worlds, but his excitement grew. He spotted the next wall, which appeared the same as the ground he'd already walked on, the mass of colorful fabric, all connected. He hit it, and his arms and legs broke off. His body shattered into countless pieces, floating away in the gel. All that was left was his soul, which entered into the plane, merging with it. Time ceased to exist. He had no name or memories. Was no longer human. He felt like everything alive in the universe was part of the quilt, connected. He moved through the strands that held everything together, toward a bright light at its center. He grew nearer, and the light became brighter. An immense euphoria took hold of him as he entered into the light and stopped before a being without shape at its center. The entity, only light, communicated to Ben without sound. Each disclosure felt like a realization Ben was experiencing on his own. The essential message was, "You are capable of leaving your body at any time and moving onto the next stage." Ben then felt he was growing more distant from his body, about to leave it permanently, and turned back. He left the light, the quilt of eternity, and opened his eyes. Everything was blurry. Much of his body, numb. He tried to move, but chains bound his arms and legs. The sound of a metal door opening and closing echoed in his head. He felt nauseous and closed his eyes. As time passed, the anesthesia wore off, and he started to form a clear picture. He was tied to a chair in a small cement room. Chains bound his wrists leading to others at his ankles. Fluorescent lights on the ceiling buzzed. There was dried blood on his clothes. Pain all over.

Ben heard the door open and close again, followed by the sound of dress shoes clacking on the cement floor. He heard them stop beside him, then slowly turned his neck. An open palm struck him across the cheek twice. "You in there, Ben?"

"Where am I?" he asked muddily.

"Well, you're not in fuckin' Peru!" said Bill.

Ben realized he was in the custody of those he'd been hiding from. He recalled the beating he'd endured and wondered if that had led him to the vision. "This life's an illusion," he said.

"What?" said Bill. He kicked Ben's shin. "Why the fuck are you in Costa Rica?" he yelled.

"Vacation."

Bill kicked him again. "Don't fuck with us, Starosta. We got a village we can burn down, a pretty girl to split wide-open."

Ben stared into his narrow, blood thirsty eyes. "You're sick," he said.

"You're fuckin' right, I'm sick. You don't tell us all, the girl doesn't walk again."

Ben cringed.

"Talk!" he said.

"I'm an English teacher on vacation."

Bill slapped him in the face with the back of his hand. "Your friend Ryan already told us. We want it from you."

Ben's eyes widened. He looked at the gray cinder block wall.

Bill hit him again. "Fuck you," he said. "You'll talk. Everyone talks." He hocked a loogie and turned to the door. His shoes tapped on the floor. A guard holding a pump shotgun opened the steel door and closed it behind him.

2001

Ben and Chi Cho tiptoed into the patch, trying to quiet their breathing, and set down four jugs of water. Sweat ran down their red necks and faces. Small plants three feet tall were spaced five feet apart, covering the patch in a sea of green. The red clay of the ground contrasted with dark soil beneath each plant. Ben and Chi Cho looked from side to side. In a crouched position, Ben walked along the edge of the patch until he reached a small rectangular box fixed to a tree. He opened its side with a key, pulled out its memory card, and slipped it in his camera. The camera chimed as he turned it on and flipped through the pictures. *"No new ones here,"* he whispered. Chi Cho nodded. Hunched over, Ben continued along the edge until he came to another box eighty feet away. He checked its card and gave a thumbs up to Chi Cho before continuing on to two more cameras. *"All good,"* he said, standing and walking to Chi Cho. He picked up one of the jugs and drank, letting out a burst of air as he took it from his lips.

Chi Cho walked to the east end of the patch and pulled up a brown tarp from under a pile of weeds. He pulled out a stack of four five-gallon pails with a pump and spray nozzle sticking out the top. Bottles and bags of fertilizer were wedged in beside it. *"Spraying or watering?"* he said.

"I'll water."

"Don't want to stand in the sun, huh?"

"No, señor."

Ben walked to the side where a small solar panel rested on the ground. Thin wires ran from the device to a ball of brown plastic. Ben kneeled down and unwrapped the plastic to expose a car battery. He unhooked the wires, picked it up, and followed Chi Cho out the west end of the patch. The shade felt good. They stopped before a watering hole. Ben set down the battery and walked out as Chi Cho emptied the contents of the top bucket, dropping the bags and bottles on the ground. He pulled the rest of the pails apart, took out a measuring spoon, and used it to pour neem oil and castile soap into the sprayer. He used one of the buckets to fill the sprayer. Ben returned with an electric pump attached to a hose. He connected its wires to the battery. It buzzed as he dropped it in the water. Then he turned to hurry back to the patch.

Chi Cho followed with the sprayer. He set it by the closest plant, pumped the handle, then sprayed the plant for a minute before moving on to the next. The aroma of neem, a nutty garlic smell, hung in the air. Ben attended to each plant for less than a minute. He sprayed a gallon and a half of water around the base to soften the soil. They carried two-liter bottles of drinking water with them as they worked.

After an hour, Ben trotted to the watering hole and disconnected the wires from the battery. He grabbed a bag of urea, jogged back to the patch, and sprinkled small handfuls of the powder around each plant. He then returned to the watering hole, dropped the urea by the other bags of fertilizer, and hooked up the battery. Hustling back to the hose, he made his rounds again, this time spraying five to ten gallons by each plant. Chi Cho was over half way through and continued to move slowly from plant to plant.

After two hours, Ben and Chi Cho put away their tools. Their shoulders sagged. Ben turned to Chi Cho as he lifted the car battery. *"Can't wait till the rainy season."*

"Have to apply the neem twice as often," said Chi Cho. *"Water will*

wash it right off."

"Oh, well. Done for the day."

"Now to work with the pineapple," said Chi Cho. *"Work never stops."* He shook his head.

"A few more hours won't kill us. Six hour work days. Five days a week. That should be the model."

Daniela was in an ocean of color, red, blue, green, and yellow. She was elated as she swam through it, riding the waves, tingling with ecstasy. A dot of light stuck out in the sea, differing from the colored waves. Daniela swam toward it and was instantly sucked from the water into reality. She was in another woman's body, a white woman's, looking out her eyes. The woman's body lay on a wet road with red and blue lights flashing over it. Her head was on the edge, chunks of gravel wedged in her scalp. Daniela wasn't alone in the body. Though the woman was on the edge of death, her soul was still there. It was as if there were three beings inside, the woman's soul, Daniela's, and their two combined. The soul of the woman was frozen from fright, and Daniela understood she was there to help. She looked out through her eyes and scanned the area. A row of pine trees seemed to glow in the distance, calling out to her. Daniela, through a type of natural, nonverbal communication, directed the woman, and they exited the body and floated toward the trees. Daniela felt calmer than she ever had.

The next thing she knew, she was back in her own body and could feel herself being carried and strapped to a chair. She felt cold steel on her arms and legs, nylon straps around her torso. Voices chattered. Her head drooped over, and she was back in the waves.

Later, she started to come out of it, slowly regaining motor coordination. A door opened and closed. She looked up to see Ron, and her head fell to the floor.

"Good afternoon, Daniela." He looked her over, seeing goose bumps and small bruises on her arms, a large bruise on her cheek. "I apologize for the injuries. My partner's a maniac. I should be able to keep him away if you cooperate." He took a small notepad from his pocket. "Exactly what is your association with Benjamin Starosta?"

Her eyes didn't raise from the floor. "I love him," she said.

"How'd you meet him?"

"Volcán Arenal. Tour."

"When was that?"

"Two years ago."

Ron's eyes widened as he scribbled on the notepad. "You've been with him all that time?"

"Yes."

"Then you're aware of his occupation?"

The grains of sand in the concrete floor danced under her eyes. "He's a scholar."

"A scholar?" Ron's tone was cynical. "And what does a scholar earn."

"Knowledge." She looked up from the floor. "Enlightenment, maybe."

"Enlightenment." He rolled his eyes. "How does he earn income?"

"I don't think he does." Daniela looked past him to the dusty walls. Black cobwebs hung from the ceiling.

"People have to work to get money."

She scrunched her face and looked in his eyes. "Americans? I've never seen one work, but they come here with lots of money."

Ron looked up. Wire mesh, black with dust, covered the lights. He lowered his head. "What exactly is your relationship with him?"

"Is it not clear I'm his lover?"

"And you two have lived together?"

"Yes."

"Did you ever notice anything unusual about his behavior?"

"No, not unusual." Her eyes narrowed as she stared at the concrete blocks. "He's very spiritual. He'd go camping in the woods, meditating, sometimes for a whole month, but he always came back."

Ron stared at her blank face. The bruise was ghastly. "He'd leave for a month? Camping?"

She stared in his eyes. "Yes. He needs nature."

"And you'd have no contact with him during this time?"

"No."

"How do you know he was camping?"

"He told me so." The chains at her wrists jangled.

"Do you know where he went camping and the dates?"

She nodded.

"Was Quebrada Grande one of those places?"

"No."

Ron noticed her eyes widen. "So you're familiar with Quebrada Grande?"

"Ben did volunteer work there."

"But he hasn't gone back?"

"I don't think he liked the country people."

Ron stared in her eyes. "Did he speak of them much?"

"No. Just jokes."

"I see." Ron slipped his pen in his pocket and closed his notebook. "Well, I'm going to let you rest a little and then I'll be back. Are you hungry?"

"No." She looked back to the grains of sand in the floor.

"Okay. Rest, and I'll be back in an hour." Ron walked to the door with a hand in his pocket, his shoes tapping. The guard opened the door and held it. Ron nodded. Daniela's eyes didn't move from the floor.

Bill and Flora were lying naked in his hotel room bed, smoking. Flora had the blankets pulled just past her breasts. Her face glowed. Bill was uncovered and spread out, his pink skin dotted with perspiration. Sun came in from a Moorish window behind them.

Bill looked pensive as he inhaled from his cig. He hit it hard, then leaned over and stubbed it out on top of a Coke can. He looked at Flora. 'Damn, she's sexy,' he thought. 'Looks so aloof when she smokes.' *"Flora,"* he said, *"I have something to tell you."* His voice was softer than usual.

She lifted his small, limp penis and dropped it. It slapped against his thigh.

"This is serious," he said.

Her smile left.

"I'm not the man I said I was." His eyes wandered to the bed. *"I don't work for an Internet gambling company."* He tugged at the sheets. *"Actually, the opposite. I work for the law, United States' Central Intelligence Agency."*

Flora slid away from him.

Bill smiled. *"Calm down, doll."* He took her by the hand and rubbed her back. She hit her cigarette and dropped it in the can.

"My partner and I were here to catch a criminal from the States. Yesterday, we did that, and it's time to return. However, I was thinking.

I'm not the young man I once was." He stared at his gut and the mass of hair running south. *"While I find the work fun, I want to relax. I'm thinking of moving here, giving it up."*

"To the Hotel Del Rey?" Flora laughed.

"No, I'm serious." His tone was grave. *"I know that I'm an old man, but I've really grown to like you."* He stroked the fingers on her hand, then looked in her eyes. *"If I decided to move here, would you live with me?"*

Flora turned and stared at the wall. Thirty seconds passed.

"I mean it," said Bill. *"I want to live with you."*

She stared at the wall for another ten seconds, then turned back. Her face reminded him of the first time they met.

"You don't mean this. You're a gringo on vacation. Go home to your wife and children."

"I don't have a wife." He emphasized each word. "*Never had the time. But I think I'm ready.*"

"If you want a wife, look on the Internet. I'm a prostitute."

"And I'm a man who buys prostitutes."

Flora rose and picked up her clothes.

Bill sat all the way up. *"Where are you going?"*

Her ass bunched up as she pulled a pair of tight jeans over her thong. She strapped her bra and pulled it over her head. "*I have to get back to work."* She picked up a tiny shirt with spaghetti straps and slid it on as she made for the door.

"*I mean it,"* said Bill. *"I think I love you."*

She grabbed a small handbag from the floor and hurried out, her heels clicking. Bill watched, his face desolate. The sound of the door shutting echoed in his head, and he heard her heels moving quickly down the hall. The smell of her perfume hung heavy in his nose. His eyes fell on the folded money still sitting on the dresser by the door.

Ron nodded and snickered as he read about Castro's intestinal surgery in that morning's USA Today. He brought his coffee to his lips and sipped, then spotted Bill walking slowly toward him. His face was sullen. Ron folded the paper. "What's wrong with you?" he said.

Bill stared before speaking. "We leave tomorrow?"

"Yep." Ron smiled wide. "Two weeks in the pits of Colombia, then back home."

Bill's frown sagged further.

"Don't be glum. There's hookers in the States, too." Ron took a drink.

"What the fuck's that supposed to mean?"

"Come on, Bill. You love this place because of cheap prostitutes and gambling. You're staying at that whore house downtown, right?"

"It just so happens, I met a girl I'm interested in. A pure woman."

Ron wiped his mouth. "Don't do it, Bill. Won't turn out."

"How the fuck do you know?"

"Never does. Just gonna fuck you up."

Bill stared at the table cloth. The fibers seemed to pulse.

"You want a coffee?" said Ron.

Bill's head didn't move.

"Café," yelled Ron. He pointed to Bill. "I was talkin' to Robert this morn. I think we're going to release the girl."

Bill looked up. His frown had morphed to a scowl.

A slim waiter then stopped before their table. He turned over a mug and filled it.

"No cream or sugar," said Bill.

The waiter nodded and quickly walked away.

"What do you mean, release her?" he said

"Let her go. We'll have someone monitor her for awhile. See what she's up to."

"I want to question her first."

"Keeping you away from her is what got me all this." Ron tapped a notebook.

"That's all bullshit. I'll talk to her. Get the real scoop." He took a large gulp of coffee.

"We have a lot of good information here," said Ron. "All the dates when Starosta came and went."

"Just not the important thing."

Ron's eyes dropped. "She can't help us with that."

"Bullshit. She's playing you for a fool."

He shrugged. "Time will tell."

"That time will be today." Bill took another drink of coffee. "You ready?"

"Anytime." Ron frowned and shook his head.

"Let's do it." Bill downed his coffee and brought the mug down hard. He rose and threw down some wrinkled bills. Ron stood and looked to the bamboo stalks above, running numbers through his head. He counted out bills and laid them in a neat pile before picking up his briefcase and following Bill out. They walked along a stone path that led around the side of the hotel. Lush green plants hung down between yellow and orange flowers. The temperature seemed to rise as they stepped on the blacktop driveway. "Need taxi?" a man yelled. The pair walked silently. Bill hit the button on his key chain to unlock the car.

"Ahh!" Ron yelled. He shook his hand. "Fuck. I touched the

rubber around the window."

"Seats are hot enough," said Bill. He dipped in and turned the A/C to high. A gust of hot air preceded the Freon-cooled blast, forming droplets of sweat on the men's foreheads. Bill reached for the radio, turned the knob, and marimba banged out as they departed.

Ron stared at the large hotels facing the main highway. Palm trees stood in front, large blue pools behind. He watched an airplane pass low overhead, and they followed a truck down an exit ramp. The road shrunk from a couple of lanes to one as they passed the airport, all steel and glass. A mesh fence separated the road from the runways. The Pan-American Highway stood above them to their right. Past the runways, there were dozens of small brick buildings. They, like the airport, were fenced in.

Bill slowed and turned off the main road. A guard checked his I.D. "*¡Pura Vida!*" said Bill, and the guard waved him through. Inside, it looked like a ghost town. Not a soul to be seen, just unpainted cinder block buildings, all one story. They rounded a corner and parked in front of one of the bland structures. The number 27 was painted in large black letters. The sun shone mercilessly as they exited and walked up the sidewalk. Ron pressed a button next to the heavy steel door and looked up at a camera. The door buzzed, and they entered.

"Welcome," a tico in uniform greeted them. "Can I get you anything? Coffee?" His accent was thick.

"We're good," said Bill.

"This is our last day," said Ron. "Just need to prod the girl some more, and we ship out with the detainee tomorrow."

"I wouldn't mind prodding her." The man raised his eyebrows.

"Me first," said Bill. He walked down a narrow hallway and opened a thick gray door. The guard inside nodded, clutching his gun. Bill pulled out his Camels and lit one, then held the pack out to the guard. The man took one, slipped it in his mouth, and Bill lit it before lighting his own. He then stepped gingerly to Daniela.

"Hello, darling."

Daniela looked up and squinted.

"What's the matter? You'll blow that gringo, but you don't have time for me?" He smiled and blew a smoke trail to the ceiling.

"Okay, honey, give us the dirt. What was he up to?"

Daniela stared at the gray brick wall.

Bill slowly moved the cigarette toward her eye. "Talk," he said, then smiled and took a drag.

"He's a good man."

"Good man, my ass!" Bill threw his cigarette against the wall. "He's a fuckin' criminal. And if you're hiding his secrets, you're one too."

"He didn't…" she sobbed.

Bill moved his face close to hers. The smoke on his breath was strong. "You better tell us," he said. "There are other ways we can get it." He reached out and stroked her hair between his fingers.

Daniela lowered her head and squeezed her eyes shut. "I told you," she cried.

Bill ran his fingers down her neck, shoulder, and arm. "It's been a little while since I've been with a tica. Hell, maybe I could get the guards, and we can all have a turn." He felt her thigh, just out of reach of her hands. "I'd hate to see this hot body go to waste." Bill leaned in, licked around the edge of her ear, and stuck in his tongue. "You wanna talk," he whispered, "or fuck?"

Daniela's jaw was locked, every muscle in her body tight.

Bill turned to the guard whose eyes were huge. "*You want to step out a moment?*" he said.

The guard exited.

Down the hall in an identical room, Ron stood before Ben. He rested his weight on his left leg and held a notebook against his hip.

"How did you get all that money, Ben?"

"What money?"

"Don't lie. Fifty thousand to that co-op in Milwaukee. The unpasteurized milk distribution in Madison. They've both been shut down."

Ron heard a large puff of air from Ben's nostrils and noticed his chest moving faster. "We know about your escapades in Mexico, too."

"I don't know what the fuck you're talking about."

Ron's eyes grew narrow. "Yes, you do. You're a puny revolutionary. Don't forget. These cuts and bruises are nothing. You can't fathom what will happen if you don't cooperate."

Ben stared into Ron's eyes. "The same that happens to the poor of the world daily."

"Doesn't compare," said Ron. "If you don't cooperate, you will be executed, but in due time. You'll wish we'd execute you a thousand times before it happens, and it could be very long if you're difficult."

"It's an illusion," Ben whispered.

"What?"

"Do what you have to to make this world a better place." said Ben.

"Answers like that won't work." Ron stared him down, then turned and walked from the room. The guard opened and shut the door behind him.

Ron slid the transmission into park and unbuckled his seat belt. The steel door handle felt cool in his hand. He stepped out, and a breeze rippled his pants as he walked to the gray building. The sidewalk was dotted with black ash and orange cigarette butts. He pressed the button by the door and looked up at the camera, waving his index finger. The door buzzed, and he entered.

"Good morning." The same tico was there in blue fatigues. His curly hair cut with perfect symmetry. "Where's your partner?"

"I let him sleep in. I'm taking the girl to the bus station, and I didn't want him harassing her."

"It was hard enough to keep my men from harassing her. Me included." His dimples swelled.

Ron faked a laugh. "Keys?" he said.

The man walked to a brown metal desk, and a screech whizzed through the air as he yanked open a drawer. He fished out a set of keys and flung them to Ron.

"Muy bien."

"Gracias." Ron nodded and showed a faint smile as he walked down the narrow hall. He dragged the tip of a key against the gray blocks and noticed a cockroach scurry into a crevice. Ron threw open the door, startling the guard, then nodded to him and walked to Daniela. He could smell a piss bucket in the corner. "It's your lucky

day." He rattled the keys.

Daniela's dour face didn't change as he knelt to undo the locks at her ankles. She watched him move to the chains at her knees and wrists. The smell of his aftershave wafted to her nose. She rotated her hands in circles and squeezed her wrists as he dropped the mess of chain to the floor. Then Daniela massaged her palms while he loosened the straps at her chest.

"This way, please." Ron motioned to the door.

Her joints ached as she rose. She moved stiffly and eyed the guard. The hair escaping his navy blue hat was the same dark black color as her own. His face the same golden caramel. In the center of his dark irises lay what? Shame? "*Slimy pig,"* she mumbled.

"Left," said Ron.

She turned down the hall and followed it to the front. There was one tico bent over a desk and another leaning against a wall, texting on his phone. They wore the same navy blue uniforms as the guard, only lighter. No thick jacket, shotgun, or bandolier. Just a pistol at their hips.

"I'm running her to the station," said Ron. "Be back in an hour."

The man with the phone looked from him to Daniela. Her hardened eyes stared back.

Ron opened the door, and Daniela stepped back as the sunlight hit her. She lowered her head and squinted, holding a hand above her eyes. Her lavender blue shirt looked as if it had been pulled from the bottom of a laundry pile. A deafening rumble passed over as a jet swooped in for a landing. Ron stepped around her and held open the door. She stared warily.

"Don't worry. I'm taking you to the bus station. Getting you a ticket home."

Daniela cautiously lowered herself into the seat as Ron walked to the driver's side, glancing at his watch. The car smelled heavily of air freshener, new car scent. A cloud rolled in, casting a shadow over the area, and a tiny bird fluttered by. Ron sniffed and smelled what he assumed was a mixture of body odor, urine, and halitosis coming from Daniela. He pressed the window buttons, they buzzed down, and the two drove out. Ron stopped the car at the gates before a guard in mirrored sunglasses waved them through.

Daniela stared at the large hotels and planes cutting through the sky. Below them, the parking lots were filled with shiny cars, people milling about in dress clothes, a line of red taxis. Her head didn't move from her window until Ron turned into the bus station's lot.

"Ten thousand enough?" Ron held out a worn blue note. It swayed, revealing a puma on one side, a portrait of a famous educator on the other, Emma Gamboa.

Daniela reached for the bill, but Ron drew it back. "You're free," he said, "but people will check on you. If you disappear, we'll hunt you, like we did Ben. No one can hide from us." He stared in her eyes and slowly brought the note back. Daniela grabbed it and got out. Ron leaned back in his seat and watched her hobble to the bus in her soiled clothes. The driver gave her an unsavory look as he changed her bill.

Ron navigated the silver Octavia from the lot. He glanced at a cab driver staring at him. 'Fuck off,' he thought, driving toward the main road. Lofty buildings stood all around. The tallest, nearly double the rest, read "Banco Nacional." It was a mix of concrete, glass, and steel. A smooth, modern high-rise lacking the charm of the older buildings below. Ron stopped at a traffic light and avoided the faces of vendors in the street who flashed their products to drivers. One with cell phone chargers draped over his arms waved and spoke quickly. Ron rolled up his windows and turned on the A/C. He turned up the radio. A couple of more stoplights, and he turned off the wide street onto Avenida 1. He hit Calle 6 where gaudy casino signs stood out against the sky. There were neon images of palms and a big, red horseshoe. Overweight Americans jaywalked, slapping each other's backs and laughing jovially. Ron crept slowly by and leaned over the passenger seat to inspect a large, pink building with white bricks bordering its windows. It was five stories high with a flat roof. A large, gold crown sat next to the red hotel sign atop it. Bill was nowhere to be seen. Ron drove around the corner and parked. He inspected the people as he walked toward the hotel. All he saw were old gringos who carried the same girth as Bill. The security guards with their wands didn't flinch as he walked by. An old man with a mustache and silver slicked back hair stood behind the desk.

"Is there a Bill Larimore here?" said Ron.

The man pointed through a doorway to the bar.

Ron shook his head and walked into the smoky room. Girls were stationed against the walls. Bill was hunched over the bar with a glass of brown liquor in hand. Ron could hear him speaking Spanish with an opulently trashy dressed woman. "*Up and left. Gave her my heart, and she killed it.*"

Ron approached one of the prostitutes. She wore tight jeans and a small shirt, a cross between a sports jersey and a polo shirt. Long dark hair hung down the sides of her shiny face. She looked deep into his eyes. "Excuse me," said Ron. "Can I ask you how long he's been there?" He pointed to Bill.

"Two girls?" she said. The woman held up her middle and index fingers.

"Never mind." Ron walked to Bill and thrust a hand on his shoulder. "Alright, Bill, time to go."

Bill slowly turned. "Hey, it's my partner. The man who thinks he's too good for places like this." Bill took a wad of colones from his pocket. "This is Candela, fabulous woman." He motioned to his side. "She's yours for the hour." Bill peeled off five ten thousand notes and held them out. The woman stared at the cash.

"Quit fuckin' around," said Ron. "It's time to go."

"Less than a hundred dollars for this fine piece of ass." Bill grabbed a handful through her lime green skirt. "You need to hit it before we go. See what Costa Rica's about."

"Is this it?" said Ron. "You leaving your dapper job with the C.I.A.?"

"I was thinking about it." Bill tipped the rest of his drink back.

"Fine by me. I'll tell Robert. I don't have time to wait around."

Bill grabbed Ron's jacket. "Wait. I'm coming. Needed to blow off some steam after the woman I love ran out on me."

Ron looked to the ceiling.

"I'll be back, though. This isn't the last of Bill Larimore." Bill handed two ten thousand notes to the prostitute at his side. *"Thanks for listening, beautiful. And remember, offer still stands."* He stiffly pushed himself from the bar and held his hands high as he followed Ron out. *"Until next time, everybody,"* he yelled. *"¡Pura Vida!"*

Ron walked through the doorway to the lobby and onto the stairs outside as Bill jaunted behind. *"Eduardo,"* said Bill. *"My suitcase, por favor."*

The man behind the desk rolled out a medium sized black suitcase and handed it to Bill. "Thank you for staying with us."

"Anytime, Ed." He slipped the man a five thousand note and headed for the door. *"¡Pura Vida!"* he yelled.

The doormen smiled as he passed. Outside, Bill looked back and forth for Ron, then spotted him at the end of the block, waving. He banged his luggage down the steps and wheeled it over.

"I'm driving," said Ron. "You're too fucked up."

"I barely had any." Bill's dress shirt was untucked, and his face was red.

"It's not just the alcohol."

"Sorry some of us have emotions." Bill slammed the trunk and plodded to his seat.

Ron looked over his shoulder and pulled out. "Bill, we all have emotions, but you have to be careful."

Calle 6 faded in their mirrors, and the towering buildings grew nearer. Bill watched a couple of school girls in navy blue pants and white button down shirts cross the street. They carried shiny backpacks.

"You're an agent. You should be able to read people."

As quickly as the roots of San Jose's skyscrapers came into view, they receded as the pair headed toward the Pan-American and the bunker by the airport. Bill watched the street vendors hocking their goods, the elderly sitting in parks, and the metropolites in their swank clothes and cars. He rolled down his window to feel closer to them. Before he knew it, they were riding down an exit ramp and being waved into the heavily secured area. Ron rolled down the rest of the windows and shut off the car.

"I'll be in in a minute," said Bill.

Ron checked his watch. "We got a half hour. I'll ready the prisoner."

Bill watched Ron strut to the door, pause for clearance, and then enter. His eyes wandered to a telephone pole to the side of the building where a hawk perched. It had a gray head with white feathers below its sharply curved beak. He saw brown and black feathers on its wings as it scanned the ground below. Its eyes were a hauntingly reddish brown.

Bill lowered the visor and looked at his eyes in the mirror. They were bloodshot, and his pupils were smaller than he'd ever remembered. He slapped at his cheeks and squeezed them, then got out of the car. A rumble came from his belly. He watched the hawk as he unbuttoned his pants to tuck in his shirt. It turned its head. Bill pulled his Camel pack from his pocket, leaned against the car, and lit one while watching the hawk study the ground. After a few long drags, he pushed himself up and walked to the building. He threw his cigarette, only half gone, amongst the other butts. Before he reached the door, he went into a coughing fit, loud, raspy sounds in his chest. He hocked a wad of phlegm and pressed the button by the door. The buzz came, and he entered.

Ron was drinking a coffee with one of the tico higher-ups.

"Buenos días," said the man.

"Buenos días, yourself," said Bill.

Ron's eyes moved over him, searching for a clue to his mental state.

"Is our man ready?" said Bill.

"He's been fed," said the tico. "The guards are making sure he's relieved himself. He will be shackled when you're ready."

"Excellent," said Bill. "How long till we go?"

"We should be getting a…" Ron paused as the phone began to ring. "Call at any time," he whispered.

The tico spoke quickly into the phone. Bill cocked his head and focused.

The officer said, *"¡Chau!"* and hung up. "Gentlemen, the plane has landed, and we're cleared. I'll drive you over in the car you've used, then run it back for you." The man turned and walked down the hall.

"You guys ready?" The man walked quickly to the front door and held it open. Ron and Bill followed. The sound of chains rattling could be heard behind them as the door slammed shut. Bill looked to the telephone pole, but the hawk was gone.

"You mind sitting with the prisoner?" Ron motioned to the back of the car.

"That's fine," said Bill. "I'm more wary of sitting in front of a prisoner than next to him."

Each man stood in front of a car door, Bill behind the driver. The metal door slowly opened, and Ben took small steps into the sunlight. Dried blood and bruises still showed on his face as he squinted to the sun. Flakes of rheum filled the corners of his eyes and stuck in his lashes. A guard next to him had a firm grip on his bicep. Another guard trailed behind, shotgun pointed at his back.

"Put him in there." The driver pointed to the seat behind Ron, and the three men got in the car. The guards led Ben over, short step after short step, then pushed him inside. Bill looked him over and then turned sadly to his window.

The driver stopped to show I.D. as they entered through a private airport gate. A small blue dot in the distance grew to an airplane as they approached, a 1973 Piper Navajo, looking in need of repair. A layer of grime coated it, and bare metal showed where paint had flaked off. Two Latin American men in dark camouflage fatigues stood outside the aircraft.

"It was a pleasure to serve you and your organization while you were here." The driver looked from Ron to Bill. "I hope you leave with a good impression of our country."

"We appreciate your assistance," said Ron. "And we'll be sure to let our organization know about you."

"Thank you, sir." The driver turned in his seat to watch Ben.

Ben looked in his eyes. *"I only tried to help your fellow ticos,"* he said.

Ron walked to the trunk to gather their luggage.

"Let's go, socialist." Bill tugged Ben out by the chains. *"Hasta luego,"* He waved to the driver.

"¡Pura Vida!" said the driver, giving a wave before leaving.

The pair looked over their new Latin American comrades. The men were of similar height and build and had the same dark features. Ron was happy to see that one had a thin mustache. He'd be able to tell them apart.

"How do you do?" said the stacheless one. His accent was thick.

"We're fine," said Ron. "Happy to get this prisoner where he belongs."

"And we are ready for another guest at our resort." The man with the thin mustache shook Ron's hand vigorously. "My name is Panfilo, and this is Juan."

"Charmed." Ron glanced from side to side uneasily. "I'm Ron, and this is Bill."

Panfilo moved to Bill and pumped his hand, then on to Ben. "Ahh, our guest? I assume with the fancy jewelry." He shook the chains that bound him. "Don't worry, my friend, we will take excellent care. Where you are going is like a… a… Club Med. You might even find love there."

He was close enough for Ben to smell the coconut on his breath. As he turned away, Ben noticed a flag with yellow, red, and blue horizontal stripes on his sleeve. 'Colombia,' he thought.

"Are we ready to go?" said Panfilo.

"Certainly are," said Ron.

"Great. I can take this mongrel from you," he told Bill.

Bill released the chains and walked to grab his bag from Ron.

"Name?" Panfilo said.

"Ben," said Ron. "Ben Starosta."

"Ben, I have a nice seat for you in the back of the plane." Panfilo made a big smile and pulled him forward. *"¡Vámanos!"* he yelled.

He pushed Ben onto the plane, and Juan and Ron followed. Bill walked up the stairs, then turned back to the city. Rain clouds were moving in. *"Pura Vida, Costa Rica,"* he said. *"Pura Vida."*

Panfilo shoved Ben past six seats with torn leather coverings to a black metal bench in back. "Sit," he said.

Ben did so, and Panfilo secured his hands to a bar running the width of the plane above Ben's head. He then knelt and fastened Ben's feet to a bar running across the floor. "Enjoy your flight," he said.

Ben flexed his back, and, arched forward, he could just see out a window. The sky was hazy. Ben thought about the fact that the windows weren't blacked out, and the agents hadn't drugged him. They weren't concerned with him knowing where he was going.

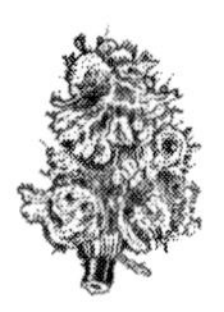

Ben's stomach bounced as turbulence jostled the plane. His arms ached. He thought about the food he'd been served that morning, salty white rice and mushy pinto beans. 'Maybe a special ingredient, too,' he wondered. 'Santorum, perhaps.' Ben tried to push the image from his mind.

Panfilo's voice was as constant as the droning of the engines. The plane's wheels touched the dirt runway. "Here we are, Club Med," Panfilo announced, like a game show host. He looked to his stacheless friend. *"You want to take these two to El Comandante? I'll bring Ben to his new home."*

Juan nodded.

Panfilo again pumped Bill and Ron's hands. "It was nice to meet you. I'll see you later."

Ron and Bill nodded, and Panfilo walked to the back. *"I hear you speak Spanish, Ben. That's good because I'm better with insults in my native tongue."*

He unhooked Ben's feet and stared at him. *"How do your arms feel, gringo?"*

Ben looked at the floor.

"Not too good, huh?" Panfilo undid the lock at Ben's wrists. *"Good for an ill born man like yourself, though. Okay. Now go!"* He shoved Ben out the plane.

Ben barely kept from falling as he went down the stairs to the dusty ground. Cement buildings surrounded the airstrip. Beyond them, a tall mesh wire fence held back the forest. Ben saw clouds in the sky and contemplated their beauty before studying the area in hope of escape. His eyes went back to the woods.

"Faster." Panfilo shoved Ben away from the plane.

A group of four soldiers stared at Ben as they approached. Panfilo kicked him behind the knee, and Ben collapsed to the ground. The four soldiers laughed.

"Get up!" yelled Panfilo. *"Walk faster!"*

More laughs came from the soldiers as Ben meekly rose and walked on, the chains rattling. After several hundred yards, he and Panfilo came upon a series of long, rectangular buildings. They looked like storage facilities from the U.S., large black numbers painted on each.

"Right!" hollered Panfilo as they passed number 5.

"Stop!" He stepped in front of Ben to open a thick steel door.

Ben thought about throwing the cuffs around his neck, like in the movies, but was too slow. Panfilo was inside and waved to someone. *"Enter!"* he shouted. *"Stop!"*

Ben went in and saw a guard walking over. He wore the same army fatigues as everyone Ben had seen on base. A large pistol at his waist.

"This is the new prisoner," said Panfilo.

"We're ready for him." The guard turned and unlocked an impenetrable steel door. The hinges squeaked as he pulled it open.

"Enter!" yelled Panfilo.

The guard stood to the side as Ben and Panfilo passed. They moved into a hall filled with numerous other heavy doors, each with a small window in its front. A buzzing issued from the fluorescent lights above them.

"The second to the end," said the guard. *"609."*

A loud click echoed as the man closed the door.

"Stop!" yelled Panfilo.

The guard walked up and opened the door with "609" painted on it in black numbers. Its hinges creaked louder than the first door. Inside was a ten-foot square room. Nothing but a bed and a steel toilet.

"There it is, Ben, your new home. Enter!" Panfilo turned to the guard. *"Draw a weapon while I unchain him."*

The guard drew the black pistol from his hip and pointed it at Ben's chest.

"I hope you like your new home," said Panfilo. *"It was designed by a gringo, like you."* He dropped the chains as he undid them, then scooped them in a pile. *"Anytime someone complains about our jail, I say, 'Hey, just like the U.S.'"* Panfilo winked at the guard, then stepped out. *"Hasta luego,"* he said. The door slammed shut.

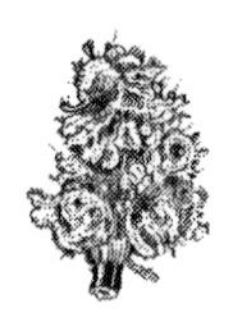

Ron and Bill stood in a small waiting room looking at signed photos on the wall. Bill inspected an image of Michael Irvin stretched out in the end zone and another of Emmit Smith in the open green.

"Dallas Cowboys dynasty," he said. "Three time champs, could have been four."

"*El Comandante* is a Cowboys fan. Watches games on satellite." Juan pointed to a photo of Hulk Hogan in his trademark yellow tee and red bandanna. "WWF, too."

Ron laughed. "Fat Elvis," he said. He pointed at a photo of The King striking a pose in a sequined outfit.

"It was right before he died," said Bill. "Show some respect." He moved on to the movie star section of the Comandante's showcase. "Clint Eastwood. *The Good, The Bad, and The Ugly.*" His eyes grew big. "Connery as Bond. Nicholson as Colonel Jessup. Man's got taste."

"Accentuated by the wood paneling." Ron ran his finger down a black line separating the veneer of the panel. The texture was rough. "My poor relatives had this stuff all through their house." He knocked on the wall. "They didn't have cement behind theirs though."

"This doesn't fit." Bill cocked his head and pointed to a picture in a red frame.

Ron walked over and looked. "Elton John?" He covered his mouth.

"He knows he is a gay," said Juan. "He doesn't care."

"Juan," a voice called from the other room.

Juan rushed from the room and returned seconds later. "*El Comandante* is ready to see you." He held the door as Ron and Bill walked in. The Comandante moved out from behind his desk. He was Bill's height and had similar girth. The gold buttons on his jacket were stretched tight. A thick beard covered his face, mostly gray with traces of black. "Commander Gonzalo Vanzuelo, friend of the United States government." He moved to shake their hands.

"Ron Numbers, friend of the Colombian government."

"Bill Larimore."

"Gentleman, would you like some scotch, perhaps a cigar?" The Comandante walked toward a table in the corner of the room.

"No, thank you," said Ron. "Unnecessary."

The Comandante had the bottle in hand.

"I'll take one," said Bill.

The bearded man poured two glasses of Scotch and passed one Bill's way. "I know you agents." He smiled. "You love your drink."

"To Colombia." Bill held up the glass and tipped it back.

The Comandante stared at him. "You really do love your drink."

"Gotta love something." Bill looked at Ron, then turned back to the Comandante.

"Aged twenty years. There are some benefits to devoting oneself to a life of armed service." He poured another splash into Bill's glass. "You have a prisoner for us?"

"Yes," said Ron. "His name is Benjamin Starosta, and we may need to keep him here for awhile."

"Not a problem." The Comandante put the scotch to his nose and inhaled.

"We're hoping no more than a year."

"But possibly no more than two weeks," said Bill.

"Nice. Nice." The Comandante nodded. "Better sooner than later." He set the bottle back on the table.

"We'll be here for two weeks for the interrogation," said Ron. "After that, a couple years tops."

The Comandante took the drink from his lips. "Who is he?"

"Marxist," said Bill.

"FARC." The word came through the Comandante's clenched teeth.

"Exactly," said Ron. "Just treat him like a FARC bargaining chip. No accidental deaths."

The Comandante's eyes cut through him. "There are deaths, but never accidental."

Ron looked behind him. An image of Troy Aikman and Emmitt Smith hoisting the Lombardi Trophy hung on the wall. "You have a place for us to stay?" he said.

"Of course. You must umpress."

Bill squinted.

"Decompress," said Ron.

"Yes. I will have Juan show you to your home, but before I let you go, I want to let you know if you need anything while you are here, anything at all…" He looked between the pair. "Our base may appear primitive, but we do have luxuries, as you have tasted." He nodded to Bill. "And we lack no necessities."

Bill threw back the rest of his drink and held out the glass. "Thank you very much, *Comandante*. Your hospitality is appreciated."

"Thanks," said Ron.

"It was a pleasure meeting you both, and I hope to chat with you later. Perhaps we can watch the TV. I have all of your stations and many movies."

"Sounds great," said Bill.

"Juan, take these men to their quarters."

Juan motioned to the door and followed Ron and Bill out. They watched him bow his head to the Comandante before softly shutting the door. The agents then picked up their luggage and walked out the next door. A green Jeep drove past, and a cloud of dust rose up. Ron coughed and fanned the air.

"This way," said Juan. He pointed away from the center of the base.

The wheels on Bill's suitcase locked up as he dragged it through the fine dust. After a hundred feet, he slid the long, black handle back into the bag and picked it up, limping as he carried it. Sweat droplets began to sprout on his back. "The temperature here's the same as San Jose," he said.

"How much was it there?" said Juan.

Bill wiped his brow. "Eighty degrees."

"Oh yes, the Fahrenheit. We can't talk weather."

"Twenty seven Celsius," said Ron. He glanced at his shoes, covered with dust.

"Yes, that is the high temperature here all year," said Juan. "One thousand five hundred meters keeps it cool. Medellín is called 'The

City of Eternal Spring.'"

"Thank God for the mountains," said Bill.

"It is good for coffee here, too," said Juan.

"Coffee, Juan?" Bill smiled. "Is your last name Valdez?"

"Ha ha. Every American ask me that."

A half mile down the road, their hike came to an end before two isolated structures. A large barracks and a small green house. Juan opened the black gate fronting the home and moved up the path. Ron cleaned his shoes on the unmowed lawn.

"This is where you will stay," said Juan. "It was built for comandantes Americans." He pointed over to the barracks. "American soldiers stay there."

Ron looked over the cement drainage troughs in the ground below the roof, then to the bars on the windows. "You worried about people breaking in?" He pointed at the bars.

"It's just the style." Juan jingled the keys as he unlocked the door, then kicked off his shoes before entering. Ron and Bill, likewise, removed their shoes and slid in on their thin dress socks.

Juan walked around the house and pointed. "There are two bedrooms, a room where you can wash your clothes, a bathroom, and..." Juan held his arms out and turned in the center of a large room that functioned as kitchen, dining, and living room. He walked to the short, stout fridge and opened it. "No food because you'll eat your meals with *El Comandante.*"

Bill was already in one of the bedrooms unpacking his things. Juan wiped dust from the top of the refrigerator. "When you two have settled in, you can come back down to the office. If *Comandante* is not in, I can help you. I should be getting back now."

Ron looked around the room, visibly disappointed. "We'll be alright," he said.

Juan nodded and moved to the door.

"Wait," yelled Bill. "I'm ready to head back."

Juan continued out the door.

"When ya be down, Ron?" said Bill, sliding into his shoes.

"Half hour."

Bill tightened the knot in his slim laces and hustled out the door like a fat kid whose friends had left without him. Ron shook his head and walked around the house. He looked to the tin roof above, then the red cement floor, thinking the place was more suitable for farm equipment. He ran his finger over a window, noticed the screen, and opened it. A soft breeze flowed in. He moved around the house opening the other windows and then walked to his bedroom. There was a twin size bed with pale colored linens, a nightstand, and a cheap wooden armoire. The light bulb above was exposed. He placed his suitcase on the bed, then shook the wrinkles from his clothes and carried them to the musty armoire. He hung his clothes, then grabbed a plastic bag filled with toiletries and laid out the items in the bathroom. The song of a highland motmot, like the hoot of an owl, rang through the house. Ron turned on the faucet, cupped his hands below it, and tossed water on his face. He then brought a scoop to his mouth, but spit it out. 'What am I doing?' he thought. He wiped his hands and walked out the door.

Daniela raised her head from the seat as the bus pulled in between two others. She waited for everyone to pass, then rose and walked off. Outside, people waited next to rundown buses and flashy new coaches. Children stood in front of stands on the station's platform, staring at candy, pineapple, and watermelon behind the glass windows. There was cooked pizza, burgers, and chicken awaiting a microwave nuke. Daniela zigzagged through the crowd and got away as quickly as possible. Taxi drivers stared as she walked through a grassy field next to the station.

Daniela stared straight ahead. She controlled her breath and focused her eyes. The grass tickled her feet above her flip-flops. The clouds pulsed. Visual snow danced in her peripheral vision, like little bubbles growing and popping. The sounds of buses from the station and children playing became faint. She blinked and looked back and forth before stepping on the black pavement at an intersection. She watched the horizon as she crossed. Two children raced down the street and ran out of breath before her. A chubby boy with beads of sweat covering his forehead lifted his shirt and slapped his belly. A little girl sat on the sidewalk and drew with chalk. She looked at Daniela as she passed.

After an hour, Daniela could see her home. She watched it grow larger with each step, and the wall she had put up to withhold her emotions started to crumble. She squinted as tears dripped from her eyes. Her lips, stretched tight, formed a straight line. The only image in her mind was Ben. She thought about the many times they'd come home together. The way he'd put his arms around her. However, images of him being beaten kept intruding. Bill kicking him on the floor. Ben in a bloody pile in the back of the car. Daniela let out sharp cries as she walked around the side of her house. A woman banging shoes together turned and watched as Daniela stretched to grab a key from under the roof, then ran to the front door. There was an intense pain in her stomach. The tears flowed harder, and she had to struggle to keep her eyes open. Finally, she pulled the keys from the door, slammed it, and collapsed to the floor, wailing. She remained there for close to an hour, moving between bawling violently and softly weeping. She eventually pushed herself up and grabbed a box of tissues before climbing into bed where she'd stay for the remainder of the evening.

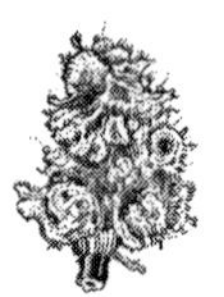

By morning, Daniela had decided she should get to Quebrada Grande to inform Chi Cho and the rest of the community of Ben's capture. She lay in bed for a long while but eventually climbed out and made it to the shower. She had to gather strength to soap her body. It seemed like one of the most difficult things she'd ever done. Minutes went by as she stood under the shower head, watching the water swirl down the drain. Afterward, she looked into the mirror and wondered if the shower had helped. She felt as dirty as when she'd entered, dirtier than ever.

Daniela felt like climbing back into bed, but dressed and went to the kitchen. Though not hungry, she forced down gallo pinto. It didn't help the pain lodged in her stomach, however. She remembered Ben talking of people who had no appetite without marijuana. Daniela never thought she'd be one of those people. *'A pain that food can't cure,'* she thought.

Daniela washed the dishes and walked to her bedroom. Memories of Ben lurked in every part of the house. He sat in each chair, wrestled with her on the floor, danced naked in the bedroom, waving his member. She tossed clothes and toiletries into a backpack, threw it over her shoulder, and walked out. The sound of her flip-flops against the floor echoed through the empty home. Daniela turned and locked the door, but the ghost of Ben had already made it out. He stood behind her, kissing on her neck. She pushed him away and moved down the sidewalk, looking at the gray clouds above. She held out her arms and let the falling mist sprinkle them. A breeze flowed through, giving her a slight chill. She saw a red taxi approaching, glanced at her watch, and flagged him down. *"La estacíon,"* she said.

The driver gazed unabashedly at her chest before pulling out.

Daniela stared at the sun breaking through the clouds in the distance. Sprinkles dotted the window, and the wipers swished them away at ten second intervals.

The driver parked next to the buses. *"A thousand colones is good,"* he said.

"Gracias." Daniela handed him the money and exited. The smell of diesel exhaust and fried food hung in the air. *"Last call for La Fortuna,"* a man yelled. Daniela looked over her shoulder and noticed the driver watching her from the curb. She became nervous and walked to the station's platform. A man sat behind a small table between the men and women's bathroom. A roll of toilet paper and a small box with change in it lay on the table. Daniela walked past him and into the bathroom. She leaned over a dirty sink and splashed water on her face, trying to wash away the black streaks under her eyes. When she walked out, the taxi driver was gone. She scanned the area and walked down to a sign that said Pital. A rickety school bus sat idling.

'The type that Ben avoided,' she thought. *'Seats too small for his legs.'*

"How long?" she asked.

"Five minutes," said the driver.

Daniela handed him a few coins and stepped onto the bus. She moved down the hard rubber aisle, passing ten ticos and a few Nicaraguan immigrants, and slid into a vinyl bench seat in back. The cry of a child rang through the bus. Daniela leaned her head against the window and waited, watching rain drops hit the ground. The engine wailed, and the bus shook as they lurched out of the lot. She watched Ciudad Quesada fade away, the tip of the church disappearing in the clouds. They drove out of the rain into bright blue sky. Passengers slid the windows down. As the bus stopped to let people off, Daniela watched high school kids throwing rocks at clusters of green coconuts. They whooped as one fell, and a boy with a machete picked it up. She closed her eyes and focused on her breathing, chanting the word "one" in her head over the rumble of the bus.

As the vehicle hooked a wide corner and came to a stop, Daniela opened her eyes to see Pital, or, rather, the shabby lot of a convenience mart in Pital. She queued up and followed everyone out, glancing around. *'Too many familiar people,'* she thought. *'He was such a showboat.'* Daniela walked down the main street and cut into an alley. Cracks showed in the paint on the cinder block walls. Some flaked off. Weeds sprouted from the blacktop. She rounded another corner and breathed a sigh of relief. A pirata sat there in an old, gray Chevette. She wouldn't have to deal with seeing the legal taxistas, those who she knew, especially Victor.

"Buenos dias. I need a ride to Quebrada Grande."

"Four thousand colones."

"Esta bien." Daniela walked around and got in. The vehicle looked freshly cleaned, the carpeting fluffed. She put on her seat belt. The driver checked his mirrors and sped out. The breeze from the windows swung the Virgin Mary dangling from the rear view mirror.

At the edge of town, the driver hit the brakes before the rough area but wasted no time getting back up to speed.

"Will you need a ride back?" The driver yelled over the noise of air blowing in.

"No." Daniela pushed the hair from her face. *"I won't be leaving."*

"You live there?"

Daniela turned from the pineapple fields to her right. *"What?"*

"You live there?" he yelled.

"No, visiting family friends. They'll take me back. Can't call them, though. No phones."

"No cell phone?"

"No."

The driver shook his head. *"They don't work there anyway."*

Daniela turned back to the fields. There was a young pink pineapple, no larger than an orange, on each plant, barely recognizable from the road. Water sat in puddles on the hard red clay between fields. There were larger pineapples in the next field, the pink hue now absent. People knelt on the ground planting in still another. And, in one more, the golden fruits swelled, begging to be picked. It all became a blur to Daniela, mixing with the old men outside the pulpería, the pastel colored homes, the concrete, tin-roofed bus stops, and the hills beyond. Daniela did notice that the pineapple processing plant outside Quebrada Grande was empty. She could remember times she'd passed it at midnight, and the lights shined brightly while people worked throughout the night. Now it was empty. She remembered Ben telling her of the Catalonian Anarchists, the ones who just took the factories from their bosses. After twenty minutes of bouncing down the uneven road, they pulled into Isabel and Chi Cho's driveway.

"It's Daniela! It's Daniela!" Chi Cho's four-year-old son, David, ran out of the house. He was on her as she stepped out of the car. She put on a smile and lifted him to her waist. Isabel stood in the doorway wiping her hands with a towel. Daniela could see alarm in her eyes.

As she grew near, she couldn't hold back the tears. Isabel took David from her arms and set him on the floor. *"Watch your brother,"* she said.

"But, Daniela." He stomped.

"Now," she said.

He walked to his brother who stared up with a dirty stuffed animal in his hand.

"They got him," Daniela sobbed. *"They got him."*

Isabel led her out to the porch and hugged her. A mix of sounds came from Daniela as she choked on tears and tried to spit out words. *"They came and got him. Kicked him on the ground. Blood."* Her voice was high and frantic.

Tears rolled down Isabel's cheeks as she rubbed Daniela's head. She looked to the doorway where David stood forlornly. *"Someone close to Daniela passed away,"* she said. *"A good friend."*

The boy stared.

Eventually, the pair composed themselves enough for Daniela to tell the story. *"There's a special place for him up there,"* said Isabel. *"And we will all see him."*

Later that afternoon, Chi Cho walked up wearing a dirty pair of jeans and a sweat soaked t-shirt. Daniela sat on the couch, blankly watching the children play as Isabel prepared food. Chi Cho and Daniela's eyes connected. Isabel looked up, dropped the knife, and hurried to the door. She took her husband's hand and led him around the side of the house. *"We should sit,"* she said.

"I already know," said Chi Cho. *"He's gone."*

"How?"

"You two wouldn't look like that if he wasn't. Besides, I had a sign

three days ago."

"What sign?"

"The day after I saw him at Poás, I went out to the patches. The biggest, healthiest plant, one that could've been the best ever, a full kilo, died. Its colas were shriveled and rotten, but no trace of mold. All of its leaves were on the ground. His favorite kind, haze." Chi Cho's eyes were glossy. *"Just tell me one thing."* His voice cracked. *"Did they kill him?"*

Tears streamed down Isabel's cheeks. *"He was alive when Daniela saw him,"* she said.

"Probably be better they had killed him."

Isabel cried loudly, and Chi Cho wrapped his arms around her. His damp shirt was cool on her face. Chi Cho sniffed and tried to regulate his breathing. *"Does David know?"*

Isabel wiped her nose. *"I couldn't tell him. Told him someone close to Daniela passed."*

"He shouldn't have to know."

Isabel lifted her head from his chest and rubbed her hands down her face. *"I'll tell him. Tomorrow."* She sniffed. *"I should go check on them, though. Daniela's got too much to deal with."*

"I'll be in in a moment." Chi Cho stared at the forest.

Isabel rubbed his back and squeezed him. *"Just come in when you're ready."*

He was still facing the woods when Daniela walked out. She could see his shoulders shaking. She placed her hands on his back and gave a tender squeeze. Chi Cho turned around. His face was red and wet. *"He was a good man,"* he said.

Daniela hugged him.

A minute passed, and Chi Cho calmed his breathing and wiped the tears from his face. *"It must be so much harder for you."*

"I haven't been able to eat," she said. *"I wanted to ask you about smoke."*

"Good idea," said Chi Cho. *"If there was ever a time..."*

"Let's get the pipe," she said. *"I'll tell you about it."*

Juan opened a thick steel door and ushered the agents into a room. Their eyes were drawn upward where, twelve feet up, the ceiling looked like that of a night club. Colored lights hung down, large speaker boxes were mounted in the corners, and a gymnasium sized heating duct ran along a wall. "This is it," said Juan. "All built by you. No more hammer and nail technique."

Below the lights, the room was drab, flat white paint over cinder block walls and a smooth gray finish on the floor. The walls were bare except for a large mirror embedded in one side. Juan unlocked and opened a door next to the mirror. He flicked on the lights to reveal a large control panel sitting perpendicular to the two-way mirror. A soft buzzing came from the machine.

"This controls everything," said Juan. He pointed to a series of switches in its right corner.

"These are for the lights, different colors, one color, more than one, flashing, more flashing." Juan moved them, and the lights on the other side of the mirror changed colors and strobed. Ron nodded with each switch, glancing between the room and the control panel.

"This is for the music." Juan hit a button with writing on it. No music played. He hit a square button and turned a knob. He squinted, then opened his eyes wide and nodded. "Yes. This is important. So you can hear inside the room." Juan pressed it, and Ricky Martin's

Livin' la Vida Loca blasted out. He quickly turned down the knob. "This is master volume." He stopped the music from entering the room and turned up the volume. The bass passed faintly through the walls. Ron and Bill saw the lights in the other room shake. Juan worked the control panel, and *Livin' la Vida Loca* was again audible.

"These are the types of music. Ricky is pop." He hit another button, and a song from India played. "Music of East." He hit another, and death metal blared. "Music of Devil." He hit one more. It sounded like a waterfall. "White noise," he said.

Bill reached in front of Juan and hit the pop music button, then one for the strobing colored lights. He swayed his hips back and forth to the beat. "We should bring girls in here."

"You'll have to talk to *El Comandante* about that." Juan shut off the music and lights, then picked up a microphone. "This is for talking through the speakers. You press this to use it. Hello. Hello," he said. His voice echoed. "These change the voice. You can slow it." His words came out deeply at a third the normal speed. "Or make it really fast." His voice sounded like a Chipmunk's. "Or, you can make it like monster." With each touch of the control panel, his voice morphed to a different horror movie villain. "These knobs are for temperature control. You can raise or lower it quickly." He turned the dial and pointed at a number changing on a small screen. "That's all I can think of. If you want to acquaint yourself with the system, I'll bring in the prisoner. He should already be stressed. We played loud music in his cell all night. The lights never turn off."

"Cool." Ron pressed buttons on the panel and watched their effect on the room. "You familiar with this, Bill?"

"Enough. I prefer the old tooth 'n' nail. You can get up in their face."

"This is better for getting in their head," said Ron. "Especially when they're sleep deprived. You can have them on the floor crying with the flick of a switch."

"Takes the fun out of it," said Bill. He picked up the microphone, cranked up the volume, and hit one of the effect buttons. "Do you like scary movies?" he said. His voice was shrill and raspy as it came out of the speakers.

"We should stop until the prisoner's here," said Ron. "Maybe change the temp. Seventeen sound good?" He turned the knob.

Bill crooked an eye.

"A little over sixty," said Ron.

"Sounds comfortable."

"It won't be for him."

Light shone on the floor in the opposite room as the outer door opened. Chains rattled, and Ben was pushed in.

"Holy shit." Bill laughed.

Ben wore an orange jumpsuit. His head, sagging, was shaved bare. Even his eyebrows were gone. He stood on bare feet and squinted.

"I like the darkness around his eyes," said Ron. "Our boys taught 'em well."

"Stand in the center. Don't move." Juan bent down and undid the chains. *"Stay there."* He picked up the mass of chains and walked into the control room. *"He's ready."*

Ron flipped open a notebook and picked up the mic. He pressed the button to slow his voice. "Okay, Ben. You have repeatedly lied to us. Now we want the truth."

Ben stared at the speakers in the corner, then the lights above.

"Where did the money come from?"

Ben looked at the mirror. It was the first time he'd seen his reflection since being captured. He barely recognized himself.

Juan stepped between Ron and Bill and hit a series of switches. Death metal boomed.

Ben fell to the floor, clutching his ears, and curled into a fetal position. 'Slayer,' he thought, pressing his face to the floor. The heavy bass rattled his organs. He couldn't swallow. Then came the lyrics. They were guttural. Ben imagined the Minotaur standing over him, yelling at him with grunts, smoke pouring from its nostrils. 'Not

Slayer,' he thought. 'Cannibal Corpse. The old one.'

The music stopped. "Did you like that, Ben?"

Ben lay on the floor in a ball.

"Get up."

He didn't move.

Ron hit the music button, and Ben scrambled to his feet, clutching his ears. The music stopped.

"You are learning our system," said Ron. "Now, where did you get the money?"

"Teaching," said Ben.

The music blasted, and, once again, Ben went to the floor. The Minotaur returned and danced over him. The music stopped, the Minotaur vanished, and Ben got to his feet.

"Lying to us is futile, Ben. Now, tell us where you got it."

"I... I... I work for a company... In Costa Rica."

Ron felt Ben was looking him directly in the eyes. "What type of company?" His voice drawled from the speakers.

"A sportsbook. Bet.com. I dealt with customers in the States by phone."

Ron looked at Bill, who shook his head. "If that's true, give me your boss's name... The address and phone number."

Ben's eyes hit the ceiling. *"Mauricio. 901, Avenida Uno, San Jose."*

"Bull shit," said Bill.

Ron again pressed the button for the microphone. "You're lying to us, aren't you?"

Ben's eyes darted back and forth. He brought his hands to his ears.

"Ben, lower your hands."

Ben's eyes moved in all directions.

Ron turned the volume up and switched the voice to a monster effect. "Now!" he said.

Ben slowly removed them to hear the white noise. He recalled sitting under La Paz Waterfall.

"I want you to crouch like you're sitting in a chair."

Ben looked around and lowered into the position.

"Your thighs should be parallel with the floor. You will hold it for two minutes. If you do it lazily, on goes the devil music."

Juan hit a button that started a timer on the panel. Before it reached thirty seconds, Ben was clutching his thighs. Perspiration dotted his face. After a minute, his posture hadn't changed, but soon Ben's legs were quivering, and his face was a mess of wrinkles.

At a minute and a half, Ron turned on the mic. "Okay. That's one minute, Ben."

Panic flashed in Ben's eyes. His muscles grew tighter. As two minutes showed, his whole body trembled. His chin vibrated, and sweat dripped from his face. He held his eyes closed as the clock hit two and a half minutes and gritted his teeth.

"Almost there," said Ron. "Don't let up. Fifteen seconds."

"He's trying," said Juan. "Give him that."

"He won't make three," said Bill.

"Almost there," said Juan.

"This is where the noise gets them," said Ron. "Causes something to snap."

Juan looked into Ron's large, saucer-like pupils, then turned quickly as Ben crashed to the floor. His body appeared not to register the impact, his legs bent in the same position. The white noise droned on inside.

"Let's let him rest two minutes." Ron smiled.

"Looks like he did after I kicked him," said Bill. He lifted a foot in the air. "Size fourteen."

Ron shut off the white noise. "To your feet," he said.

Ben slowly got up.

Ron shut off the mic and held out a notebook to Bill. "How do you say this name?"

"Jerónimo."

Juan nodded at Bill's deft pronunciation.

"Not Geronimo?" said Ron.

"Give me the mic." Bill grabbed it and flicked it on. "Ben, who's Jerónimo?"

They watched Ben's eyes grow, like waxing moons. Ron snatched the microphone. "Yes, we know about him. Ryan didn't like you working with the Zapatistas."

"He lied," said Ben.

"We'd heard of a shipment of guns to the Chiapas. Then we find out you were there at the same time."

"Lies," said Ben.

"No, you're all lies. But we'll stop that. Strip naked."

Ben stared in the mirror.

"I said strip. Or face the music."

Ben undid the jumpsuit and dropped it to the floor. Bruises showed on his gaunt body.

"You're going to do the exercise again." Ron pressed the button for the white noise, and Ben looked to the colored lights above. "Get in the position. Two minutes."

Ben dropped.

"Legs parallel with the floor," said Ron.

Bill winked at Juan. "Bet he can't make a minute thirty."

"I would not take that bet," said Juan.

"Two to one odds?"

"No, thank you." Juan looked from Ben to the timer. It read twenty eight seconds. Ben's legs shook, and his face was stiff.

"Might not make a minute," said Bill.

Juan watched it tick to forty three seconds. Ben's legs were swinging wildly, and his face showed the pain. His cock swung like a pendulum. Juan saw his legs pause and then watched him collapse to the floor. He stuck his fingers in his ears. Ron hit a couple buttons and cranked up the metal.

"Use the lights, too," said Bill. He reached up and turned on the white strobe. "There we go." He moved his arms rigidly up and down, imitating a robot, then glanced at his watch. "Almost time for lunch.

Wanna leave him there?"

"I don't know how safe that'd be," said Ron.

"Perfectly safe," said Juan.

"Is the Commandant ready for lunch?" asked Ron.

"We can see."

"We should drop the temp a little." Bill turned the knob.

Ron raised his brows. "That's fifty four."

"Sure is," said Bill. He hit another button, and colored lights flashed.

Juan checked the door separating the rooms, and the three left the noise and flashing lights behind. They ducked and shielded their eyes as they walked out onto the gravel.

Ben lay on the floor, eyes shut, and ears plugged. He drew his body in close as the temperature dropped. He began to shiver. He opened his eyes and stared toward the mirror, his teeth chattering. 'Fuck them,' he thought.

Ben stood and picked up the thin orange garment. He slid it on, his joints moving stiffly. He then looked in the mirror and started to jump in place, holding his hands over his ears. The colors flashed. He began to run in circles, clutching his stomach. His intestines writhed. Lightheaded, he stopped and rested, hunched over and stared in the mirror. "You're not even there," he said. "You're not there!" He jumped up and pounded the mirror, then stepped to the door. The handle wouldn't turn. He walked to the door that led outside and tugged on it. The music bumped in his head. He stepped back and gave the door a kick, then another. It didn't move, and he walked away limping. Ben sized up the mirror, thinking he might be able to break it. 'Only another locked door on the other side.'

Ben leaned against the wall and thought hard. He looked at the floor, tuning out the colored lights that danced there, then scanned the room slowly. There wasn't a free object anywhere. He looked up. The colored light came from small black rectangular boxes mounted to thin metal rods. A different color of light, red, green, blue, or violet, flashed from each box. The beams shot from inside the boxes and hit a small mirror. The mirrors moved back and forth, causing the light to jump. Electrical cords hung down farther than some of the lights. Ben looked around the room again. The grunts of the death metal vocalist continued to resonate, not one word comprehensible. Ben walked to the corner of the room, stood facing it, and placed one hand flat on each wall. He pressed in and jumped, slapping his feet against the walls. He slid to the floor. He tried again with no success. The image of the Minotaur came back, pulling the lyrics deep from his belly and shouting them out. 'The door knob,' thought Ben. He studied the ceiling above each door. A loop of cord hung lower above the door by the mirror, and he walked toward it. He grabbed the upper hinge and held it tight as he jumped up to the knob. Pain shot though the arch of his foot as he landed. He eyed the cord, bright lights moving around it, then jumped. His fingertips brushed it. 'I've dunked,' he told himself and jumped back onto the handle. He focused on the cord, controlling his breath, and leaped. This time he got his fingertips over it. His arm jerked as the cord pulled tight. Then it snapped, and Ben hit the floor.

Ben rubbed his face and stood. He looked at the black rectangular box, no longer flashing, and the cord that dangled below. He gave it a pull and watched the rod above bend. He wrapped his hands around it tightly, hung from the cord, and felt his body slowly lowering. The rod bent sharply, and he hit the floor. He then got up, took hold of the rod, and pulled on it until he freed it from the ceiling. Then he grabbed the rectangular box and ran a finger over the mirror. He held his body tight and twisted the black box free of the rod. He let out a huff and glanced around the room. The music now seemed non-existent, just a throbbing pain against his eardrums. Ben then walked to the door with conviction. He held up the black box and brought it down on the door knob, shattering the glass rectangle. Pieces of it fell to the floor. He looked where the rectangle had been and pulled out the longest sharp piece. Then he dropped the box and walked to the center of the room. He looked up at the ceiling, then stared into the mirror. He held his arm out and pointed the tip of glass at his neck. His forearm and bicep were flexed tight. The door flew open, and Bill ran straight for him. Ben stood like an animal in headlights as Bill's shoulder slammed into his gut. The piece of glass flew. Bill turned him over on the floor, twisting his arm behind his back. The music and colored lights went off. Ben felt his face being pushed into the floor and heard the sound of chains rattling as someone ran into the room.

Ben walked through the desert, naked, carrying a jug of water. His mouth was so dry he couldn't swallow. Each breath dried it more. The words "I believe I must die" echoed in his head in a cartoonish voice. He coughed and watched dried pieces of his throat float away in the breeze. Birds descended from the sky and pecked at his body. He then jolted out of sleep to a repetitive trance beat with the words "I'm blue da ba dee da ba die" playing over it. A pain pounded in his head, like an intense hangover, and the dream faded. His throat burned.

'What time is it?' The fluorescent lights buzzed. They were surrounded by wire. 'No getting that glass out.' There had been a thorough search of his cell after the previous day's incident. He was on suicide watch.

A small door screeched open, and a tray of food slid in. *"Comida, gringo."*

Ben scampered from the bed and nearly fell as a wave of dizziness passed through him. He grabbed the tray and listened for the guard to lock up. Then he sat on the bed and stared at the food. Rice and beans. Water. He slowly got up to avoid dizziness and dumped the food in the toilet. He then poured the water over it and flushed. 'Forty eight hours,' he thought. He set the tray on the floor and lay back down, trying to mellow the pain in his head.

The same dance track repeated itself several times before the stiff lock on the cell door clicked. Ben sat up, and the room became blurry.

"Buenos dias," said Juan. *"Your friends have a surprise for you today."* He knelt and fastened the chains. The thumping was intense.

Ben's mind went to Daniela.

"¡Venga!" Juan tugged on the chains, and Ben sprung up. They rattled as Juan led him outside. The sun almost knocked Ben over. Juan gave him a shove, and the pain in his head increased. Dust wafted up as Ben drug his bare feet across the gravel.

"Stop," said Juan. He eyed Ben as he unlocked the door to the interrogation room. Ron and Bill stood around a long, plastic board. Nylon straps hung from its sides. Three buckets of water sat on the floor.

"Howdy, Ben," said Bill. "Check out your new bed."

Ben stared as Juan undid his chains. The board was tilted at an angle, a head brace at the lower end.

"Now, Ben, you know what this is," said Ron. "It can be avoided if you come clean."

Ben looked at the buckets of water, thinking how his plan of dehydration had been foiled.

"Anything you'd like to tell us before we strap you in?" said Ron.

"I know nothing," Ben said dryly.

"Sounds like you need water," said Bill. "Now lay down." Bill shoved him onto the board and put his head in the brace. He pulled a small black hood over Ben's face. It went halfway down his nose.

"Everybody's gone surfing," Bill sang as he and Juan fastened the straps.

The nylon dug into Ben's skin. He tried to move his limbs. His whole body was immobile. There was a slight rush of blood to his pounding head. Then he heard a splash of water and droplets hitting the floor.

"Open your mouth," said Bill.

Ben clamped his jaw, but Bill ripped it open. "Dumb bastard," he said. He forced a wet towel into Ben's mouth. Ben could feel the fibers against the back of his throat. He flailed, but the straps held tight. Bill pinched Ben's nose shut until he gave in and lay still.

Ben felt a stream of water pour over his face and stop above his mouth. The towel expanded, and water dripped down his throat. Each drip caused him to choke, but the towel prevented him from breathing. The board shook as he struggled. His lungs burned, and he pictured the water collecting there. The water stopped dripping, and the towel was pulled out. Ben wheezed and coughed, feeling as if he'd swallowed a hot coal. As he started to catch his breath, the towel was forced back in. 'Relax,' he told himself. 'Relax.'

The water splashed in Ben's face and then began to run down his throat. He tried to swallow it but choked. More water ran down his throat as Ben managed to delay his gag reflex. He could count to five before choking. The towel was pulled out, and Ben went from coughing to wheezing, then close to normal breathing.

"Going to talk?" said Bill.

"Nothing," Ben cried.

"Wrong answer."

The hood was brought up so it only covered Ben's eyes. Then Ben felt a piece of plastic pulled over his face. It covered his nostrils and lips. Breathing became difficult with only a small hole over his mouth. Ben felt the hole with his tongue. Then water came pouring through. He tried to stifle his gag reflex as the water poured in. It came faster than before. Even when he choked, water came through.

The water stopped, and Ben hacked. He felt someone restrict the air by plugging the hole with his finger. The person pressed it and released, like he was playing a flute, and Ben choked with each press.

Again came the stream of water. 'Relax,' Ben told himself. 'Relax.' He managed not to gag, and the water flowed through the tiny opening. '*¡Pura Vida!*' he thought. He lost sensation.

Bill stopped pouring the water as Juan covered the hole in the plastic.

Ben didn't move.

Juan plugged and unplugged it.

"He's not moving!" yelled Ron.

Juan pulled off the hood. "His eyes are still!"

Bill stared into Ben's throat. He could see water.

Juan tore loose the straps from Ben's upper body, Ron from his lower. They picked him up and moved him to the floor. Bill stared at the paleness in Ben's face.

Ron locked his hands over Ben's chest and began pushing and releasing every few seconds. Water bubbled from Ben's mouth. Bill stared.

"Help me!" Ron yelled.

"He's gone," said Bill.

"He hasn't answered the question yet!"

"Two minutes without a breath, clinically dead."

Ron kept pumping. "Call a doctor!" he told Juan.

Juan ran to the other room. He frantically went through his keys to open the door.

"Ask for a defibrillator," said Bill. *"Electricidad para su corazón."*

Water stopped coming from Ben's mouth, and after every fifth push, Ron blew a breath into his mouth. Juan ran back in. "Doctor's on the way. He's bringing electricity."

"I'll meet him outside." Bill walked to the door and reached in his pocket. He pulled out his smokes as he went. A shadow covered the ground, and Bill looked up to see a cloud hiding the sun. He left the door open a crack, leaned against the building, and lit one up. The sun returned, and Bill looked to the hills. The leaves of the trees glistened. He exhaled and saw someone running toward him. It was a man in green fatigues, carrying a black case. As the man grew nearer, Bill saw he had a smooth baby face. Bill stomped out his cigarette and held open the door.

The doctor ran in and tossed down his case. *"Move him from the water!"* he yelled. *"Over here."*

Juan grabbed Ben's legs. "We have to get him away from the water."

Ron hoisted Ben's shoulders, and the two dropped him in front of the doctor.

The doctor felt for a pulse, then held his cheek over his mouth. He opened the black case, and the defibrillator beeped as he took it out. *"Stand clear."* He held up the ends and then pushed them into Ben's chest. Ben's body shook. The doctor held them up and then pushed them back down. Thump. He repeated the action. Thump... Thump... Thump.

Ben's body began convulsing. *"He's breathing,"* said the doctor. "*But seizuring.*"

"Brain damage," said Bill. "That's why he's shaking."

"Fuckin' great." Ron looked at Bill.

"Don't you fuckin' put this on me."

Ron turned and walked out.

The doctor stared into Ben's pale face, then turned to Bill. *"What do you want us to do with him?"*

2007

Isabel dried the last dish and took a seat next to Chi Cho on the couch. Every few seconds he'd flip the channel. *"Stop here,"* she said. *"Shakira."*

Chi Cho glared at her.

"You know you want to watch her."

Chi Cho shrugged and set down the remote. He glanced at the clock, then out the window. The sky was bluer than he'd ever seen it.

There was a knock at the door. Chi Cho flicked off the TV and got up. Isabel stood behind as he pulled back the curtain next to the door. A gringo hippie stood outside. He was the same height as Ben but had long hair and a goatee. A blue-nosed pit bull stood to his right, and an overstuffed hiking pack covered his back.

Chi Cho opened the door. *"Charles?"* He brought his hand out slowly.

"Of course," said Charles. *"You are Chi Cho?"*

"Sí." Chi Cho pulled on Charles's hand. *"Come in."* He motioned to Isabel. *"This is my wife, Isabel."*

"It's a pleasure," said Charles.

"Charmed." She stepped forward, and the two exchanged a kiss on the cheek.

Blue sniffed her leg, and she jumped back.

"You don't have to worry about him," said Charles. *"He's a mouse."*

"Biggest mouse I've seen."

The hiking bag hit the floor with a thump, and Charles slid into a seat onto the sofa. He kicked the bag. *"Three hundred twenty thousand dollars."* He reached in his pocket and took out his orange, yellow, and blue glass pipe.

Chi Cho stared at Charles's face. *"I have to talk to you. About your brother."*

"I got the message from Daniela. Tell her I'm sorry for not responding. The news left me dumb." Charles finished packing the bowl and took out a lighter. *"So was he killed, captured, or both?"* He put the pipe to his lips and lit it.

Chi Cho's eyes widened. *"He and Daniela were captured, it was the last day of July."*

Charles erupted into a coughing fit. *"They got Daniela, too?"* he wheezed. He wiped his eyes and held out the pipe. *"I didn't get that."*

Chi Cho grabbed the pipe and took a seat next to Charles. Isabel sat on the end. *"They released Daniela,"* said Chi Cho. *"Everything comes through her."*

Charles narrowed his eyes. *"Strange they'd let her go."*

"We're happy we didn't lose both," said Isabel.

On cue, Charles bent over and hacked. Chi Cho and Isabel glanced over, and the dog stared at his master.

"I'd seen him that morning," said Chi Cho. *"Met him at Volcán Poás. He was in good spirits. They were waiting for him when he returned. Daniela said they traced him through books he'd ordered."*

Charles shook his head. *"Our father always told him those books would be the death of him."*

Isabel handed the pipe to Charles and let out a tiny cough. Charles examined the bowl and hit it. He then got up, tapped it into the trash can, and started to pack another. Chi Cho and Isabel stared at the glass piece as he stuffed it. Then they gave each other a look.

"I had a vision of Ben about a week after that," said Charles.

Isabel and Chi Cho's heads snapped up.

"I thought it signaled his capture, but I'd been on acid at the time. I

don't take acid signs too seriously." Charles pressed the pipe to his lips and lit it. He passed it quickly before whooping. *"From the vision I thought Ben died. He spoke to me."*

"We all experienced it," said Chi Cho. *"It's when we assumed he'd passed."*

Charles stared ahead. His pupils grew. *"Makes sense. It seemed so real."* He lit the fresh bowl. *"I guess it's better than being a prisoner."*

"Guess so," said Chi Cho.

Charles held out the pipe, wincing to stifle a cough.

"No, thank you," said Chi Cho.

Charles "wooed" with his last cough. Isabel stared at his wide nostrils as he took a deep breath.

"I actually wanted to talk to you about the visions," said Chi Cho. *"Ever since Daniela had her vision, she's wanted to take over for Ben, keep the Anarcho Grow alive."*

"I wouldn't know what to do without it," said Charles. *"It's the only steady thing in my life."*

"It's dangerous," said Chi Cho. *"But something significant can come from it."*

These are his mountains and skies and
He radiates
And through history's rivers of blood
He regenerates
And like the sun disappears only to reappear
He is eternally here
His time is near
Never conquered but here

—Rage

Epilogue

Bogotá, Colombia

A tall white man with short hair walked down the sidewalk. There was a distant look in his eyes.

A fruit vendor smiled as he approached. *"Hola, George,"* he said.

"Hola," said the white man.

"Going for lunch?"

"Lunch," said George. He walked by the fruit stand and into a restaurant. Dirt showed on the tile floor. A television played in the corner.

"George, where have you been?" A woman walked from behind the counter.

"Park," he said and sat at a table.

"I have your gallo pinto." She carried a plate and set it before him. *"One egg and plantains."*

The white man smiled, and the woman retrieved a glass of juice and a coffee from the counter. She sat across from him. *"I have tamarindo for you today."*

"Tamarindo," George said slowly. He stared into the glass.

"What are you doing this afternoon?"

"Park."

"You love that place."

"Park," he repeated.

The woman sipped her coffee as the white man finished his food.